I0672373

Pure
Intention:
Book Two
of The
Felled

Pure Intention: Book Two of The Felled

Ryan S. Leavitt

Cover art by Sutthiwat Dechakamphu

Copyright © 2023 by Ryan S. Leavitt. Published July 2023. First edition. All rights reserved. This is a work of fiction. All names, characters, events, and things in this work are a product of the author's imagination. Anything seemingly similar existing outside the author's imagination is entirely coincidental. Reproduction in whole or part of this publication without express written consent is not okay. It means a lot for you even seeing this and giving this a chance. If you enjoyed this tale, please consider leaving a review wherever you purchased it.

To report typos or offer any other general feedback, please e-mail: ryansleavittscifi@gmail.com

Visit my website: www.ryansleavitt.com

Table of Contents

Foreword

If you're seeing this, then most likely you've already gone through book one of this series, *Never Going Back*. I'm so grateful to have you back. No doubt you must be itching to know what happened after that previous cliffhanger.

With that I mind, I won't hold you up for too long. There is one thing I think is important to mention. You might be forgiven for assuming the Sleeping Sickness is some kind of allegory or stand-in for COVID-19. It isn't. I began writing The Felled in 2016 and many of the themes present were already concertized before that particular hyperobject emerged.

I felt it was important to make that distinction. This series was finalized during the pandemic, it is not at all about it.

Lastly, here are the chronological ages of all the POV characters as available:

Lyda, ?
Gabriel, 12
Carlos, 15
Kalyna, 16
Will, 17
Siannon, 26
Callum, 48
Mark, 54
Sali, 124

Dreaming of screaming
Someone kick me out of my mind
I hate these thoughts I can't deny
You will take their body parts
and put them on the wall
And bring the dark disaster

-System of a Down

EPISODE 7
Tendency to Form a Sphere

Prologue

In the oldest of tales, water could stop an evil entity's advance. Malevolent forces were unable to cross a flowing stream or withstand contact with the substance. Water, sacred for its hand in the formation of known life, would give a cornered hero relief. What pursued was not defeated in those moments, only forestalled.

Siannon was being chased. As she barreled down a path, the trees thinned away into a clearing. With the shade departed, she was unshielded from the broiling sunlight. It would be over, one way or another, once she got to the ocean.

Siannon was not alone. Uriah and Cassie were just up ahead. They all hailed from the same fallen settlement, the moon outpost of Rula. How far they were from home, thrust randomly on this sequestered island. They would often see the moon in the sky. Some nights it was so small she could fit it pinched between two curled fingers. Last night the moon had been a waning gibbous, looking insubstantial. Back on Rula, Earth's visual presence had been enormous. Yet to Siannon, the planet had been of so little consequence back then. The moon had been bigger in her mind. How foolish she'd been.

Evil is not an entity in its own right. Rather, it is a privation of good, the deacon had said during a sermon years before. Siannon was falling behind. Her friends were both gifted with augmented physiology. Siannon was supposed to be like them, but a mishap during her mother's pregnancy left her worse off than an unedited fetus. Prone to chronic pain, her nervous system was a failure. *A perversion of the natural,* in the deacon's speech.

"We're so close," Cassie managed between breaths.

Uriah sped up, the knowledge revitalizing his steps. Siannon would later come to believe it was that motion that activated it.

A whizzing sound came from behind, crescendoing as it passed the two girls by. A flash of spinning light overwhelmed Siannon's retinas. Against her immediate instincts, she had to stop running or risk falling over.

Uriah cried out. The agony was too great for words to form.

Blinking fiercely, Siannon's vision soon focused as the light source petered out. It had toppled Uriah over, and he was clasping his right leg with both arms. The ground took in the blood from Uriah's gaping wound. How was there already that much blood? Siannon looked at Cassie. The girl shook her head.

"It's a Spicket," Cassie said. Turning away, she resumed running. "We need to keep moving, Siannon."

"Please, I need help!" Uriah implored. He writhed, arms flailing out. With the pressure gone, a torrent of red seeped out of him. Siannon watched the Spicket burrowing deeper into the boy's skin, poking out of his calf. It was a horn-shaped metallic blob, an unstoppable projectile. Once inside, it spiked out while shredding everything: skin, muscle, bone. The weapon would mangle Uriah's entire leg beyond repair in under a minute. And if Siannon was stupid enough to intercede, whatever part of her tried to extract the Spicket from him would latch itself onto her. It was a weapon made of nanotech: self-replicating destruction.

Siannon sped away until Uriah's cries were just another thing of the past. Had she covered so much ground that she was too far away to hear him? Or could a Spicket silence a man that quickly?

The soul's gravest offense, the most heinous sin of all is...

The burning in her lungs intensified as she tried to catch up with Cassie, who had already made it onto the beach. Tears came for Uriah, though they came at the expense of her focus—

...to leave this world of immolation, the deacon had said, *is to eternally brand one's self with the consciousness of evil. God takes life in His own time, and it is never through the mortal sin of suicide. He only gives you the option! The choice... to be damned.*

Siannon's dire circumstances had softened her stance against suicide. The past would not help her, she had to remain alert in the now. And yet the memories would not relent. She parsed through bits of them chewing, concentrating.

Consciousness of evil. Siannon had thought a great deal about that phrase since being driven off Rula. The two words *seemed* distinct to her. But were they mutually exclusive? Were less conscious beings more evil? That didn't seem right. Siannon

4

thought the opposite was true. As consciousness evolved, so did evil alongside it.

Screw the deacon. Anything was better than captivity again. Let her be a privation of good, if it meant she got to suffer less.

Siannon saw Cassie hit the water and swim out. The plan had been to hold each other under. So much for that.

The thing that followed them was a tank-like vehicle. Siannon hadn't gotten a good look at it, but she could hear it crunching through the jungle. It came wheeling onto the shore as she at last made it to the water and off her ailing feet.

The frigid waves made Siannon shiver. Her mind flashed to just moments before, as the beach had been littered with bodies: dead or dying soldiers in similar measure. People with *guns.*

That would have been so much easier than this, Siannon thought as she forced herself underwater. The vehicle was coming. No use even thinking of doubling back.

Around her, the world was ending. A gradual conclusion that had started many years before Siannon had ever been born. It was as if there was not a square mile of the planet at peace.

Now would come the resistance. The biological mechanisms in no way related to her higher desire to avoid capture. As the caustic seawater invaded her, she couldn't help but go up for air. No! She had to do this before that thing could get her. She coughed and went back under, arms vacillating between helping and harming her intentions.

Siannon was growing tired. It would be over soon... the conscious experience of it, at least. Her body would give out, her panic would dull. Then the thoughtlessness would come. No longer able to breathe, she knew she could do this, she could get away from this nightmare. She'd—

Something hard bashed against the back of her skull. Terrified, she thought it was a Spicket; but no, it was some other monstrous apparatus, clawing her out of the water. It unfurled and wrapped around her chest.

Back in the air, she convulsed, seeming to levitate. To imagine all that resistance amounted to nothing short of more torment.

Her awareness dwindling, Siannon knew she had failed. *They* had her, and so her life would be theirs. Evil had braved the water just for her.

Chapter One

1. DEPOSITION OF THE TESTIMONY OF CARLOS
SUÁREZ

A.   This is such a small room.

Q.   It's interesting how you
continue to point that out. Each of you
has your own story, your own recollection
of what happened in there. Do you know
you're the only one who remembers passing
through the Erstveil on your way back?

A.   You'll have to help jog my
memory. It's kind of hard to pay
attention.

Q.   Oh. Well, that's disappointing.
We are talking about the resultant
structure that appeared after Lyda did
what she did. The Erstveil.

A.   Right. Yeah. Well, Lyda said
something about—think of it as a barrier.
She hit the L'rias hard, but she didn't

kill them all. Instead, she destroyed the ones who were an immediate threat to Arqa and Flight Division. Boom, ships gone. After that, Lyda erected that thing. They couldn't reach Arqa if they wanted to now. It blocks them from crossing. I guess that is what she called it, the Erstveil. I couldn't tell you why.

Q. So Lyda found a way to use B3?

A. It really is a small room. Arqa too. Arqa is a tiny speck.

Q. Carlos, Carlos, wake up, man. Now I'm going to ask you a hard question. Why do you think you made it back? As opposed to some of the others?

A. Well, she—

Q. What?

A. I don't know. I mean, it all seemed like chance to me. Some people,

their actions, their emotions set off
something inside that place. B3 made
mirrors of ourselves. We weren't told
anything about that part. Did you know
about it? We were completely unprepared
and still haven't been filled in. I never
thought we were so small. Something big
is right.

    Q.   You're referring to B3?

    A.   (No audible response.)

    Q.   We still don't understand how
you think you made it out of there okay.
Carlos, you've got to answer all of my
questions if you ever want to be let out
of here.

    A.   (No audible response.)

2.

Lifting his head up from the deposition on the holo-screen, Callum felt a sinking feeling in his chest.

The encounter with B3 had left everyone on Arqa nonplussed.

The group who'd returned from the alien structure had been isolated in the Gaze Room for weeks. First had come examinations, then the questioning. He had been the one to conduct that. There were many disturbing events he'd heard about, but Lyda's transformation unnerved him most of all. She came back years older, while only having been gone for a few days. It was almost time to disclose to the children what Arqa's true mission was.

Callum stood outside of the sealed-off Gaze Room. The sound of Lyda's tantrum was muffled but audible. Today everyone would be released besides her.

There had been several anomalies reported on Arqa the day they reached B3, including Callum's pursuit of Congo. He wondered if that had been in his head. He never did catch that dog.

He had to keep reminding himself there was nothing supernatural taking place. B3 was real; it was there. It was just such a difficult thing to wrap his head around, the scale of it. How it came to be and what it was capable of.

Stephen exited the Gaze Room, his eyes darting back and forth. He was peering at Callum's shoes when he said, "Another great fuckin' day."

"Thanks for giving her the bad news," Callum said. The two men walked back toward Stephen's quarters.

"What are you doing here?"

Tension had arisen between the two after Stephen had read a copy of the depositions. He grew furious over Callum's clinical and dispassionate questions. It hadn't helped when Callum explained he was only following the captain's orders. "How is she, Stephen?"

"Let's talk about how she *should* be first: dead. The doctors assure me that three weeks of sleep deprivation would have killed anyone else. Yet physically, Lyda is fine." He peered at Callum. "You never asked her about the sleep. Why is that?"

"It was not germane to the objective. I was told to get an accurate account of what happened in B3. That's all."

"Her being in there, it ruined her."

"It's trauma, Stephen. She's improving. She'll sleep again."

"Lay off. It's much more than that. That place put something of itself in her and—I don't know how to help her."

"Just being there for her is all you can do."

"She's like a morose teenager now. She feels betrayed. I tried to tell her she shouldn't have snuck away like that, but it's hard to be mad at her."

Craig popped into Callum's head, but he pushed those thoughts away. "I know it's hard. Her mind has gone through a drastic change."

"Do you think I would have brought my wife and daughter on this ship if I knew this was the cost?" Stephen asked. "We were not properly briefed about any of this. Us guys, we weren't supposed to see B3. I—if I had any idea of what would become of my family—"

Impatient, Callum blurted out, "We're alive, Stephen. Lyda's alive. What more do you want?"

It looked like Stephen was about to charge at him. Callum relished the opportunity. But the man held it in. "Captain Sali misled us."

"We went to B3 on little more than a hunch, Stephen. You know that."

"Do they really expect us to migrate there? After the disaster we're still picking up after?"

"We're far from a decision like that, but I'm sure if you wanted to stay on the ship, you could."

"The captain can't keep giving us half-truths," Stephen said flatly. "Sali's the one you should be interrogating, not these kids. It's cruel to expect the truth out of them when we haven't given them the same."

"Deviating from the process would be unwise, Stephen. And watch your mouth. You know we're being monitored."

"I have a right to protect my daughter!"

A morbid thought crossed Callum's mind: *Not at the expense of the mission.*

The two men rounded a corner. A group of technicians were taking an air duct apart for repairs. "The captain is going to brief Flight Division today. With some, but not all of the facts. You know that's how it had to be. From what we gleaned from the

Bobbin. The other thing is… listen so, I'm going to question Leni some more later. That's the reason why I bothered you: is there anything you wanted me to ask her?"

Stephen scowled. "No. I already told you. She's not the one we need to question. The woman plays with tarot cards. Acts like she's the assistant manager of chaos itself. She's making up stories, Callum."

"What about the bug that day? The pseugra malfunction? Lyda's vision? You think that was all some sleight of hand?"

"Leni's phoney. Pretending she's connected to some great source or whatever."

"Why is it so hard to believe she might know something useful about B3?"

Stephen groaned. "I'm too tired for all this. Look, I'll just tell you it's a good thing she's locked up. It's better than nothing. But taking her at her word is dangerous. She doesn't have the mission's interest at heart."

"Do you?" Callum asked.

"I should be asking you that. After all, everything you cared about losing is already gone. Am I going to turn out like you? Wooden and emotionless? You're not human, you're science incarnate. I'd say that's Arqa's real aim, huh? Too far gone to stop."

"Too far gone to be stopped," Callum corrected.

Chapter Two

1. DEPOSITION OF THE TESTIMONY OF LYDA HALL

Q.   What happened in B3?

A.   (WITNESS throws her chair.)

Q.   You still don't want to talk?

A.   You keep us in the Gaze Room. As if I could be contained.

Q.   So you're upset about that? We have to ensure you and everyone exposed to B3 didn't bring back something harmful. Until then, we cannot allow you to rejoin the general population.

A.   I was the one who saved you all, and this is how you thank me.

Q.   Rest assured, we are appreciative. But I fail to understand. How did you save us, exactly?

A.   I already answered that question. Don't act like I haven't. B3 contained a dormant source of power I was

able to influence. It acted on my behalf.
Out of my desire to see my home safe.

Q.   Then why didn't you take care of
all the L'rias? Only some were—

A.   Why didn't I slaughter the rest
of them, you mean? That's what I did, say
it. Slaughter.

Q.   I couldn't disagree with you
more. Imagine what they would have done,
had they reached us. Perhaps you're
feeling guilty? Were you hoping to scare
the rest of them from any thoughts of
retaliation? It didn't work, Lyda.
They're not afraid. We need to
exterminate the rest of them.

A.   It was a hard enough decision to
do what I did. It… changed me and I'm
never going to do that again. Let someone
else do it. You won't make me!

Q.   What if the L'rias find a way
through the Erstveil?

A.   When you take life, you become
death. The way I did it... I was made to
feel what they felt. I sensed all that
life going away. Going to nowhere. For
them, it was a moment they hardly had time
to process. But me? I'm still
remembering the thoughts of the dying.
The density of their feelings, they have
conquered me. I am not growing, not
maturing. I am dying. How many years did
B3 take from me? Your tests say my body
aged five years. What else? My mind, my
innocence… both scattered. I can't give
it what little essence I have left.

Q.   That leads to my next question.
Can you channel B3's energy without being
there, do you think?

A.   (WITNESS nods.)

Q.   We need verbal yeses or no's,
Lyda. Remember?

A.   Yes. Yes, I can.

Q.   So basically, you're actively
holding it back, your connection. You
could, hypothetically, attack the L'rias
again?

A.   Yes. But like I said, I won't.
I can't. There is only one thing I will
do with my connection to B3 now.

Q.   And what is that?

A.   You know, Mr. Benito.

2.

The Bay Line was filled with members of Flight Division,
including those who'd gone to B3. Sali stood next to Tanya Lucio
by the podium, playing with her buircraft. The device had games,
comprised of patterns she had to recall and reconstruct. She never
thought she'd live to see B3, but Arqa had arrived far ahead of
schedule. The best of humanity had conspired so that Sali could
shepherd her people onto the bridge. The bridge that had
somehow outstretched itself to them.

"Everyone's here," Tanya said to Sali. "Look at him."

Mark and Rayna approached. They were both dressed in formal wear. Mark was wearing the tie he'd kept hung up outside his door, with a white shirt and an acorn vest. Rayna had a nice purple dress on, with a matching bucket hat. Sali furrowed her brow.

"Big day," Mark said, performing a mocking genuflection.

"Let's get to it," Sali said, pocketing her buircraft.

"Hang on," Rayna said. "I see some fresh faces, which makes sense because we've lost some people in Flight Division, but..."

"What is it?" Mark asked.

"That one, is he in Flight Division now?" Rayna was pointing to someone in the back row. Someone Sali hadn't noticed until then. Will. He was speaking eagerly to the people next to him.

"Will? Flight Division? No way."

"He's not supposed—" Tanya began.

But Sali was already crossing the distance to shoo the boy away. She grumbled, then said, "Oh, you've got to be kidding me." Mark had already shown up late and now this.

"Will, why are you here?" Sali asked her grandson.

"Oh, hey Grammy. I'm ready for my briefing."

"Wrong," Sali said. "This briefing is classified. You need to leave."

The boy grinned as he got up, making for the exit. But then he doubled-back, rushing to the podium. "Yo, what's happening Flight Division? Fact one: I have had telepathic conversations with Gabriel. It happened, I'm not crazy. 'Cause I'm not the only one, who else, who—"

Tanya shoved Will, preventing him from saying more. "Do I have to escort you out?"

Will's cavalier attitude fell away. "Seriously? This is the first exciting thing that's happened in weeks and you want to exclude me? Even when I said I want to help?"

"You can best serve us by going away," Tanya said.

"Did you hear what I just said?"

"We don't care right now, Will!" Sali snapped. To Tanya, she said, "Look, he might as well stay and hear this. Sit down, Will. And keep quiet. If you cause any more disruptions, you will be dragged out of here."

17

The issue managed, Mark and Rayna positioned themselves by the podium.

"Do you need any star charts for this, Mark?" Tanya asked.

Mark waved a hand dismissively. "Not at this time. With something like this, we'll have to rely on our old friend the metaphor."

"Very well," Sali said. Approaching the podium, she addressed Flight Division. "To those who braved B3, we welcome you back to Arqa proper. You have my deepest gratitude for your actions in keeping this ship afloat. You have questions, and today there will be answers. I appreciate your patience. Mark, if you would?"

"Yes. Thanks, Sali," Mark said, taking her place. "Many of you are not sure who I am. I've felt it was prudent to lie low over the years. Sometimes it's safer to keep certain information to yourself. My name is Mark.

"We've been debating for many years how best to disclose certain information to you. After much deliberation on the matter, I'd like for you all to please close your eyes. That's right, everybody. Eyes shut. Listen to the sound of my voice. See that wondrous illusion of a void. Chemicals in motion. A mind working to contemplate what exists beyond itself. For those of you who have seen B3, you might note some slight similarities in the way the colors dance for you now. Before the mind, there was life itself. Before that there were inorganic molecules, clustering to form stars. There are many stars. They come in all varieties. Overall, most of them are unremarkable, seeing as there are so many. Billions upon trillions. All classifiable, fitting into certain boxes. We revered our own solar system's star. For a long time we've known that it was pivotal in creating favorable conditions for life as an emergent property. Thus, a concerted effort was made to find another star that could do the same thing. Being a star, the sun will one day flicker out and life on Earth will be untenable. We needed a long-term plan to find another place.

"That search got disheartening. In every direction we looked, we could find no star like our sun. One that supported life. Was it our paltry instruments, unable to cover the distances needed to make such a discovery?"

Sali spaced out, processing the significance of this moment.

The decisions that had led her here, the sacrifices... the uncertainty. She reached into her pocket and got the buircraft out again. The wellspring of her psychological continuity. Her safeguard against the consequences of time.

"Keep those eyes shut, I'm not finished just yet. For a very long time, nothing was forthcoming. Then we got lucky. We began tracking this new star's rotational cycle. In our own galaxy, no less. Periodically, there would be erratic dips in the star's light intensity. An aberrant finding, mind you, but not entirely unheard of.

"Put simply, something was blocking the light of this star. And how unpredictable the dips in the light were! It couldn't have been a planet or comets. Those rotational events fell short in explaining the data. If it had been a planet blocking the light, the duration of the dips should have only been a few hours. These light dips went on for days or weeks at a time, with no consistent pattern. Whatever was blocking the light was not strictly circular. Or singular, for that matter. You may now open your eyes.

"From the time we began observing, the dips got to be more drastic. From the variables in duration and brightness, we concluded that whatever is blocking the star must be as large if not larger than the star itself. A baffling discovery, to be sure. After debunking every known astrophysical conclusion, we had to admit we had stumbled upon something new. Our hypothesis was that it had to be something undiscovered and we sent probes to the area. To our astonishment, we discovered a remnant of a derelict extraterrestrial relic—some technology not created by us.

"On Earth, humans harvested the power of the sun by way of photovoltaics. Capturing the sun's heat and converting it to electricity. That process, though a step up from previous forms of energy cultivation, can only capture a tiny percentage of the sun's energy. This alien structure was built in space by a civilization *millions* of years ahead of us. It is what we'd call a Dyson Sphere. A module assembled around this star to harvest solar energy for use by this alien race.

"The star in question is intact, but the Dyson Sphere has been torn asunder. We found a piece of this old Dyson Sphere floating around a vast distance away from the others. We came to learn that it could be explored. The confirmation of this discovery is what first triggered Arqa's mission. We call this isolated portion of the Dyson Sphere B3."

Murmurs overtook the room. Tanya silenced them.

"Now I'm sure you're assuming the L'rias built B3. Get that out of your head. They didn't. We call the builders of B3 the Prior Race. They're an entirely separate species. We know much less about them. Given the evidence, I think it's safe to say the Prior Race reached their own Technological Singularity. Created a non-biological intelligence. In doing so, they accomplished what we have not. Though it is dormant, we believed the answers we sought for the survival of humanity and all life were within. The nature of this thing is very hard to describe. It is, though defunct and drifting, very much habitable. Not only that, but while inside, one can go on indefinitely without eating or sleeping. Though we do not yet understand why. Another thing we know (though, again, not the how) is it has *pulled* us to it. Arqa's propulsion could not have made it this far out on its own merits. B3 knew we were coming. It has helped us along, creating some kind of bend in space-time. Instead of the hundreds of years it was supposed to take us, it took thirteen. But the L'rias hopped on this cosmic express lane after us. The good news is, we don't think B3 cares for them very much.

"If you're wondering why are you only being given this information now, well... it was always known you kids would need to be the ones to enter into B3 first. We have discerned various messages and imperatives left behind by the Prior Race. Let's just say the way we did it was the way we had to do it. Inside that place are secrets mankind hasn't the intellect to even ask about." Mark paused, then threw up his arms in a sudden fit of enthusiasm. "So I hope you're all ready for some fun! The next step in the process I just mentioned is a second expedition into B3, which I will be leading."

Chapter Three

1. DEPOSITION OF THE TESTIMONY OF CARLOS SUÁREZ

A.   Yes, I said it was a blur. Most everything was a blur.

Q.   Most?

A.   I remember little things. It was traumatizing. The room we were in, if you could call it that, it was—it, like, folded up. As if it wanted to crush us. Can we take a break?

Q.   Listen so, you have to answer my question completely first. You don't understand how vital this information is.

A.   Quit fucking with me. So what if I don't answer? Things couldn't be worse for me as it is.

Q.   You seem on edge. We believe sharing your experiences will make you more comfortable. Help you process. Is your proximity to Lyda the issue? All you need to do is answer all my questions and we can be done with this. We can get you away from her. Your current attitude is only going to prolong your situation.

A.   Fine. What do you want to know?

Q.   Would you say you feel threatened by Lyda?

A.   Look, I've known Lyda for a long time. I had to help her get gum out of her hair once. She was a good kid. But then, that day in B3, it was like she got possessed. I suppose it was for the best, right? At the time, when she left us, we had no idea how screwed Arqa was then. At the time—you know, I've already told you this, it feels like we're going around in circles.

Q.   Do you think you are, Carlos?

A.   I know I am.

Q.   Even though you have limited
memories of what took place?

A.   It's—I don't know. It's like I
fell asleep.

Q.   But you had to have been awake
to pilot your Spaero and return to Arqa,
correct?

A.   Yes.

Q.   You said it's like you fell
asleep.   Like the Sleeping Sickness?

A.   I didn't have the Sleeping
Sickness.

Q.   What you imagine it'd be like,
then?

A.   Look, the best I can do is tell
you, I mean—there are some things we know
for sure now. Reeve, Eric, they died.
The rest of us, we found a way out.

Q.   Millie too, right?

A.   Oh, right. Yeah. Well, like I said already, that happened before. That was the first thing that happened in a long list of fucked-up things.

Q.   You said the place was like a maze. But you must have found your ship again somehow. So you got lost, then you found your way back?

A.   I think Lyda got a hang of that place. As my uncle would say, "it took a shine to her." I think, if Lyda hadn't been there, maybe we wouldn't be having this conversation. That's what you're really asking, right? If Lyda hadn't been there, we all probably would have died.

Q.   Now it seems like you're telling me Lyda isn't dangerous. Which is it?

A.   After what she did, the power

she channeled, we both know I can't say she isn't dangerous. I mean, it was self-defense though, right? She had to save Arqa. We couldn't have just let the ship be taken. Then me and the others, we'd be trapped on B3 forever, although...

Q. What? Please finish what you were going to say there.

A. I don't think Lyda would have minded that. Staying, I mean.

Q. Say more about that.

A. I already did. You asked me these questions yesterday. She was trying to find her mother.

Q. So she never did?

A. I don't know, did she? I don't recall seeing the lady myself.

2.

Carlos was processing Mark's explanation. Was that what Miss Siannon had been trying to tell them that day in the classroom? What Leni and Uncle Antonio had been rebelling against? He hadn't even heard from his uncle since after getting back. There was doubt as to if he ever would again, considering the man's part in the mutiny. Carlos hadn't been privy to his uncle's activities, though they'd asked him all the same. As much as he wanted to feel sympathy for his uncle's cause, he couldn't stop thinking about Paiyan. Leni had done that. As if losing people from the L'rias wasn't bad enough. It should have never led to such extremism.

The last few weeks in the Gaze Room had been horrendous. They slept on cots, all the while knowing Lyda was there, fuming and thrashing, unable to sleep.

The dim light on the side panel of the transport flashed as Carlos trailed the line with his fingers. He was squished in with Trisalyn, James O'Malley, Connel, Theo, Vanessa, and Mark's assistant, Rayna. Oliver was piloting the transport. As far as he knew, Lyda was staying behind. That made him nervous. As disconcerting as her presence was, having her on this expedition would have made him feel safer.

Today, the mission was to get the Spaeros they had found upon landing and drive them to Arqa. They needed every ship they could get.

Mark was a very elusive man. Carlos's uncle had told him that Mark was best avoided. Then there was Rayna. Carlos had seen her around before, though this was the first time he'd seen under her veil. With those scars, he could understand why she usually concealed her face.

Trisalyn was the one to cut through the oppressive silence. "Rayna, Mark said we don't know a lot about the builders of B3."

Rayna nodded.

"Will you tell us more?"

"Don't give me too much credit. I'm like you. See, I didn't know about B3 until that day either."

"Well, what was it he called the builders of B3?"

"The Prior Race."

Carlos and Trisalyn had grown closer over the past few weeks, stuck in the Gaze Room together. She was now the highest ranking person in Flight Division, below 2nd LT Lucio.

"How do birds know how to migrate?" Rayna asked in return. "How does an infant know to swallow water without choking? Life learned how to get what it needs a long time ago. The how of it is an uninteresting, meaningless question to ask."

"Real profound," said Connel. "But what else you got?"

Rayna frowned at him. "Humanity wanted to survive a devastated Earth and B3 became the answer. Given the evidence, Mark believes the Prior Race lived and died, most likely millions of years ago."

"Is there a connection between life on Earth and the Prior Race?" Oliver asked.

"We haven't established that concretely. From my personal beliefs, I think all life is connected throughout the universe. We seem to be in a closed system. So it makes more sense to me that if it popped up once, it probably spread as opposed to popping up in multiple isolated instances. Though I can't dismiss the latter since, once again, I'm working off of beliefs here."

Oliver furrowed their brow. "When I was in B3, I didn't feel one with the cosmos. It was very unwelcoming."

"We're morons for going back," James O'Malley said.

"Yeah, that sounds about right," Theo added.

"Guys, it's going to be fine," Rayna assured. "Trust me. Mark is very into self-preservation. He wouldn't go anywhere, let alone permit me to join if he didn't feel safe. Just remember what he said at the briefing: conjure up overall good vibes."

It was the same advice that Lyda had given. Maybe if Carlos followed it, he'd walk out of there. No, of course he would. There had to be no doubts. The other members of Flight Division were entering B3 for the first time. They had to be more nervous than he was. It was on Carlos to set the example. "Mind over matter," he said.

"Well said," Rayna said, tilting her head and smiling at Carlos.

"So what about the L'rias?" Carlos asked. "How do they fit into all of this? Did they do something to the Prior Race?"

Rayna shook her head. "No, the Prior Race was much older and more advanced. The L'rias were trying to prevent humans from reaching B3. You know why now. It's our only option to beat them."

He peered out of the window as the conversation went on without him. Space hadn't looked the same since they'd reached B3. It was still black, but just a tad bit brighter outside. Periodically, a series of ripples pulsed across the sky. The netted structure known as the Erstveil. It stretched out beyond B3. To where the L'rias's ship was waiting.

Carlos's mind wandered back to what it always did: girls. He'd been wondering if he had a shot with Trisalyn. That was his motivation. Why he willed himself to be positive and have a successful mission. Maybe from now on, Carlos could enjoy himself.

Chapter Four

1. DEPOSITION OF THE TESTIMONY OF LYDA HALL

A.   You said how do I feel about it all?

Q.   Yes. This hasn't been an easy experience for you. For any of us. How have you been feeling? Better since that day? Or worse?

A.   I don't know. How should I be feeling?

Q.   When you returned to the group in B3, Oliver wanted to hurt you because they thought you were responsible for all the unfortunate events that had transpired. Is that right?

A.   Precisely.

Q.   Were you?

A.   No.

Q.   The others said Oliver went to slap you and you didn't even flinch. Is that true?

A.   I knew they weren't going to follow through with it.

Q.   They couldn't carry through with harming a child?

A.   (WITNESS shakes head.)

Q.   Lyda, I'm going to keep reminding you about giving audible responses. Shaking your head isn't enough.

A. Yep. I could tell.

Q. Wow. Was it like you saw the future?

A.   Almost. I had a feeling, more like.

Q.   That's really interesting. Incredible, really.

A.   I wouldn't say that. I resent it. But now, all that, it's a part of my

```
life. My words. My feelings. I'll have

to manage. I lost Josie in there. Just

when I thought I had that place down.

It's so funny to me. If I was the one in

charge of things around here, I'd be

prohibiting myself from ever going back to

B3.
```

2.

Last time, B3 had pulled Carlos in harshly. This time, the landing was smooth, with Oliver in control the entire time. Carlos savored the tranquility. After disembarking from the transport, he looked around. This was the same place as last time. Where he had found the others and the ships. Where that monster had murdered Millie.

It's fine, he told himself. *She got hysterical. You survived. You will again. It's all going to be alright.*

2nd LT Lucio ordered everyone into formation. Carlos couldn't help but disengage from Lucio's words to watch Mark, who was doing cartwheels with Rayna. So B3 was just one part that had broken off from a Dyson Sphere. He wondered what it had been like when it was whole and drawing power from its star.

"Private Suárez!" 2nd LT Lucio called out.

"Me?" Carlos asked. "Oh. Uhm…"

"I asked what your assessment was. You with us, Private? Mind on the mission!"

He wasn't sure what to say. "The landing, well, it was different from before. Better. I liked it more. I knew what to expect now, see."

"Wow," Mark said. "I never thought I'd see it with my own

eyes. Let alone bounce around in it." To 2nd LT Lucio, he said, "Don't be so stiff, Tanya. Military decorum is a futile sentiment in here, I told you that. Let the troops marvel. Let yourself marvel! I know we have a timetable, but I'd say a moment to take all this majesty is in order, don't you?"

"Marvel all you want, Mark," 2nd LT Lucio said. "We have things to do. Please continue, Private."

"Right," said Carlos. "So last time, it felt like being captured. I didn't want to come here. B3 parked our ships then we reconvened. Saw these other ships. None of them would take off, so we ended up exploring. Lyda did that thing she did and when we came back, our ships were operable again."

"Mark has suggested, as ridiculous as it sounds, that all we have to do is will the ships to leave and they will."

"I mean, it's worth a try," said Trisalyn. "But like Carlos just said, when we first got here, we weren't able to get any ships off the ground. Why was that, Mark?"

"I like to think it was your collective shock and confusion," Mark speculated. "Keep any of that out of your mind as you try again. Before, it was Lyda's certainty that helped you navigate and ultimately leave once her task was done. Hold fast to the certainty of your success."

"Does anyone from the first expedition have anything else they want to add before we extract these ships?" 2nd LT Lucio asked. "O'Malley? Vanessa?"

No one did, so they fell out, splitting up to attend to different Spaeros. Carlos approached Mark, who was now working on a holo-screen. "Hey, I'm sorry to bother you, Antonio is my uncle. What's going to happen to him?"

Mark's jubilation collapsed into a sour expression. "Your uncle did a bad thing. But I'm not the one who gets to say what will happen to him. Someone back on Arqa has that answer so please, don't dwell on it here. We've got to keep that anxious energy to a minimum, so stay on task, mate! Look at it this way: we're here. You're already halfway done! Now, please shoo." Mark waved him off, returning his attention to the holo-screen.

Carlos was about to say more, but Rayna stepped between the two of them. "You heard the man. Carlos, Mark is very busy right now. Breaking his concentration could make us all float, freeze, or choke. He's trying to find out the source of B3's life support systems."

"What?" Carlos asked incredulously.

"She's being sarcastic, but her main point of me being preoccupied is true," Mark said. "Good day. See you back on Arqa another time."

Rayna swept an arm over Carlos's shoulders and led him away. "He was very patient with you. Lucky you, catching him in such an auspicious mood. I can tell this place suits him."

"Rayna, what are you doing?" Mark asked as he unpacked some folders from a backpack. "You need to stay near me."

"I'll be right back. I have an idea of how to start these Spaeros. It'll take two minutes and if it doesn't work, well, I'll be back."

The man growled but said no more.

"Mark doesn't like people," Rayna explained to Carlos. "Everyone's got their character flaws, right? Anyway, it's best if you didn't speak to him ever again. Oh, wait, no. That's not it. Better put, if *he* has to have a word with you, have it, but no more."

"Who are you to tell me I can't ask about my uncle?" Carlos asked, trying to wrest himself from her arm. She reinforced it and he gave up. No telling what a struggle back and forth with the girl would do in here.

"Oh, no, on the contrary. You can do as you like. It's just Mark is also doing as he likes and I am telling you that includes not being a conducive receptacle for your questions. I was informing, not forbidding you."

"Whatever." Carlos realized they'd been walking for some time rather close together. "I won't bother your boss. You can let go of it. And me."

"Of course, sorry." She relinquished her grip. "Anyway, what's yours?"

"Huh?"

"Your character flaw?"

Carlos thought immediately of how horny he was all the time. That was best kept to himself. "It seems like you're going to get in trouble, Rayna. Maybe you should go back?"

"Uh-uh. Remember what I said? I have an idea. I have a feeling you'll have no luck."

"Hey, what makes you say that?"

"I worded that poorly, oops. Look, let me try a thing, okay?"

"Fine."

They reached an unoccupied Spaero.

As he opened the hatch, Carlos looked down at her. They stared at one another for a moment. Carlos felt awkward. "So, what's your idea?"

"Just get in this one and wait," she said.

Carlos did as the girl asked. The engine started, but the ship wouldn't move, as if some unidentified force was keeping it fixed in place. Just like before. He put on the vis-cap and scanned the area. The infrared cam was the same interface as any Spaero from Arqa. He saw swaths of heat signatures and engines from the ships, but nothing was getting off B3's surface.

He suddenly thought back to before. The first time in B3.

"Any good?" Rayna asked from below.

"Negative," Carlos said. He felt glad she was there. The thought of being alone in here discomforted him. Wait, maybe that's why she actually went off with him. Maybe she preferred to be around him because of his previous experiences. Wasn't that the consciousness he had been projecting since landing? Could she have picked up on it? That's how it had felt last time, with Carlos himself being drawn to Lyda's energy.

Something crashed below him.

"What are you doing?"

"I spilled a toolbox!" Rayna responded. "Hang on, I'm coming up."

"Wait, you can't do that, there's no room."

"Just wanted to check in," Rayna said, her head poking through the aperture just under him.

"Did you hear me? You won't be able to get much further."

"Maybe if you scrunched."

"Scrunched?"

"Made yourself smaller. A little ball or something like that."

"Did you want to try that idea you had? I can get out, you

know."

"Uhm…" she said, advancing further into the cockpit. What the hell was she doing?

"Rayna, wait. I want to get out. Don't you see how cramped this cockpit is?"

"Oh, sure!" She made her way back down, and Carlos slid out of the seat. As he descended, he felt a hand grabbing at him, fumbling around until—

"What are you doing?" Carlos asked, his cheeks going flush. One of her hands had clamped down on his groin.

"I already told you, I'm checking in. remember?"

He could feel a primal stirring within him. The hand didn't move. He didn't know what to do besides feel a wave of nervous. But in that wave there was also desire. Something he'd wanted more than anything else. No one had ever touched him there before.

Then she let him go. "Oops, I'm so sorry. I didn't see where I was reaching. Are you okay? Here, come on down." Rayna rushed down the ladder.

"Okay?" Carlos asked shakily. He made his way out of the cockpit. "Come off it, you meant to do that. You saw what you were doing."

"No! Of course not. I'm super embarrassed. What did I do?"

Carlos's mind sped through an explanation for her behavior. Her denial irritated him. "You held your hand way too long for that to be an accident!"

"What? What was I touching?" Rayna had an oblivious tone to her voice. "Just come down. I'm really sorry."

Carlos took off the vis-cap and did as she asked.

While descending the ladder, Rayna jumped up to grab him. The weight of her caused him to lose his footing. The two of them went tumbling to the surface below. It wasn't a far fall, but Carlos didn't have time to brace himself. He landed right on top of her.

Scrambling up, he caught a look of amusement on Rayna's face. That angered him. Quietly, Carlos said, "Stop, stop. There are people around. We need to get back to work. Why are you giggling? That hurt, you know!" He surveyed the immediate area.

There were a few Spaeros nearby, some people milling about, but none were paying any attention to them.

"No fun? No games?" Rayna said as she sprawled her limbs out on the surface of B3. It dispelled any ambiguity in her actions. She had a nice body. Why hadn't he seen her in this way before?

He had to snap out of it. He got up, but she remained on the surface.

"What are you thinking right now?" she asked, her hand pulling one of his arms back toward her. "It's normally a very private thing, isn't it? No need to be bashful, Carlos. This place brings out the truth, wouldn't you say? What's the use in hiding it?"

Looking away from her, he said, "If you must know, I'm feeling anxious. It's not playtime, you heard Lucio and Mark. We have to try and get these ships out of here and go back home."

"Maybe they did say that. Thing is, I'm a terrible listener."

The way she had said that deepened his feeling of uneasiness. He stepped away from the girl still splayed out below him. Then the place he was in *changed*. Instead of the room with all the ships, Carlos found himself in an abnormally familiar location: the space where he'd go in VR to meet with Faeleen.

"Hey Carlos," Rayna said, standing up while patting her hat off. "Good point about the people. Is this better? Just us, alone again. Yeah, so sorry you haven't heard from me in a while. It's been pretty busy the last couple of weeks, hasn't it?"

Chapter Five

1.

Will and his Grammy exchanged tense looks. "Before you start in with your little spiel," Will said, "would it be possible if we could just skip it? I have a feeling I know everything you're going to say. But you might be surprised by what *I* have to say. Let's switch it up, just once. I'll do the talking and you do the listening. How does that sound?"

"No," she said sternly. "I'm not awarding recalcitrance."

"I know. Look, I need you to tell me how I can do the most good! Especially after that encounter with Gabriel. How'd he do that? B3? If you have any idea, you need to tell me. How did he talk to me if he was vitrified?"

"Gabriel has some connection to B3," his Grammy explained. "I understand little beyond that."

"But you had some idea of it? All this stuff I heard earlier, about not telling us, it hurts."

"It was never supposed to concern you in your time. This has been a sudden change for everyone."

"But when you learned we'd be approaching this thing much sooner, you *still* didn't tell me. You acted like Gabriel was crazy and put him away. What the hell?"

"Hysteria is a very dangerous thing. Our best chance for survival was to leave Flight Division in ignorance. That is what we were instructed to do. Send children to B3 that first time without telling them what it was."

"I'm not a child, though. I'm older than most of them. You could have told me."

"Everything is happening like it's supposed to," she assured him. "There is a plan laid out by the Prior Race we must follow." His Grammy summoned a holo-screen. "And yes. You are almost an adult. But you're still not fully mature and—"

"Fuck off!"

"Use anymore of that earthly language, and I won't speak with you at all. This anger you're feeling, it's quite unfounded. Let me remind you: I keep us alive. Yet you keep doubting me."

"You don't keep *all* of us alive. Paiyan and all the other dead kids could have told you that."

"We are in a war. Enough foolishness. We are trying to stop the L'rias at any cost. That had to happen so that the rest of us could have a chance at survival, a chance B3 has granted us."

Will balled up his hands into fists. "Maybe so. But Gabriel told me B3 is more dangerous than the L'rias. And I get the feeling he knows more than you do."

"No, Will. You're mistaken."

Will resisted the urge to lose his temper again. "It's always someone else's perception that's off, isn't it, Grammy? Well, you said it yourself: you don't have control over the situation. Jeez, it's like, I don't want to be fighting with you. I just need you to know something. I don't think I can trust you... the way you act is just disgusting to me."

"There is no other option, Will. You keep forgetting the fact that we had nowhere else to go. No future. B3 gave us hope. It was proof there was life out there that had accomplished what we need to: artificial general intelligence. Earth was only a starting point for our species." His Grammy brought her hands close to her chest. "You know what? I don't need to justify my decisions to you. Why am I wasting my time? Your trust is not as important to me as your life." Will could tell she was struggling to keep her composure. This was a rare occurrence. He'd reach past her outer layers, the 'Captain Sali' persona into her being, the woman beneath the leading. That person seen less frequently as he got older. "Oh, Will," she said, forlorn. "I had this same conversation with your mom a long time ago."

"What?" Will asked, taken aback.

"She died for nothing. Refusing to trust me, she ran out into an unsafe mission I told her not to take on. Remember Will, ignorance is permitted only until the point where you notice it. Deliberate wrongness is the most dangerous earthly notion there is."

Will snapped. What audacity the woman had, to reduce his mother to a cautionary tale. Where he saw an orderly corner or a decorated shelf, he overturned it. His woman did not stop him as he rampaged her office, only watched, seeming indifferent to it all.

"I accept your anger," she proclaimed. "And I still love you. B3 will nurture you long after I'm gone. And someday, you will understand."

His mind went to the horrors he'd felt at that first glimpse of B3. She must be insane. This entire ship was led by mad scientists tampering with things far beyond them. That's what Arqa was. And Will never had a choice in the matter. He was born into this, raised to think it was all normal. This realization brought Will to tears. He left, bound for anything to keep his mind away from the understanding she would not give.

2.

Callum detected a musty odor as he set down a chair just outside of Leni's cell. "How'd you get that in there?" Callum asked, waving his hand to redirect the smoke tapering through the air from several incense sticks. It had little effect.

"I had to do something to cultivate the proper energies," Leni said in a low voice. "These lights are not up to my standards."

"Okay, okay. Listen so, we have let the kids out." He sat down.

"To return to B3. Not much of a consolation."

"Yeah, well, you mentioned you'd be more cooperative once we let them out," Callum reminded. "We've been grinding you down for weeks, and credit where credit is due, you haven't budged."

"You *could* always torture me, you know." She snickered. "But keep in mind while my body may be held, my spirit cannot be arrested." Leni was exhibiting many signs of spacesia. She'd always been eccentric, but Callum had to keep reminding himself that Leni had orchestrated a hostage situation, and had somehow controlled Siannon's body. The details of that were being uncovered. Supposedly, it was a device crafted by Antonio Suárez, made unbeknownst to those on Arqa. Siannon had been the first and hopefully only victim of that thing. "It's like I told you. I want to cooperate." She looked directly at him. "I want *us* to cooperate."

"You know what you need to do to make that happen,"

Callum said.

Callum leaned back in his chair as she met his eyes enthusiastically. "You want to know more about Gabriel?"

"That'd be a great start, but you know I'm far more interested in Dominique."

"Oh, I love talking about her as well."

"Go on…"

Leni brought a hand up. Looking as if she were about to touch him, Callum set himself further back. She snickered again. "One thing for another." She got up, spreading her arms out to embrace the bars. "But first let me explain to you something of great importance."

Callum relaxed. "Go on. What are you waiting for?"

"I know what you think of me. Your assessment. But doesn't Sali have a bigger body count than me? Not that I'm bitter! The universe decided I should be here, so here I am. And I know you yourself have more wiggle room after experiencing B3. Even so, you're nowhere near where you need to be. It's really sad. Maybe that's why Congo kept running away from you." He hadn't told her about that. "Yes, I'm not who you thought I was at all. You're still processing that. In the meantime, I'll answer your bad questions today. On the condition that you bring Siannon out of stasis. I need to see her here, in the flesh."

Callum shook his head. "Nope. Out of the question. You were controlling her."

"That was a temporary hold. Her body has long since digested the mechanism that Antonio used. She's her own girl by now. I just want her free again."

"What you did, it was too much for her to handle. She asked us to be vitrified, we didn't make her. Don't you think she deserves a rest?"

"No. Life's tough. She'll get over it. What she needs is to be alive, not sitting in a tank. How I hate vitrification. It's worse than death."

"I would have to disagree with you there." Callum brought a hand to his cheek and dug a fingernail into the flesh.

"This ship is suffering without Siannon, Callum," Leni said. "Don't you miss her?"

Callum grunted. "Stop. It's not happening."

"Everything you wish to learn from me, I got from Dominique. About B3." She gave him a quizzical look.

"And where did she get that information? Were you both working against Arqa's interests this whole time?"

"Hardly, Callum. Dominique is a mother first. She wouldn't do anything to put her daughter in jeopardy. No, don't be ridiculous. We're not some spies of the enemy. We were people escaping, genuinely drawn to Arqa's mission. But as time went on, we saw the impurity of what we'd been told. Dominique was always further out in the atmosphere than I was. But she's not around. Let me tell you about Gabriel. He is clairvoyant. A power that activated that day in the Gaze Room."

"Clairvoyant?" Callum asked. "What's that mean?"

"The simplest way to put it is he can see beyond his immediate physical surroundings. Beyond his senses. He can remotely transmit his awareness to other places. With intense focus, he could do more. All this by the means of B3."

"Dominique explained this all to you?"

"Which she learned in dreams. Most of it came out like babbling. So hard to discern. You think I'm bad? Try getting something out of her when she was in one of those trances."

"Leni, did she tell you she was going away? Or where?"

Leni looked down. "No, Callum. I know we like to have our fun. And I lie at times for my safety, but this bit is the truth."

"Why volunteer that you sometimes lie?"

"I've said enough. What's to become of Siannon?"

Callum crossed his arms. "She's your friend. I get it. Although, she did betray you. Is waking her up your idea of vengeance or something? What's your angle?"

"For all my negative traits, spitefulness is not one of them. I forgive Siannon. She's her own woman. She believed stopping me was the right thing to do. In turn, I feel leaving her in stasis is wrong. Make the call. Give her her life back."

"You sound guilty for how it turned out with her."

Leni shrugged. "Guilty of what Dominique told me to do."

Frustrated, Callum said, "Look, I just want us all to be on the same page. Don't we want the same things? Consider Lyda. All the risks she took to find her mother."

"That unfortunate girl. Cosmic powers without context. That's it. You've disturbed me. I am taking a talkfast until I know Siannon is back in commission."

Just when we were getting somewhere, Callum thought.

Chapter Six

1. DEPOSITION OF THE TESTIMONY OF CARLOS
SUÁREZ

A.   Can I ask you something?

Q.   No, Carlos. This is your
debriefing. We're here to get
information, not give it. Now then, what
became of Eric?

A.   He was split in two. Each of
them was talking to us, claiming that he
was not the replica. It was stressful.
I'd taken care of my own replica by
myself. That's about when Lyda came back.
Looking years older. Her clothes were
ripped up, she'd grown right out of them.
Trisalyn shared some of her own. It was
really weird seeing Lyda like that. She
hadn't been gone long. I can't say,
between a half-hour or maybe an hour? She
was… taller.

Q.   I asked about Eric, Carlos.

A.   Right. Right. Of course. It was Vanessa. She just went ballistic. She jumped at him with a knife, slitting his throat. Then she did the same thing to the other one. Both bodies bled out as you might expect. We thought her doing that would cause some reaction from B3, but I think it was—like almost as if it was spent after Lyda's attack on the L'rias.

Q.   So both Erics, when they died, they seemed human?

A.   Yes. It wasn't like with my replica. I believe they both were Eric. The place had cloned him somehow. That didn't matter to Vanessa. It was too weird for her. Lyda seemed very displeased with Vanessa's actions and almost left her behind.

Q.   But you all reached some agreement? I mean, everything's been peaceful since then?

A.   Lyda scares me now, but at the same time, I feel bad for her. By the way, we don't have peace.

Q.   What do you mean by that?

A.   It's all appearances. Things seem peaceful, placid. They're not. As long as we're near B3, things will never be peaceful. We're just far enough away from the facts to see the real picture. Like Earth. From a distance, Earth would appear peaceful too, I bet.

2.

"You're Faeleen?" Carlos asked. He was afraid to look away from her. Examining the building behind him and the sky above left him stupefied. It was just like the VR on Arqa, only a little different. They couldn't be in VR, neither of them had on viscaps. Yet everywhere he looked, the simulation was crisp, with no sign of the prevailing structure of B3.

Rayna nodded. "You won't find a single detail off in this projection. It's just like where we used to meet." Her mouth did not move, but he heard her voice again. *Privacy is quite a tricky thing to hold on to here in B3.*

It was possible for a person to send a thought via their IC to another's IC. It was like a mental text message. Only, ICs didn't work in B3. That message had not been via IC. She had sent a thought *straight* to him telepathically. "No, no, don't do that!" he protested. "Talk to me normally."

"Fine."

"Yeah, so this is all too much right now. I can't—"

"You never suspected me, did you?" Rayna stomped her foot onto a patch of grass next to the sidewalk. "I'm so good!"

"No," Carlos admitted. "I never thought it was you. It's not like I see you around."

"I know. You don't think of me at all. I get it. We've lived on the same ship most of our lives and we weren't ever properly introduced. Well, I was tired of feeling isolated! So I reached out to you. Took a little tweaking, but I have a lot of downtime."

Carlos struggled to maintain his composure. "Please, wherever we are, take us back with everyone else. We don't want to be alone in here. Something bad could happen. When people freak out in B3, things, they—" Rayna brought her left hand up and reached for his face. Carlos recoiled. "Rayna!"

"Carlos, freak out to your heart's content. Don't withhold a thing. We're in a special part of B3 that you haven't seen before. And nobody's coming to make you feel better but me, so take that for what it's worth."

"I don't know how you're doing this, but I want to go back to the others. They've got to be worried about us. This is—this is wild. Lyda wasn't even able to change the space around her like this."

The girl let out a high-pitched laugh. "Come on, Carlos. All you ever wanted was sex. You pleaded for it constantly. To see who I was in person. To get out of your responsibilities in Flight Division. It took me some time, but you're welcome. Truth be told, I didn't think you'd be this ungrateful. Maybe this will help?"

She slowly began undressing.

He'd been so vulnerable with Faeleen... Rayna. What an idiot he'd been! This girl was out of her mind. "But you mocked me. You know? We were supposed to meet that day and you left that awful drawing of me in that locker. Then I never hear from you again! What was that about?"

"You were the one who was unreachable. How was I supposed to catch up with you when you've been quarantined in the Gaze Room?"

"You hurt me a lot doing that," Carlos said. This was all wrong. Rayna, the scarred girl now naked and approaching him. When she caressed his neck, he braced himself against the building's wall. Then he shifted away, the two of them leaning against the wall side by side.

"Again: I thought this is what you wanted," Rayna said. "I went through a lot of trouble for you. All based on your begging. Now your begging has a different quality."

"Just bring us back and we can talk more later."

"Ah. Well, consent is important. Are you just concerned they'll find us in the middle of things or what? They won't. No one will be able to until I want to be found."

"Just... why now?"

"When else? You want to try sneaking around the ship and getting caught? Mark keeps tabs on me. He can't do that here. If you want what you said you did all those times, it'll need to be here. So?"

"Okay. Listen: this is very much a case of too much, too soon. It doesn't exactly put me in the mood. Rayna, I saw people die in here... you know, when things got too intense. Emotions amping up. Do you get what I'm saying?"

Rayna slid in closer, wrapping her arms around him. There *was* something arousing about her, but when she tried to take off his g-suit, Carlos squirmed. "Just concentrate," she said. "We have to do it now. Think! Mark and the others don't know I can project a place like this."

"He doesn't?"

Rayna shook her head. "If we go back now, he'll make some dumb rule. And I have to follow his rules... like no more juggling."

Carlos hated this. He had grown to resent Faeleen, assuming it had all been a cruel prank orchestrated by one of his classmates. But now that he knew it was Rayna… he did pity the girl for having to be alone with Mark all the time. But those feelings didn't matter while she had this power over him. If he couldn't go through with what she had in mind, would she lose her temper?

"There you go again, Carlos!" Rayna said with disapproval. She returned to telepathic thought. *Your emotions are spilling all over me. I can hear everything you're thinking. Yeah, Rayna, the weird girl. Covers her hideous face and squeaks more than she talks. When I was Faeleen, I was much more attractive.* She scowled, stepping off the wall and putting her g-suit back on.

Carlos brought up his hands in defense. "This isn't fair. I deserve to have my thoughts stay in my head. How come I can only hear yours when you want me to?"

"I'm smarter than you. Get it? Yes, power over you is right. And no, I don't want to lose my temper. I just can't believe you'd chicken out on me at the moment of truth."

He tried to think clearly. How had she done all of this? Well, they were in B3, so she must have willed it. If he willed that he was back with the others, then maybe—

"That won't work," Rayna said. "Your intentions have to be stronger than mine."

"You want to keep me trapped here more than I want to leave?"

"Exactly." She poked his nose with a finger. "Meaning there's a part of you that wants it. Wants this."

"Duh! I want it, just not here."

"I just told you, it's here or nowhere."

"Well, I don't know what you expect me to do. You know how I feel."

"After all those weeks of complaining. 'Oh, I don't want to die a virgin, we could be gone any minute.' Put your money where your mouth is!"

"You can't pressure me like this. It's wrong."

"Oh, and when you were pressuring me whenever we'd meet in VR, nothing was wrong with that?"

Before Carlos could defend himself, Rayna hushed him.

"You upset me back then, Carlos."

"So it's eye for an eye?" Carlos asked.

Rayna paced away from him. He watched her butt in the g-suit, his mind grinding against madness. "I know what this is *really* about. You can't get away with half-truths in here. It's disappointing. You wanted—" Rayna snapped her fingers and the Faeleen avatar took her place. She was nude. "I can do it, Carlos. I can look like this while you fuck me."

"RAYNA, ENOUGH! I'm not cool with this, okay? Okay?"

Rayna frowned. "Is that not good enough for you? How about?" She snapped her fingers again. A cloud from the sky descended, morphing into a sphere of bright light. He thought he heard the sounds of an angelic chorus.

When the sphere made contact with the street, it dissipated to reveal someone in a g-suit laying down. Carlos couldn't believe it. "That can't be—is that really Kalyna?"

"Yep. Safe and sound. You had a crush on her before, right? Not me. *Her.*"

Carlos rushed down to check on the girl's condition. "Kalyna, are you okay?" he asked, shaking her. She was breathing, but not conscious. He noticed some burn marks on her cheeks.

"She's been through a lot, a bit worse for wear. Not as much as me. My scars are permanent. Hers will heal. See, B3 spared her a horrid fate."

"I can't believe it. Her family is going to be so happy. 2nd LT Lucio reported her dead. How is she alive?"

"This is who you really want, isn't it? More your speed?"

"Excuse me?"

"You don't have to admit it. I know."

"Rayna, you just did something amazing. We need to get her back to Arqa."

"What is it about her and not me?"

"For one, you're pushing my boundaries. It doesn't matter who it's with, I don't want to lose my virginity in B3. Now take us back!"

Rayna only gazed at him in puzzlement, then changed from the naked Faeleen form into her actual body. Thank goodness she was not longer naked. "Not just yet." She wagged a finger at him. "Human history is much darker than you could ever imagine. You're acting virtuous now. Say I was to leave? Keep the two of you in here, in this little pocket. You wouldn't starve or sleep. She would be your only comfort. Her body. How long would it take, do you think? I mean, to change your tune? Lots of frightening possibilities there."

"What the fuck is wrong with you?" Carlos asked with unrestrained hostility.

"Hmm. Not a smart idea to ask such a stupid question. I'd say I'm socially awkward. Anyway, it's just a thought experiment. I'd never actually do a thing like that. But you still need to answer me. Answer me, respond thoughtfully, and we can go."

Carlos felt utter revulsion. He stood back up. "I would never violate someone like that."

"You watched her once, though. With her friend. Yes. That Felicia. They didn't know. But you stared. And you took the staring home with you like a present. You owned a part of them they didn't give you willingly. You little sneak, you still rub yourself off to that stolen moment that wasn't for you. Trying to sprinkle that beauty onto your own loneliness. Just admit it wouldn't be that different... you'd do most anything you could get away with. Say it. Then we can go."

"Fuck you!" Carlos yelled.

"That's what I wanted. Get to be outrageous. Let's spice this place up." Rayna formed fists. "Do you want to hurt me back? You won't love me now that you've met me, but I can defend myself against you." She punched the air near him. "Physically, philosophically." The fist melted away as she brought her fingers to his chest. "Sexually."

"Rayna. Please. I just don't want anybody to get hurt. If I just agree with you—"

"Genuinely," Rayna said through clenched teeth.

"Genuinely..." Carlos said. He was fighting against a lump in his throat. "What is it? You want me to say humans are evil or something?"

Rayna nodded. "The evil in yourself, you shouldn't fear it simply because you can't hold it back. We have inherited B3. It's not for the narrow-minded. The Captain Salis of the world. Just look at Kalyna here! They left her for dead. This girl is just a few years younger than me. Arqa did nothing for her. Humanity saw fit to see her go. All for lofty ideas. And yet B3 spared her. Her and you, Carlos."

He felt like their conversation was becoming productive.

"At last. Your undivided attention. I know what people really think of you, you know. But their opinions don't have to matter, only mine is valuable if you'd just let go. Will you be with me here and now?"

"Rayna, I'm sorry, but no."

She shrugged. "Eh, you can't fault a girl for trying. I guess there's evil across the spectrum, huh?" She giggled.

Carlos tried to laugh along. "So can we go now?"

She stopped. "I dunno." She did a cartwheel while letting out a "Whee...." After she righted herself, she said, "So what if I told you I made a mistake and didn't know how to get us out of here?"

"Then I would say you and I just need to focus on getting back. If we just combine that intention, then maybe—"

"That's a terrific idea! Only, maybe I don't want to do that. Because then you might oust me for the Faeleen antics and all this stuff now. I mean, I made you afraid for your life. And to think you were SO MACHO before all that."

Above them, the sky chipped away. A curtain of darkness made it harder for Carlos to see the VR city. He steeled his mind, imagining himself long gone, light-years away from Rayna and her enchantment. "Rayna, please bring the sky back. I'd never do this to you. Please stop. I'll do whatever you want."

"Tsk, tsk, tsk. Man, it's really difficult to trust you with the present dynamic we have going on. One more time: I know what you're thinking. I can calculate the difference between what you say and what you mean."

"Was your life on Arqa that shitty you have to be like this?" The only thing Carlos could perceive now was the sound of her voice. The VR projection no longer seemed there. They were now in some kind of void.

No, I'm—it's just rough being rejected by a loser such as yourself, Rayna said. *I even tried to be the better person and bring you someone you wanted.*

More telepathy. He refused to respond like that. How he wished someone, anyone, would come to help him. Though Lyda's way of navigating B3 had been unpredictable, at least she hadn't done anything like this. "Yes. Kalyna. I want her. I want her safe and sound. That's it."

"Masturbate, right now. I think that's a fair compromise here."

"No."

"Well, let's bring up precedent: when you cut out of formation during the second battle, thinking you'd be dead soon, what did you do? You were plenty turned on then. You just kept going and going until you passed out. You didn't even bother to clean yourself up."

"Get out of my mind!" Carlos demanded. The darkness dominated everything around him. He couldn't see Rayna, Kalyna, or the city.

"For all this duality and hypocrisy, I'd say a time-out is in order," Rayna said. "Please don't be glum, though. Everyone's got to go away sometimes."

"What?" Carlos asked in a panicky whimper.

"It's just, there's a lot of really mature stuff that's going to be taking place moving forward, and I don't think your head's up for it. Maybe later. Heck, maybe you'll find your way back. That'd be a first, though."

"No! Stop, stop. If you do that, when they find me, then you'll be in real trouble!"

Though he could not see her, he knew she was shaking her head. "The next step is going to be astonishing. In the meantime, I'll just say we got separated. Even if you did somehow escape, it'll be he said, she said. They'll be so overjoyed when I have Kalyna back. They prefer her to you. See, she's an asset to Flight Division. She'll fight to the death. Not like you."

"This is all a joke," he said. "You've been joking. It's your sense of humor. Rayna, you can't do this, you—"

"Peace out; sincerely, your secret admirer."

And with that, it was done. No more words back and forth.

In the times to come, Carlos would wonder; while the moments stretched out beyond ways to measure them. Things like, what if he had not been himself? Spoken more eloquently, acted differently. What if he'd gone along with Rayna? Or better yet, killed her before she had time to prevent it (it would sicken Carlos, how that particular fantasy lent credence to her theory of humanity). He wandered aimlessly in that realm of hypotheticals and what ifs, remaining trapped.

Epilogue

Through his ceaseless trance, Gabriel would come to Lyda. Not physically, but as a voice in her mind. An encounter of his essence originating from the cryo chamber. He was all admonishment and sorrow, sympathy and severity. It was all so tiring to Lyda.

She had not slept before going to B3.

Blowing bubbles wasn't fun anymore, but it was meditative. An activity of distraction. It made it easier to ignore his voice. Though it wasn't always a sure thing.

"Why don't you bug someone else?" Lyda asked.

I care about you Lyda, Gabriel said. *Everyone is worried about you.*

"Worried about what I'm capable of, not how I'm feeling." She blew a large bubble. When she was satisfied, she swished her wrist until the bubble was free. Then she recaptured it with the wand, blowing a second bubble that combined with the first. She repeated the process. They were spheres, like stars, like planets. Why did the universe have a tendency to form spheres?

Her sheets and hands were a sticky mess, the bubbles never getting too far beyond her. Like all those minds she'd ended. Voices expired, trapped in her head. Desperate cries she could understand, piercing any chance of lucidity. And the one she hadn't dealt with.

The adults had *lied.*

B3, luminescent and strange.

You kept Arqa safe, Gabriel told her. *Now they're just returning the favor.*

"My mind is the threat." She could see him at the edge of the bed, even though he wasn't there. He seemed different. Well, so was she. "You were supposed to be in a lot of trouble, you know."

You too. You too, Lyda. Your dad was planning on grounding you. Not like this, but you understand.

"They're trying to convince me to kill the rest of the L'rias," Lyda said. "I don't think they're going to let me leave here until I do."

It wouldn't work, even if they made you try. She watched

Gabriel closely then, index finger out. He poked a bubble, and it popped. It looked as if his projection had touched it.

"You've been asleep a bit longer than I've been awake," Lyda said. "If this keeps up, I think they'll vitrify me, too." She shuddered, her muscles stiff from their sleepless exhaustion. It caused the container of bubble solution to tip over. Lyda watched Gabriel set it right.

"Wait, you're here?" Lyda asked in surprise. "Your body?"

"Mhm," said Gabriel. "In the flesh."

"You're awake again. I—I'm so out of it. What's going on? You were just a voice one minute ago and now—" Lyda felt moments and colors, hints of her preternatural connection to B3 that took her away from this discovery. To the other times Gabriel had communicated to her, only to realize this time, this was different. But she hadn't notice. What else was escaping her perception?

"You're the one who's been out of it for a while, not me." He snatched the bottle of bubbles out from under her. The doctors had told her what kind of havoc sleep deprivation had on the body. Fresh memories don't form. Hallucinations came in their place. "They let me out not too long ago. This is the first time I've checked in on you in person." Gabriel blew a stream of bubbles. "You just forgot how to fall asleep."

"I remember sleeping and dreaming, but every time I try now…" She reached out for the bottle. "Give those back."

"No problem," Gabriel said.

It *was* better having them back. So much better. "My mother, she said, don't think of it like falling… falling asleep. Flying asleep." Something was happening. "Are you?"

"Shhh," Gabriel said. "Rest." He closed his eyes. She did the same. Tears came. "Thank you, Gabriel. I'm sorry, I've been entirely irritable."

"We have the opposite problem," he said. "I was vitrified for weeks, and you couldn't fall asleep. I'll be taking these bubbles off your hands."

"Deal. Deal. Watch out… for the other shapes. There are some bubbles that aren't spherical, you know." Each successive thought she harbored became smaller and simpler. Her mind needed this. She would feel better after. Maybe B3 had not entirely extinguish the child in her after all.

Somehow, Gabriel had lifted her. Freed from weeks of all the guilt, confusion, and hatred, Lyda Hall vacated the waking world.

EPISODE 8
Condemned to Be Free

Prologue

The Nook was bustling with activity. It was early in the month, so many people were there using up their meal passes. Gabriel had accumulated several since his placement into the cryo chamber. He shuffled through the line, deciding on a double portion of lemon tahini tofu tacos.

His life since coming out of vitrification had been a muddle. Most of his time was spent in physical therapy.

He was so upset at what the adults had done. Why had they treated him like he had spacesia? All he'd been told was it had been 'the only way'. It was the unknowing that bothered him the most, the lack of specifics. Unknowing of things in his mind, unknowing of where his power came from, all of it. He was trying to be patient, as the captains had assured him things would become clearer soon, but it was hard.

Gabriel found the table where Trisalyn, James O'Malley, Theo, and Will were eating, far off from anybody else.

"It's your grandmother, Will," Trisalyn was saying as Gabriel took his seat. "Everyone falls in line with her."

"Is it?" Will asked. "Maybe you're right. Still—hi, Gabriel."

"Hi. Sorry if I interrupted something." Gabriel wasn't sure what else to say. These people had never invited him to eat together before. Until today.

Trisalyn smiled. "Little dude, we thought it was only right to make sure you were up to speed with everything that's been going on, considering how dirty they did you."

"Hmm. My foster parents already did that."

"No," said Theo. "Forget that. It'll be different from our perspective."

"Go on." Gabriel picked up a taco, taking a small bite.

James O'Malley pounded his fists on the table, rattling the dishes. "Hardly any grown-ups have been to B3. Trisalyn and I have been twice now."

"Lyda said you were there," Trisalyn said.

"Yeah... talking with her," Gabriel confirmed. "I know this sounds like a cop-out, but that's all really hazy."

"She said you tried to talk her out of it," James O'Malley said.

"Out of using it to attack the L'rias. What's up with that? Did you want to die? They would have taken the ship, moron."

"Forget about that, James," Will said. He turned to Gabriel and asked, "Do you remember talking to me?"

Gabriel gave him a blank stare, then looked down at his food. "No."

"It happened, Gabriel. The day we reached B3."

"It's like asking me to remember a dream. I feel like, when I first woke up, it was all there. What I had done, where I had been. So many places. But since then it's been harder and harder to remember. None of you have been put under before, but you must know it messes with your memory. And I shouldn't have any at all, since I was technically asleep. And yet... yeah, somehow I had this awareness. Will, you should be telling *me* what I said that day. I've already asked Lyda what I said to her."

"You're such a liar, Gabriel," James O'Malley said.

Gabriel had never liked James O'Malley. The boy had occasionally bullied Craig for being shorter than him. "If you're going to be like that, I can eat somewhere else."

"You heard about Kalyna, Gabriel?" Theo asked. "You talked to her too, helped her against the mutineers."

"I heard about that," Gabriel said.

"But you don't remember anything about it yourself?" James O'Malley asked.

Gabriel shook his head.

"I'll bet. You really want us to believe you know nothing? We thought she was dead, but it turns out she was in B3 all along. Trisalyn and me, we think that place is going to take us away, one by one."

Gabriel sighed. "Look, I have a feeling about B3. An intuition. It's not like you said. We have to beware, but it's not some monster that wants to eat us."

"Mark said it is if we think it is!" James O'Malley said, raising his voice.

"Then why would you think it's going to do bad things to us?"

"We just want to be safe," said Trisalyn.

"Then tell James not to make stuff up."

"Your feeling about B3 is just as made up as mine," James

O'Malley countered.

Trisalyn jabbed James O'Malley in the shoulder. "Quit being such a pest. We want to help each other out. We need him, remember?"

"For what?" Gabriel asked apprehensively.

"They've written Carlos off. He's missing, but I don't think anyone is trying to find him. We only found out after we brought the extra ships back to the Bay Line."

"Mark and some others are still there, though," James O'Malley pointed out.

"He's running tests," Theo said. "He doesn't give a shit about finding Carlos."

"We heard," Will said in a low conspiratorial tone, "you might be able to look. That's what you do, right?"

"I already tried," Gabriel said. "I haven't been having any luck..."

"What if you're too far away? What if you were already in B3? Would it be easier to look then?"

Gabriel shrugged.

"That's why we asked you here, Gabriel," Trisalyn said. "We're going to B3 to look for Carlos."

Gabriel shrunk in his seat. The thought of going into B3 filled him with dread, mostly because he could tell they were planning on sneaking a ship out of the Bay Line to get there. It seemed to be part of his ability. An intuition to pick up on more than what was said in conversations. "I feel like the only reason why they aren't looking is they're worried about losing more people."

"Think of it, Gabriel," Will said. "Imagine how miserable it would be, lost in that place. We can go there, ask Rayna. She might be able to point exactly where she saw him last before they got separated."

"She's attached to Mark at the hip," Theo said.

"Maybe we could make her," Trisalyn suggested.

"Just how far are you all willing to take this?" Gabriel asked. "I'm not some code breaker for B3. Even if I could project myself to search for him, I wouldn't know where to begin. That place is gigantic. And then... look, there's just too many conflicting interests at play here. And I appreciate being included, but since I got up, I haven't been at a hundred percent. I don't understand what I'm capable of. And I'd prefer not to be at the center of any mischief, all things considered."

"No good options, as usual," Will said. "I hate feeling powerless. We thought… if we had you helping us, we'd have a fair chance of finding him. This isn't how you were when you were talking in my head. What happened?"

"I couldn't tell you, Will. I don't know."

"Okay," said Trisalyn, "so we can't rely on Gabriel. We can't rely on the adults to authorize the mission. It's just us. Great. Fucking wonderful."

"If you just wait, maybe Carlos will come back," Gabriel offered. "Maybe Mark's team already found him and they're drinking tea right now. It's only been a few days since he went missing."

"This meeting is for people who care about Carlos, so why don't you buzz off?" James O'Malley asked.

When no one came to his defense, Gabriel got up despondently. "Whatever." He left them behind, finding another place to sit so he could finish his meal. What they said he could do and what he knew he could do were different. Still, he wanted to know what they were planning. From the other side of the room, he projected himself to hear their conversation.

"—had to snatch a ship, we could," Will was saying. "We'd only need a bit of leverage."

"Oh?" Theo asked. "What did you have in mind?"

"There's a secret about my grandmother. See, she has this—"

Gabriel returned to his body as he felt an ominous current of energy. Anxiety welled up in the boy, and he knew something bad was going to happen. Before he had completely returned, the Nook fell into disarray: people were keeling over all around him. Gabriel made for the exit as an alarm blared through the ship.

A notification on Gabriel's IC followed: the Sleeping Sickness was back.

Chapter One

1.

"It doesn't matter," Sali was saying over her IC to Captain De Plez. All along, her grandson's eyes watched her intently. "She has us looking like fools. If enough people listen to her, this hysteria will be unstoppable. I won't have that happen. She has two options: tell us what's happening or die."

"An execution?" Captain De Plez asked.

"Yes," she said with vigor. Leni had taken responsibility for the return of the Sleeping Sickness. With no understanding of it, Sali had to take the woman at her word.

"Grammy!" Will shouted out.

She waved a finger at him.

"Sali," Captain De Plez said, "we have no reason to believe killing her will put a stop to the Sleeping Sickness. If she's the only one who understands how it happened—"

"I told you," Sali said, "I don't care."

"You're going to need a majority, Sali. This is against the charter."

"What, are you working with her or something?" Sali asked coldly.

"No, of course not. It's just... are you trying to prove her right about what she's been saying? We need to find another way. She has... more supporters that have made themselves known. They stormed into the cryo chamber and extracted Siannon. They took her to the classroom and they're not letting anyone in."

"How many are there?"

"Nearly three dozen."

"I want the identities of each mutineer. Are they holding Siannon hostage or what's the deal?"

"They have specified that they want Leni freed and for the both of us to resign."

Sali bristled. She'd been so fixated on the enemy. That was how Leni had moved under her and started this mess. Thanks to the Erstveil, the enemy was subdued. Sali had to concentrate on stopping the mutineers. Only, it was a delicate issue. She wondered how many people were already out of commission because of the Sleeping Sickness. That was bad enough. But three dozen passengers away from their duties to post up in the classroom? The ship could not sustain that kind of neglect for very long. And if it came to combat, that would exacerbate things even further. "Give the mutineers in the classroom one hour to surrender—"

"They have weapons, Sali," Captain De Plez said.

"No. How? What kind?"

"Homemade projectiles... maybe explosives too."

"My order stands. We have no other option but to engage them." She paused, the fact of the matter bringing her great anguish. "Where did we go wrong, Manuel?"

"Ma'am, speculation like that is for later. Is there anything else?"

"No...." The best thing she could do was try to get more sleep. "Will and I will be safe where we are. In the meantime, it's still your shift."

That settled, she turned to Will. He was pacing. Not too long ago, they'd had a conversation about how Will had never faced any legitimate crisis. The boy took a pen off of her desk and began chewing it. "If it was Leni who reactivated the Sleeping Sickness, why didn't I get it again?"

"I have no idea, Will."

"Grammy, I wanted to apologize to you, about how... disagreeable I've been to you lately."

"Sit down. It is time to relax."

Will did as she asked.

"A leader sometimes has to make these kinds of decisions. Of who lives and who dies. I established this community as a nonviolent one. It breaks my heart that I've failed, but... I won't let them intimidate us."

"This mutiny, it's only a few people."

"Even so, they're *our* people."

"Well, you can't let them hurt the mission, right?"

She wondered if there were any doctors or nurses in the classroom.

"You gonna be able to sleep?" Will asked.

"I think so. Fix me some tea, Will?" The boy nodded. She smiled at him. "I don't enjoy when we fight. I'm glad you're here. Thank you for apologizing. Today is awful. But the future will be brighter."

"I know, Grammy."

After the tea was ready, Sali went to lie down. Will sat beside her bed. "Promise me you won't leave these quarters?" she asked him.

"Yes. Grammy, I've been working on a project. I think you'd appreciate it. Maybe not right now, but I'm tired of keeping it to myself."

"Oh?"

"It's a chronicling of Arqa's journey."

"Tell me more."

"Not now, Grammy. You need to rest. When you wake up again, maybe De Plez will have taken care of all of this."

She nodded, knowing full well that things would be worse when she woke up again.

2.

Regulators dragged Leni out of her cell as Callum scrutinized everything he saw. He had an electrical scan of the area done. Nothing besides the surveillance camera came up. All the while, Leni just looked on in amusement, though her face looked haggard and her hair was unkempt.

Callum didn't know what to do with the woman. She'd outwitted him, time and time again. If she did what she'd claimed, he couldn't do anything about it. "I got to say, Leni," Callum said as the Regulators shoved her back into her cell, "I'm fed up with my life revolving around you and your games."

"Your suffering," the woman said passively, "it's like a pregnancy. You are in turmoil now. But soon that strife will lead to the birth of something beautiful. You can't imagine it, but one day this confusion must end."

"What are you trying to do here, anyway?" But that was a stupid question. She wasn't going to cooperate, she didn't need to. How had things devolved to this point? Maybe he could have had

Captain Sali and Leni sit down together. Mediation. He'd done it for some high-profile people back on Earth. He'd been good at it. Speaking, convincing, connecting. What had happened? The years had taken his old touch with others away from him.

"I couldn't sleep at night anymore knowing what was happening to our children, Callum. And not just Flight Division. B3 is not meant to be used as a weapon. I had to do something. It's meant for good vibes only."

"These followers of yours, the ones in the classroom, with those homemade guns."

"Yes?"

"Are those meant for good vibes only too?"

She had no response to that.

"What about the Bobbin? None of this is part of what the Bobbin prescribed!"

Leni smirked. "Sali's interpretation has been misguided."

"What evidence do you have of that?"

"You know, Callum, it's not too late to switch sides. Well, I dislike the idea of sides here. But there are. There's working in accordance with B3 and there's abusing it."

Callum furrowed his brow. "It said the first expedition into B3 *had* to include children."

"Callum, I know you've been tortured with indecision. But for what you do know, you need to choose once and for all. Now."

"I'm not joining you."

"That is a sorrowful thing to hear."

"You're going to have eyes on you from now on. I'm watching you. You don't get to make a single move anymore that I don't see."

"Watch me all you want. I have asked to be released, yes, but I don't need your help to do it."

"Stop," Callum said.

"You sure are slow on the uptake. Stress, I suppose. Fine, I'll explain it slowly. My collaborators in the classroom, that's a smokescreen. I knew Sali wouldn't release me for anything. No, she'd sooner see it all burn down. I suppose I shouldn't be surprised you forgot about our conversation regarding Gabriel. You remember what he can do, right?"

"You said he can project himself to other places. Travel beyond his body."

"And I said he was capable of more. *Much* more."

"So?"

"You put him away for awhile, but he's in play again. If you don't get him off the chessboard, one of my friends will get him. You'd better go find him before they do. Gabriel can teleport objects. Like say, if someone was locked in a cell. He could get that person out."

No, Callum thought. *Oh, shit!* Callum rushed frantically out of the room.

Chapter Two

1.

Mark couldn't remember the last time he felt so challenged. He sauntered through a large tent erected for his stay in B3.

"Ceaseless activity, goodness! Not that I'm bitter, though an occasional break may soon be mandatory. In the meantime, Rayna, I need to know what you think. Who is this girl? This Kalyna? She's the real thing, not some clone, but how is she still alive? I'd deeply appreciate your opinion and—" He stopped. Rayna had no response to these things, as she was a recent victim of the Sleeping Sickness. She lay in a cot by some medical equipment that monitored her brain activity and vitals. Mark was hoping he could snap her out of it, snap her consciousness out of it through his need to know. "Kalyna. She speaks to the others as if she believes this is the land of the dead. It most decidedly is not! Oh, why must we each find the other out of commission at the most inconvenient moments? Fine. Let's sail on; go over what we know. The enemy shot down Kalyna's ship. We know before that Gabriel used his power to reach out to her, offering her the crucial insight needed to resolve the Jun situation."

He looked at his slumbering assistant. "Rayna, she was *protected* somehow. Thing is, I'm not too worried about that. She'll level out soon, I'm confident of that. I hope you'll wake up sooner. You're the one who found her. That, or B3 disclosed her presence to you. Which is it? Each possibility leads to vastly different outcomes. The right solution will lead us to everything else."

Mark stopped in front of a chair with a duffel bag on it. "This first though, right?" He interlocked the fingers of both his hands to crack them. "Stress versus strain, I think so." Then he called out, "Bring in the rotisserie!"

Felicia entered with a tray. On it was an entire roast chicken. Mark salivated at the aroma. It had been too long.

"This is disgusting," Felicia said.

"Your honesty is indefatigable," Mark stated. "Set it down there. You may never see one of those again. It's the last one I

71

stowed. Are you not even somewhat fascinated?"

"Eating meat is an earthly notion."

Mark tore off a wing as he sat down. "Kids," he said with derision. "Now then, several of our personnel are down. We have already sent back the ships to Arqa. Just in time for a new mutiny, that's just great. And then we have this variable of Kalyna. Say you were in charge of operations here. What would you do?"

"Are you asking me because you don't know?"

"Give me some suggestions here. I'm not really a decisive person. To be honest, it's a wonder I'm still alive at all."

"We need to do whatever it is you came here to do, I would say." Felicia turned away from him, visibly disgusted as he bit into the meat of a wing. "So whatever that is. If we were to pack up and go back to Arqa now, we'd just be putting ourselves in the firing line unnecessarily."

"You're saying you feel safer here than there?" Mark leaned forward. "Carlos hasn't just gone fishin', you know."

"I *feel* safer here," Felicia said. "It's dazzling, wandering around in here."

"Agreed. You mentioned you were close to Kalyna. She's acting funny. Have you talked to her?"

"I haven't. We got into a fight after that first battle. I'm worried about her. I love her, but I was sent here on a mission… and—"

"What?" he asked.

"Now that I'm part of all this, I'm realizing how careless I was to her. I can be self-absorbed." Mark could relate. "That's why we fought. But when I was drawn into Flight Division, I started to understand things from her point of view."

"Less self-discovery, more problem-solving," Mark said. "Look, without Rayna, I'm just a little off-kilter." He sucked the marrow from his meatless bone.

Felicia raised an eyebrow. "What makes her so special?"

"She listens to me."

"You know, everyone out there is very leery of being here. I'm sure if you go out there and tell them the next steps, tell them to be calm, they'll all listen to you."

Mark picked out a small piece of bone from his mouth and

tossed it on the floor. "I know. I just didn't want to proceed without her. There's a long trek ahead of us. I'm not afraid to go, but I am afraid of leaving Rayna behind. We just got to a good place too, after a series of disagreements." He set his plate aside. Rayna was supposed to try chicken for the first time in celebration of their arrival to B3. He'd had to refreeze the leftovers for her.

"Not much we can do for them, right?" Felicia asked.

"If I'm *really* lucky, I can make it so the Sleeping Sickness isn't a problem for us anymore. I just can't do that here."

"Then I don't think you can wait anymore," Felicia said firmly.

"Well said. You've been surprisingly helpful. Sounds like we both have things we have to do, but don't want to."

Felicia laughed. "If that's you telling me I need to go talk to Kalyna, I'd prefer not to."

"I'd rather not do as you say either. Let's split the difference and do it anyway, then hope that doesn't make things a whole hell of a lot worse."

2.

When Siannon woke, she did so forcefully, as if having just fled a nightmare. Those initial breaths out of vitrification brought on a coughing fit. Her hurried thoughts were indecipherable. The stiffness in her muscles, normally a challenge to navigate, felt compounded. Gooey cryo material surrounded her body, and her limbs shifted uselessly within it. Her vision was shoddy, sensitive to the lights above, and so she shut her eyelids. She was shuddering, hopelessly ripped from peace.

Her last memory returned to her: being controlled... possessed by another. Every motion had been directed from somewhere beyond her nervous system. In that time, she almost hurt Callum Benito, but he had overpowered her before she could do what her operator wanted. Was there more after that? No, she couldn't say.

Unknown people were tending to her, speaking in hushed tones. It filled her with dread—what was happening on Arqa? *Was* this still Arqa? She dared to open her eyes again, seeing cryo technicians. Further out beyond them were people carrying guns.

Siannon recognized she was in the classroom.

She connected the dots from there: these were mutineers, following Leni's orders. One of them she recognized. A cryo technician named Mina. She was on a holo-screen. When they made eye contact, Mina approached her.

"You're back," Mina said in a delighted voice. "It can come about no other way."

"What is going on?" Siannon asked. "Because to be honest with you, I'd rather go back under." Her voice broke up as the burden of her experiences washed over her. "I don't want any part in what's next."

"That's not exceedingly helpful to hear," Mina said. "Leni has gone to great lengths to see you back. She initially petitioned the captain on your behalf, but that obviously didn't work, so she put matters into her own hands."

"But I don't wish to be back," Siannon said.

"But she's going to heal you."

"Heal me?"

"Your body, your constant pain. Yes."

"There's nothing that can be done about that," Siannon said. "It's part of me—congenital—never mind that. I thought Leni was in prison."

"Leni cares about you very much, Siannon," Mina said, seeming to admire the woman. "In attempting to rid this ship of Sali's brutality, Leni has invoked the powers of B3, reactivating the Sleeping Sickness in a select number of passengers. Soon, this ship will no longer be Sali's to jeopardize. Karma is a wheel that is turning for us."

"But I—I went against Leni before, she knows that. That I didn't want to be involved with any part of what she was doing. No matter how nasty Captain Sali was, this, this is going to cause Arqa to collapse altogether!"

Mina remained calm in her words. "Leni isn't mad at you. She expected you to go against her then. She *wanted* you to do everything you did. Inadvertently, you're the reason Leni will stop Sali. Arqa's true potential can now be realized."

Siannon sighed, watching the people bustling about the room, pretending to be soldiers. These people were not soldiers. They were electrical engineers, biologists. Just what was it about Leni that would convince them to become so radicalized? "How many people are following Leni's orders as of now?"

"We have a modest group of collaborators, but with Leni's ultimatum, we will undo all of Sali's damage. We were brought to it that day, Siannon. What was supposed to take generations made itself known to us much sooner than the Bobbin ever suggested. Leni says B3 brought us all here for this purpose. We are moving towards life, along with B3. Siannon, help us. You know Sali's led the children into abject slaughter. She is only a woman, and she is ailing. Captain Leni is tuned into a greater intelligence, far beyond any of Sali's neural modifications."

"*Captain* Leni?" Siannon asked incredulously.

Mina nodded, pleased with herself.

Siannon groaned. She felt her legs growing restless, the desire to get up and walk. Little point in that.

"Don't withhold. Why do you withhold aid from the person who has offered to save you from suffering?"

"I told you, what's wrong with me can't be healed."

"Open your mind. You were told you'd never live to see the day Arqa reached B3. But you were told of what B3 held: brilliant wisdom, unconditional love. Humanity's redemption from failure. Some have already touched down there. You can too. But that's not how Leni intends to solve your problem."

Siannon was growing livid. Before her rage could burst forth, another cryo technician Siannon knew named Di interrupted. "Siannon, you have a visitor."

"If it's Leni, tell her I'm not helping her, accidentally or otherwise," Siannon said, her body jerking from a jolt of pain.

"No, Leni is... still in holding." Di looked at Mina.

"We were getting to that," Mina said.

"Hold off. We've had something urgent come up."

Di soon returned with the last person Siannon expected to see: Will.

"Uhm, hey," the boy said. Will frequently looked away from Siannon to the people with guns orbiting him.

"What are you doing here?" Siannon asked. Mina and the others slowly cleared the area. The group huddled by the door, their conversations too quiet for Siannon to make out. "I was under the impression I was being held hostage. How did you get past them?" He couldn't be—no.

"P'shhh, you don't give me enough credit. I'm the captain's grandson. Mutiny or not, are they really going to beat me up, shoot me? I don't know, looks like those things would be more likely to backfire anyway. I saw it in their faces too, they know. Yeah, I told them as much." He chuckled. "I'm kidding. I hope they didn't hear me just now, they're super unstable. What I told them was I needed to know you were safe with my own eyes before my grandmother would come to the negotiation table. So, do you feel safe and sound?"

"Uh... how long has it been since I was put under?"

"Less than a month. She knows you're a victim here, by the way. She appreciates you staying loyal and all that old junk. And yes, I already told her how little her sentiment would be worth to you."

"Oh, Will, it's really not like her to have you get involved in something this risky." Siannon began wheezing and spat up a nasty bit of phlegm mixed with cryo material. "I know. I'm gross right now. Sorry. You really should be going now."

Will's usual quick delivery fell into a low drone. "I can't leave until—I get it's a bad time... but it's never going to be a good time. I came here because it feels like the last chance I have to talk to you."

"Will, things look bad, but please don't be so grim."

"I decided to come down here and reaction be damned, I have something to tell you. It can't wait till later."

"What is it then? Let's have it."

Will stared at her for a few moments before going on. "You know. You've been the only one who sees me, you know that, don't you? I mean, if you haven't pieced together by now that I'm in love with you, I'm going to feel pretty dumb."

Chapter Three

1.

Gabriel was sequestered with his foster family in their quarters. They were safe for the moment, but Mrs. and Mr. Avery were fighting about what to do about Mr. Benito's imminent arrival.

He lived in a cramped room of bunk beds with two other orphans and his foster parent's biological daughter, Olivia. Olivia was awake, but Emma and Elias were in their beds, hit by the Sleeping Sickness.

Olivia watched Gabriel. She was still too young to understand what was happening.

"Can we even trust Callum?" Mr. Avery asked.

"Don't start that up again," Mrs. Avery said. "What choice do we have? We knew something like this could happen."

"Huh?" Gabriel asked.

The two ignored him. They fought so much... whether it was the best injection site for Siranis Fluid or how their quarters should be arranged, the two disagreed about everything. What he had to say was of little concern to them. He didn't know why he bothered.

Gabriel heard someone knocking at the door.

Mr. Avery stepped in Mrs. Avery's way. "He could be a threat. Why chance it?"

"Dennis, Callum is coming to prevent other people from taking advantage of Gabriel. We've talked about this."

"Hello?" Mr. Benito asked from outside.

"Just let him in," Gabriel implored. "You know Mr. Benito."

"Nobody's themselves anymore," Mr. Avery said gruffly, bringing his arms up to block his wife. "Not since B3. Not what I signed on for at all. Uh-uh! You get away from that door, Terri. I'm the one who got us tickets to Arqa. These are technically my quarters."

"Daddy's quarters!" Olivia reiterated.

Gabriel saw a look of hurt on Mrs. Avery's face. Olivia was too young to understand the context of what she was saying.

"You won't stop us, Dennis," Mrs. Avery said. "We are moving Gabriel to a safer location."

"You're right, of course," Mr. Avery said. "But—"

"Gabriel, answer the door for Mr. Benito."

The boy did as he was told. Mr. Avery had a fierce expression, but didn't stop him. "He's not part of the mutiny, dad." He tapped the side of his head. "I've watched him. I know which side he's on. Okay?"

Mr. Avery looked perplexed. "Gabriel, are you certain about him?"

"Yes." Gabriel jumped forward to open the door.

Mr. Benito entered suddenly. "Hi. Gabriel, quick, put this on." Mr. Benito started fiddling with a black bar he'd gotten from his jacket, which grew and expanded into what looked like a vest. Nanoarmor.

It fit over Gabriel's body and continued to spread, eventually shielding the boy from his neck down to his toes. "Wow!" he said.

"We need to get out of here. The fighting's already started and they'll be coming for him. Who's joining me, who's staying?"

"Dennis is staying... I'm a better shot," Mrs. Avery informed the man. "You've got something for me?"

Mr. Benito reluctantly handed her a railgun.

"Where are we going?"

The plan was to meet Mr. Hall and Lyda, who was still asleep.

The parting of the Averys was heart-wrenching. There was no telling if they'd ever see each other again. But there was precious little time. It amazed Gabriel to see Mrs. Avery kiss Mr. Avery goodbye, their previous acrimony gone.

Mr. Benito had one last thing to ask of Gabriel before they risked venturing out. "Listen so, we need to be sneaky and hopefully avoid any confrontations on our way to Lyda. The mutineers want you. The best way to keep them away is for you to use your clairvoyance to look ahead and give us the best path forward. Can I trust you to do that for me, Gabriel?"

Gabriel nodded.

"And if trouble is unavoidable, will you help me keep us safe?"

The boy nodded again, only much slower than before.

2.

"I only told you because I have a new rule about unspoken things as of today," Will said. "Namely, don't have them."

"Great, then let me reciprocate," Siannon said. "We're nearly a decade apart. I've changed your diapers. I'm in a vitrification pod. Our ship is in shambles. Oh, and let's not forget, should none of those other disasters be sufficient: I do not feel that way about you."

Her reaction was less than ideal. "It's like I said. I just had to get it off my chest. Whatever." Will was feeling as if he'd made an error in judgment. The risk he'd taken certainly wasn't worth this.

"Fine. Acknowledged. I'm sorry things aren't different. Now that you've got that out, you should leave."

"I—I don't know, Siannon. I don't want to leave you here. What Leni did to you, that was some messed-up stuff. Did the L'rias ever do anything like that back on Earth? It doesn't seem like something we should be capable of."

"Did your grandmother mention something about that?" Siannon asked.

"Forget her! I'm against her as of today."

"Will! Don't talk like that. I thought you told me you weren't with these people."

"I'm going with the current. She had the chance to let me in. I just wanted to know why. Why hide every conceivable aspect of Arqa's mission from me?"

"Just because she made a mistake, that doesn't mean you turn against her. She still has most of the population's support. And you know... Will, she loves you, but if she knows what you've just said, she wouldn't give you any mercy."

"How can still you defend her? Huh?" Will kicked over a tray and medical equipment fell onto the floor. "This fucking place is driving me crazy. Look at how you ended up. All because that lady is a shitty leader. Leaders need to be accountable for every mistake."

Leni's supporters came rushing over at the sound of the commotion.

"It's alright," Siannon said. "Will just tripped. Clumsy as

always."

Will gave her a venomous look. "You're supposed to be the only one who treated me with any respect."

The mutineers went back to what they'd been doing. "This is not the best place for a tantrum. I'm trying to keep you from getting hurt." She detached a pouch of empty Siranis Fluid from her side. "Do you realize what Leni will do to the captain if she takes power?"

Will gulped. "Leni wants people to stop dying."

"That's what everyone wants, Will."

"My grandmother had a chance to do the right thing, and she didn't. She was supposed to get us away from the L'rias. She didn't. She was supposed to protect Arqa's crew. She hasn't. Carlos went missing, and no one cares. Leni does."

"Even if that's true, how many more people are going to die while Sali resists? Huh? What about that? Think this through, Will. There's no going back if you join Leni."

"That's the best part, Siannon. I know for sure that, this time, my grandmother is going to surrender."

Siannon looked unconvinced. "What would make you say a wild thing like that?"

"Because of me," Will offered gleefully. "I tricked her. You know her little toy, the buircraft? I waited until she was asleep and pried it off of her. It wasn't easy, but I did it. See, I gave it to the mutineers. They let me see you when I offered it to them."

Siannon gasped. She scrambled to get out of the pod, breaking her statuesque position. "Will, tell me you still have it."

"No," Will said.

"But you realize… that device helps regulate her psychological continuity, don't you? At her age, her mind is too fragile to keep itself together."

Will smirked. "I know! That's the glory of it. She'll start forgetting her appointments and she won't be able to serve as captain. This is a good thing, Siannon. Like I said, she'll have to surrender to get it back."

"No, Will, it's way more than that. Without that device, Captain Sali won't be able to function. All of her memories and abilities are contingent on constant proximity to the buircraft. The longer she's without it, the more her cognitive function will decline. Her brain depends on that device."

"I don't need this explained to me, Siannon. It's already done." Will had *known* what Siannon was telling him. Only, when he'd taken the buircraft, he blanked out on all the details, glossing over them. He did that sometimes. His focus had been on fury, and on needing to get to Siannon.

His actions were self-defeating. This *was* bad.

Chapter Four

1.

Swirling lines of color danced all around Kalyna, odd formations and patterns her eyes had never seen before. Every direction she looked she could see them, like an all-encompassing shore.

Once she was content with that mind-boggling wonder, she retreated into the tent she was sharing with several others on their expedition.

Taking her back to Arqa hadn't been an option. And since her injuries were superficial, they expected her to contribute.

Kalyna was alone. It was dark in the tent, which she liked. A small dose of B3 went a long way. Too much threatened her fragile sanity. All she wanted was to crawl back into bed. Her nose itched and she resisted scratching it.

"It's me, Kalyna," she heard Felicia say from outside.

"Alright, what's up?" Kalyna asked in response.

Felicia meandered in. Kalyna was very skittish, wrapping a blanket tighter around herself. Then she turned to face Felicia. "You don't exactly make for pleasant company lately. You know that, right?" Felicia had her cornered, their old roles reversed. The threat from before was something Kalyna didn't have the heart to follow through on any longer. Violence seemed so gratuitous to her now, which made her an awful soldier. "Yeah. Not to be like that, though. I mean, I'm just worried about you. We're stranded here for the time being, what with the mutiny and all. The good news is, we have Mark. He has a handle on things around here. It's incredible." Felicia approached Kalyna. "Can I?" She pointed to a chair.

"I don't care," Kalyna said, laying back into her cot.

"I just wanted to tell you how sorry I am. I didn't know what you were going through last time. I was oblivious. Well, not anymore. I'm in Flight Division. I get it now. I was petty."

"Of course, make peace with your mistakes. I wonder what mine was?" Kalyna stared at her hands. "You still don't know what I went through. You feed Mark chicken. Try fighting against the L'rias."

"Rayna found you alive and well. Everyone on Arqa was mourning you. It was awful, Kalyna. But it's incredible, you're incredible. B3 saved you—"

"Or maybe it was Lyda."

"Either way. Something kept you with us. I think I know why that is. Think about it! Your sister came on this expedition too, to assist Mark, but she's incapacitated by the Sleeping Sickness. You're meant to take her place!"

"Brenda is a kinesthetics specialist," Kalyna pointed out. "It's not as if I could pick up her workload."

"Mark needs help more than ever."

"What is he doing here, exactly?"

Felicia shrugged. "Why don't you ask him? I mean, you worked with Brenda a lot. It's like robots or something, right?"

"Yep."

"Forget all that for a second though. We used to be best friends."

"So?"

"You still trust me, don't you?"

"Nope," Kalyna said, as she curled her fingers around the back of her head.

"Mark's getting ready to traverse beyond the campsite. I'm going to stay behind in case anyone wakes up."

"That guy creeps me out."

"We aren't getting back to Arqa anytime soon. I was thinking we might as well help him to pass the time. The guy is off, no doubt about it, but it's not *so* bad. You'll get used to it."

"I can't imagine being out there for a long stretch of time," Kalyna said.

"That's not the Kalyna I know," Felicia countered. "Come on, it'll be an adventure." Kalyna frowned. "See what Mark is up to, at least. Where's that annoying overachiever?" Felicia then had the temerity to laugh, albeit nervously. "Before, you'd jump at a chance to do what Brenda does. Look, Mark's got an idea of how to stop the Sleeping Sickness. I know you want to get your sister back."

She has changed, Kalyna thought. "This place, it's so huge...

and Carlos is lost out there somewhere. Aren't you afraid of that happening to you?"

"I'm more afraid of us not being friends again."

The sappiness of it compelled Kalyna to smile. She got back up from her cot to face Felicia. "What the hell? Don't be like that. I asked you a serious question."

"I'm being sincere. You know me. Sure, maybe this place could eat me alive. There's that and then... like I said, there's the feeling I had when I thought you were dead. Thought I'd never be able to fix things with you. And look what happened. Thanks to this place, I at least got to try."

"That's very touching to hear," Kalyna said.

Not long after, Kalyna found a brush and attended to her hair for the first time since being found. *I want my sister back,* she thought. *I want to see my dad again. I want peace. To see Arqa again. To find out I'm still alive... and why.*

2.

It was a grueling journey to meet with Stephen and Lyda. Callum and Terri Avery had to resort to lethal measures to protect Gabriel. But thanks to Gabriel's clairvoyance, Callum had the jump on his adversaries. The boy could tell Callum when trouble was around the corner, providing them with an advantage each time a confrontation was inescapable.

Callum was currently talking down the sole survivor of his latest firefight. The railgun in his hands was strong enough to kill anyone with as little as a single shot. He remembered being given this weapon at the start of their journey. It never crossed his mind at the time that he'd ever need to use it. No, not with Captain Sali's enlightened crew.

The sole survivor was taking cover behind a large panel that had fallen from the ceiling, still dangling from above.

"You know who I am, right?" Callum asked. "Listen so, Arqa doesn't have a backup crew to speak of. You know it, I know it. I get the feeling both of us want to keep doing what we need to do to keep this ship afloat. Tell me, what is your role on this ship?"

A woman's voice shouted out, "I'm a mapper! I generate

projections of our vectors to steer us toward the least concentrated areas of external debris."

"So you and your friends there, you're prowling the halls to... how do you map space if you're holding a gun?"

"We were sent to wait outside of Captain Sali's door by Leni. She has to come out eventually."

"That's not happening anymore. I hear you, you know? If Captain Sali's leadership got us to this point, I totally get it." Callum remained firm in his shooting stance.

"You're not going to let me live after we just tried to kill you."

Callum mumbled in agreement. "I'm sorry. How much longer do you want to drag this out?" He kept expecting her to try running away, but she didn't.

This was their last obstacle. Stephen was waiting with Lyda in a secret storage room not marked on Arqa's schematics. Callum had to do something. The panel wasn't even protecting the woman.

Just then, the woman cursed and darted away.

"Mr. Benito," Gabriel said from behind him. "I tried something and it worked."

"Don't come any closer," Callum said.

"But I got the gun," Gabriel explained. "I tried, like you said, Mr. Benito. Pulled the gun right out of her hands and into my own!"

"Damn, kid!" Callum said with gusto. The mapper was right, of course. He couldn't let her capture Captain Sali.

He fired a single shot, a plasmoid round tearing through the woman's back.

The body fell. Callum carefully approached her, ready to shoot again if needed. After ensuring the woman was dead, Callum called out to Gabriel and Mrs. Avery, who were not far behind.

A few minutes later, they convened with Stephen. There, Gabriel attempted to wake Lyda up with his clairvoyance.

"It's like she's not there," Gabriel explained to them after coming back into himself. "Like she's empty. It's her consciousness. It's somewhere else. Lyda fell asleep here on Arqa, but that's not where she is. Maybe the Erstveil, but I can't reach there."

Callum was hoping maybe if Lyda woke up, so would everyone else. With nothing else left to do, Callum decided enough was enough. "Gabriel, we should have told you all of this sooner," Callum said. "Now things have gotten out of hand. You're going to hate what I have to say, and I'm going to keep reiterating this: we thought we were making the best decision."

"Callum, do you have to do this now?" Stephen asked. "I'm afraid of how my IC is going to react just with you explaining it."

"Same..." Terri said. She looked at Gabriel. "Isn't this going to get you in trouble with the captain?"

"I'm not hiding it any longer. You two should keep yourselves occupied so you don't have to listen." Their ICs were programmed to jam any mention of the truth.

"I wish she was awake," Stephen said.

"I tried," Gabriel said to the man. "I really did. She's... I don't know. I don't know if I can't do it or if she won't let me. I can't tell."

Stephen patted Gabriel on the back. "Thanks for trying," the man told him. He and Terri went to go listen to music at the other end of the room.

Callum put away his railgun, regarding a confused Gabriel with concern. "I first saw your eyes at the end of the world—wait, no. I don't want to start it there. First, I need to ask you, what happened on Earth?"

"The L'rias," Gabriel said. "They invaded our planet. Scoured our atmosphere, killed most of us."

"Mhm. And then Arqa escaped. But the L'rias found us. And they attacked Arqa. And when they did, they used human ships, didn't they?"

"Yeah, they did," Gabriel said.

"We doubled down, panicked by their return. We told you kids that the enemy was an extraterrestrial one. That was only a story. It wasn't true, Gabriel. We've, as with this mutiny, been fighting against ourselves. Do you understand? The L'rias never invaded Earth, they don't exist. Their atrocities did. But those acts were committed by humans.

"Back on Earth, we had this holiday, Christmas. We'd tell our children that a magic man named Santa Claus would come to every house and bring gifts. It was a kind of noble lie. The gifts came from parents or another relative. They just gave Santa the credit. Because it was better to distort reality. To make the world seem *better* than it really was. As Arqa was establishing itself, Captain Sali crafted the story of the L'rias for similar purposes." Callum took a second to gauge Gabriel's reaction. The boy had no words. All that mattered was knowing more. "As adults, we decided that most of you kids were too young to remember how it was. To remember we fought other humans, who simply had different beliefs from us.

"We came to B3 to escape a ruined Earth. All the devastation we told you about from an alien invasion, we did it ourselves. To the planet. It was easier to feed you images of alien monsters. Leni, everyone in revolt right now, they thought keeping the L'rias lie was wrong. The problem was, most people on Arqa have their ICs programmed to prevent them from explaining what I'm telling you now. They were happy to have their ICs fixed up in that way. The feeling went that deep because at the time, we thought it made a lot of sense. This was years ago. Back when we were confident the enemy would never find us. But I killed those mutineers, and that's what they died for. I'm in the chain of command, so I don't have the same ICs restrictions as the general population.

"It all leads back to B3, another thing we didn't tell you about until we were able. A place of immeasurable potential. And you are connected to that potential, Gabriel."

Chapter Five

1.

It was official. Captain Sali was giving up control of Arqa to the mutineers. Siannon couldn't believe it. The news came directly from 2nd LT Lucio, shouting angrily from the corridor outside the classroom. "It's unconditional," 2nd LT Lucio was saying. "Do you hear that? You got your way. So there's no need for any more fighting."

As things were settling down, Siannon was telling Will more about the consequences of his actions. "Your grandmother is very old. Arqa's last captain, Dremon, recovered several artifacts originating from B3. The Bobbin and what your grandmother refers to as the buircraft. The Bobbin is how we first learned about B3. It contained specific instructions for reaching and entering the structure. As for the buircraft, well, that's the only reason Sali has circumvented the effects of aging."

"So what you're telling me is I've killed her then?"

Siannon sighed. "Her mind has been in jeopardy from the moment you left her. Without it, she knew she couldn't lead. And she knows the mutineers won't just give it up now that you've given it to them."

"No…" Will said. "I just needed to see you."

"A fine job of that you did, Will. Now what will you do? You can't go back to your grandmother. You might never see her again."

"That's… I hate to say it, but that's probably for the best. I didn't mean for any of this. If only she'd been straight up with me."

"It's not that simple. I wish it was."

Will hopped from his seat, calling out to the mutineers. Begging for the buircraft back. He broke down in front of them, his pleas futile. It was horrific for Siannon to watch.

Just then, Siannon felt light-headed. Perhaps she needed to rest more. After all, she was in recovery.

Will rushed back to her. "Siannon, we have to do something. I screwed up and I need to take it back."

"But it's already done," she said, yawning. A call was coming in on her IC. But it was weird... the ID was blocked. That had never happened before. "Hello?"

She saw Will fine one moment, standing over her, rambling about something, then a veil of blackness curtained her vision. She blinked, but things remained as they were. Something was wrong. Like when she'd felt her body being invaded before.

"NO!" Siannon cried out. No one answered on the other end, but there was a pulsing, a rhythmic pattern. What was happening? Her senses had been dropped into a void.

She felt pulled into some noumenal realm beyond the daily intake of Siranis Fluid and exercise. Beyond the drama of five hundred people trapped in a ship light-years from Earth. Briefly, she was above it. It was liberating. Joyous.

She tried to speak. To say, "Evil defeats itself." But she was away from her mouth. This lack of control and physicality unnerved her. But before the formlessness could overwhelm her, Siannon was drawn elsewhere. Struck by pain. She was grounded in her normal senses. The pain was in her forehead. She was on the floor of a bathroom. This was not where she had just been. Where was the classroom? Where was Will?

Disoriented, her hands went to caress the site of the pain. It was isolated. The rest of her body, normally sore, felt fine. Only, her hands—

They were different.

She ambled up onto her feet; her form making itself known in a mirror. She watched hands rubbing an aching forehead. A body that was not hers yet moved when she moved it.

She looked into the mirror's reflection. At a face. It was not her own... it was Leni's. Siannon burst out of the bathroom and saw she was in a prison cell.

2.

Stunned, Gabriel listened intently.

"As you know," Mr. Benito went on, "on Earth, I was pretty famous for speaking. I had it pretty good, even when things went bad for everybody else. The world was grappling with ecological

90

devastation, mass migrations. People without homes or resources just turned into animals. Civilization couldn't maintain itself. The death tolls that came pouring in each day were staggering.

"My wife and I had enough resources to survive, but that existence was challenging in its own way. After a few years of seclusion, I heard from the core of Arqa's leadership. Captain Dremon, Sali, Dr. Coulton, Mark. They explained it simply: Earth was to be left. Left to rot, left to die. I couldn't dispute that. I was told about the Prior Race, B3. The plan to steal Arqa. That's right, Gabriel. Arqa didn't belong to us. We were utterly consumed with the hope of one day having our descendants reach B3. That meant fighting our way to freedom. Even the idea, the intention of taking Arqa was enough for me. Anything after that was just icing on the cake.

"One night, we were storming a military installation that housed the genetic samples we'd need to ensure future population diversity. It was one of the last things we did before seizing this ship. Getting in was the easy part. We lost a lot of soldiers on the way in. Too many to get back out. They were pinching us, cutting us down. We held off as long as we could, but we were sure we were done for.

"On the second night holed up in that facility, help came for us. Only, it wasn't anybody affiliated with Arqa. Most of the fighters we had were on this mission. We watched in amazement as this new faction made an exit point for us. Someone had come to our rescue. Together, we fought back the enemy. These newcomers were mysterious. Many of them wore veils that concealed their faces.

"When the enemy was neutralized, one of them informed us that our peaceful departure was only possible with their permission. Their English wasn't great, but the transaction was made clear. They told us if we brought this baby with us to Arqa, they would join our efforts. Facilitate our escape. All for the low, low price of a single ticket to Arqa.

"We never knew who these people were. Where they had come from. Why they saved us. They gave us only the baby's name." Mr. Benito nodded to Gabriel. "It was you. I realize now that these people must have also known about B3, been affiliated with it in a way we didn't know. I'm sorry. I understand that was a lot to take in all at once."

"Well, thanks, Mr. Benito," Gabriel said half-heartedly. "I mean, you're not wrong. This is a lot. So on the other side of the Erstveil, there's a ship that came from Earth. Full of other humans?"

Mr. Benito nodded. "These people, on the other ship… from their perspective, we are terrorists. We caused a lot of damage on our way out. It's all relative. We thought we gave them the slip, that there was no way they'd pursue us this far out. Maybe it was all they could do to commit themselves to destroying us, aftermath be damned."

Epilogue

"Is this everyone?" Mark asked.

"Yes, sir," the short boy said.

"Drat. Suppose it's now or never." He paused, realizing he had been working with this boy for days. "Your name is?"

"I'm Stewart."

"Cool. You're going to get everyone in formation and recite the pledge."

"But that's supposed to be done by the highest ranking member present."

"Well, that'd be me, and I'm telling you to do it."

Stewart set to work as Mark tried to manage his disappointment. Here he was, about to see the culmination of his life's work. *Whoo-hoo*, Mark thought mildly.

The group did as instructed:

> *We of Arqa are not the last*
> *Earth behind us, we seek to thrive*
> *Through science and sanity*
> *Without dogma or superstition*
> *The elevation of consciousness*
> *May beckon being unbound*
> *Evolution without conflict*
> *And a galaxy to share our virtue*

"Awesome," Mark said. "Okay, so we've had a few setbacks since arriving. It wasn't my plan to venture out with such a small team, but I'm done with sitting on my hands." He sized up the group in front of him. Some were children from Flight Division. Hardly qualified to gather any meaningful scientific data. That being said, there were a few heavy hitters from Arqa. Dr. Pelham, Erin, and Arqa's head nurse.

Mark knelt to pick up a duffel bag. He pointed at the short boy, whose name had already slipped his mind. "You, you're going to be the guy who carries this. Believe it or not, it's the most important job." The boy reached out to grab it. "Not yet," Mark said, snatching it away. "First, I need to make sure you understand

93

I'm not pulling your leg. Then you can tell me if you're truly up for it. Let's see now..." Mark rifled through the bag and took out a neon green balloon. "That is definitely not what I meant to grab, but I will need someone to hold this."

"I got it," Kalyna said, standing in formation near the short boy.

"Great, great, take that away then. Next we have..." Mark pulled out a bouncy ball. He dropped it and caught it when it came back up again. Then he held it in his palm. "Can someone hold this?" No one jumped at the chance. Mark looked at the kid in between the short boy and Kalyna. "Boo!" The kid flinched. Mark smiled. He then paced back and forth to address the line-up. "People, my assistant is down, as are other key people I was banking on to do my thing. We can't wait for them, as we have a problem that needs solving immediately. Are you volunteers or involunteers? Because this next step is going to require your undivided attention and full commitment." He took out another object from the bag, another unintended retrieval. "Like, see this acme whistle? Who'll hold this whistle?"

Everyone jumped at the chance.

"This is the kind of enthusiasm I don't want to be checking for from here on out. Great, great." Mark paced in front of the formation. "Now it's time that you know exactly why we're here today. Well, when we first got here, we were scavenging, right? We took those Spaeros that were here and got them back to Arqa. Then what happened? Well, we got them, but your buddy Carlos went missing as that one," he pointed to Kalyna, "made a surprise comeback. In hopes of getting him to turn up, we're going to reactivate this station. As you know, the space we occupy is a piece of something greater. The whole was abandoned and subsequently came apart. But in its heyday, this place harvested so much energy that even now, countless years later, the residual power has been enough to regulate this place for our purposes. Think about it! We have the right temperature, the right elements, the right gravity. How is that possible? This station is producing it.

"It has read us, in a way. There are some more things I need you to understand about B3. What you see all around you and wherever you go is most likely not this place's actual shape. I don't want to freak you out too much, but I doubt B3 is, physically speaking, strictly three-dimensional. Wherever we stand now is safe enough, but be aware there are ways to become trapped in areas beyond your geometric comprehension. Are you following me? It is most important of all to never imagine yourself lost. Always project an assumption of knowing where you're going. And where is that? To access more of this station's stored energy."

Mark unloaded the entire contents of the duffel bag onto the surface, and there was a loud clanging sound of a heavy object hitting the ground. "You," he said, pointing again at the short boy. "See that piece there? Pick it up."

The boy did as Mark asked. Mark gave the group a moment to take it in. The boy picked it up in disbelief. "What... am I touching?"

Instead of answering him directly, Mark addressed the group at large. "This, people, is the Bobbin."

The Bobbin appeared as a stony gray sphere, floating and bouncing within a transparent box. The inner sphere changed, becoming a rhombus, then a rectangle. "Among other things, the Bobbin is capable of something incredible: this thing will, when put in its proper place, restore this station to a semblance of its former glory. For a time. And that's exactly what we need to do if we want to survive."

EPISODE 9
No Further
Fact

Prologue

TWO YEARS AGO...

Arqa's atrium was the most spacious part of the entire ship. It was a wide open area that bisected the ship's two main sectors. Being a liminal space, activities that resulted in congregation or congestion were prohibited.

But that restriction only made it all the more enticing for the children to brave the risk. Two such boys were currently playing a game of tag. Gabriel was it. They knew at any moment the sight of their actions could mean the game was over and Gabriel would be victorious. Some of the grown-ups didn't bother with stopping them, but Craig knew each step he took could be his last before the game was cut short. It seemed like no matter what he did, Craig couldn't catch Gabriel.

The boys had been best friends for half of their lives, having been introduced based on coincidentally having the same middle name: Emery. From the day of that revelation, they had assumed it meant they were related, though not in the traditional sense. They decided anyone middle name of 'Emery' was their brother. They had yet to find any more siblings on Arqa, but they imagined there had to be at least a few more.

Gabriel stuck his tongue out at Craig. Craig waited for a group of people to pass beyond his intended path. Clear once more, Craig advanced, seeing Gabriel languish without concern. This goaded Craig. "You're gonna get it!" he declared. "Not only am I gonna tag you, I'm gonna tag you with my butt. Then you'll really be defeated." Craig would often jump down on Gabriel's desk in school, buttocks first. During the descent he would shout out, "Booty powers!"

Craig never broke the desk, but once he had misjudged his trajectory and landed past his target on the ground. Nothing had been damaged but his pride.

Craig was outspoken. Quick to get loud. Gabriel was much quieter by comparison. His primary hobby was reading, while Craig's was interrupting said reading. Making people laugh was when Craig was at his happiest, and Gabriel loved his sense of humor.

It was true that Gabriel did, at first, find Craig irritating, but that didn't last long. Indeed, Craig's tendencies had made Gabriel several degrees more extroverted—though the converse was not true. They had grown up together, an inseparable pair.

Craig told himself to stop worrying about getting too tired—to stop thinking he'd never be able to catch Gabriel. Though, to be fair, that might have been his father talking. He was so good at reevaluating Craig's problems in life. Craig could go to him with anything and his dad would reshape the sentences, sometimes with different words, to show Craig that what he thought was a bad thing was actually a good thing. How if he could push past what he thought his limits were, he'd be showing progress. Improving.

A bead of sweat dripped down Craig's temple. It was working! He was getting closer. Gabriel seemed to be tired from running. All Craig had to do was fake his friend out somehow. Trick him with some zig-zagging maneuvers and close the distance between them before Gabriel had time to react. Gabriel's running devolved into more of a jog. But before Craig could seize the moment, he fell. Something awful from a few days before had come back: a stomach ache. Between panting, Craig moaned. A wave of nausea followed. He sank down onto his back. His hands, as if magnetized, went to his stomach. He felt his throat convulse, and he resisted the urge to do what he knew had to be next. Still, vomit came out of his nose and his mouth. Beleaguered, the best he could do was tilt his head as it was happening. He became soaked in his own vomit.

When he looked up, he saw Gabriel.

"Get up," Gabriel said. "What's a matter? Is it your knee?" Craig had torn his ACL playing soccer a year before.

"No. I... uh..." Craig said, feeling as if he was slipping from consciousness. More people came to his side... they were calling for help.

"No, no, don't move me," Craig pleaded. "I feel sick." There was this agonizing throbbing in what felt like his brain.

"Craig, you got puke all over you, you can't just lay in it," Gabriel said.

Craig knew his friend had omitted an important detail about that. Craig was young, but he'd thrown up before. This time was different: there was blood visible in the bile. Craig had just enough strength to pat Gabriel on the shoulder. "Hey. You're it."

Chapter One

Kalyna could not take her eyes off the Bobbin. There was something about it that was even more enchanting than B3 itself. The object seemed unreal, like something only found in VR. Seeing it change in real-time gave her this comforting energy. As if everything was taking place only for her benefit.

Colors danced across the surface of the Bobbin, all the while altering itself to unpredictable geometric configurations, some of which Kalyna had never seen before. It would go from one shape to another at different durations, flowing in accordance with a source unknown. The Bobbin did not have a fixed form, it shifted in time.

She had many questions, but she restrained herself. The others were pelting Mark with their own. "You could never really touch the Bobbin itself," he was saying. "The box you're touching is a dense field of energy; impossible to pierce."

Kalyna straightened her posture, taking in a deep breath. For most of her life, she'd been in proximity to that thing. This is why Arqa had made for B3. Why she'd fought in Flight Division. The Bobbin was the key to it all.

"Okay," Mark said, "now that we're clear on that, let's move on." He placed the Bobbin back in the duffel bag with care. "Now you, stuff everything else back in there."

"Yes, sir," Stewart said.

Kalyna's attention shifted to the group: Erin, Stewart, Oliver, Dr. Pelham, Johnathan, Zaid, Dr. Lorn, Jin, and Vanessa. Each of them listened to Mark, spellbound.

"Now, several of you have been in B3 before," Mark said. "You reported that you were attacked?" He looked over at Stewart. "Keep that bag off the floor from now on, please."

"Sorry!" Stewart said, blushing while he scooped the bag up.

"What was I just saying?" The man muttered under his breath. "Mhm. Mhm. You over there." He strode over to Vanessa. "Vanessa, was it?"

"That's correct."

"You've been here before?"

"Oliver and I have, yes."

"And you reported a feeling that… what was it? Something else was here, watching? Reacting to your mood?"

"That's right," Oliver added.

"Uh-uh," Mark said in admonishment. "We're hearing from her right now."

Mark urged Vanessa to go on with the impatient rolling of a hand. "This place has some type of awareness," she said. "Creatures. They killed Millie. Reeve. Now Carlos. If we ever find him, I doubt he'll be alive."

"Don't be so certain," Mark said. "Of anything. Look at Kalyna. She's been here the longest of all, and she's fine. Physically speaking." Kalyna scowled at him. What was that supposed to mean? "Not only is that impressive, it also messes with your assumption of hostility."

"Excuse you?" the woman asked, glaring at him. "You weren't here when Lyda abandoned us for that oval thing. Or when we first landed. It was a living nightmare."

"I see what's going on. You just can't help yourself. It's a matter of trauma. I ask you, if you become traumatized by something, is the damage always irreversible? Darn, wish our Psych was awake to answer that. Oh, well."

"You expect me to put my guard down in here after everything?"

Mark groaned. "Just trying to explain post-traumatic growth. Your guard is pointless because if there were monsters that wanted you right now, you could do nothing against them. Fortunately for you, there's nothing coming. Now, why is that? I think this demonstration could enlighten you. Remember: undivided attention." The man dashed out beyond them, then patted the surface with his hands. He rose, elevated by something unseen. Going on all fours, he climbed up into an invisible structure. When he was about twenty feet above the others, he said, "Break formation and gather 'round. Now, I doubt you can see it yet, but I am halfway up a tree right now. Okay? Get that through your heads. Do you see it?"

Upon being told it was a tree, Kalyna did. Where there had been nothing seconds before, a birch tree appeared all at once under Mark. The man was grasping onto a thick branch near the top of it.

"You there," he said with a raised voice, pointing to Vanessa. "What kind of tree am I on?"

"A willow."

"Okay. What if I told you I was on a palm tree?"

"I still see a willow tree."

"Well, I imagined for myself a palm tree," Mark contradicted. The tree lowered, growing in reverse back into the surface. Mark scampered down it until it was gone. "All that to show B3 is receptive to intentionality. Write that down somewhere. Thoughts become things here, to a certain extent. We're all gifted with the power of perception. Of will. Intelligence, consciousness. Whatever you want to call it. Vanessa, and you there; you were brought in not knowing where you were. So you had pre-installed fears you projected. No wonder scary things took place. You're back and nothing is attacking you because there are others here who know better. This place does not have creatures waiting to snatch you up. It is a lifeless structure made to harvest energy from a star. That said, it can use that energy to manifest your inner state. You saw nothing just then, I'd wager, until I suggested to you that I was in a tree. Am I right?"

"Yeah," Vanessa said.

"But we had contrasting views on what kind of tree it was?"

"Correct."

"Both trees existed concurrently, with respect to our individual perceptions. And you could say the same for every tree each of you saw. None of us saw the same tree. What you saw was a construct of your perception. In here, we need oxygen. That in mind, oxygen is produced. We need to explain something by climbing a tree, a tree appears. And if we persist that something means to do us harm, eventually it will. Thoughts can become things here. Is that clear?"

"No," Vanessa said. "Because then we could just desire that Carlos come back or the Sleeping Sickness ends."

"This place isn't a wishing well. It's receptive to intentionality. There are no absolutes, only probabilities. Were you here alone, bereft of the information I just gave you, I've no doubt that something would come and attack you. This is one problem we'll face. Our collective vibe has to be both monitored and managed. We can't, as a group, dwell on negative thoughts. Accidents can happen as a result. Which is why it's best you leave the heavy lifting to me. Do as I instruct, no matter how ridiculous, and we should, I think, evade all peril."

"How do you even know all of this?" Oliver challenged.

"We learned about B3's workings from the Bobbin. The only threats we face in B3 are threats from one another. And our own fears."

"I fought for my life in here," Oliver said.

"Yeah, what was it you fought against?" Mark asked with condescension. "Do you remember?"

"It... looked like me," Oliver said, deflated.

Mark looked around at the others. "Ladies and gentlemen, are we beginning to understand?"

"Millie wasn't attacked by a reflection of herself," Vanessa said. "Some monster tackled her."

"That's what you saw, but what did Millie see?"

"She didn't say. She was having a mental breakdown."

Mark rolled his eyes at her. "Okay, so good rule of thumb: avoid mental breakdowns in here. B3 is a mindscape. If we treat this place like an incomprehensible alien deathtrap, that's what it's going to be. If we treat it like a paradise or a research facility to augment humanity's future, I believe it will also be that."

"What if..." Oliver started, "What if I can't see this place as anything other than a nightmare? Like rationally, maybe I can concede to your argument. But emotionally..."

"I have a temporary solution for that," Mark said. "We just need to get in sync. Back at my tent, I distributed vis-caps that will interface with your ICs. Everyone put them on now."

Kalyna put on her cap and, to her surprise, the bright and swooshing surroundings of B3 became a road... a highway.

"As we proceed, you will be guided by what I show you," Mark said. "I will project the path. As I am able, you will see what I see and, to a much lesser degree, feel what I feel based on my consistent verbal updates. Everyone, take a moment to adjust to my view, walking with the caps on."

After a few minutes of adjustments, Mark continued. "I don't have a great fix on where we're going. The only thing I'm certain of is it's many, many miles from here. I plan for us to be away from camp for a few days. We have a long journey. Remember, the Dyson Sphere we stand upon is the largest consciously constructed object we have ever come across. It must have been larger than the size of the star it once drew power from. Though we stand now on only one node of that entire operation, realize B3 is still humongous. It's much too large to scale with our feet or a ship and it was not built in such a fashion. An greater intelligence than our own must have seen to it. What that means for us, however—"

Kalyna felt the road beneath them sink. The floor broke under the group and they were free falling. Kalyna had no bearings, nothing to hold on to. She looked down. Below there was a floor of stalagmites!

"Testing, testing," Mark whispered. Relative to her, the man was upside down as they fell. "To be clear, I don't like being ignored. So I thought we should begin with a difficult example. Could everyone stop screaming? We're getting closer. Look!"

Kalyna dared to look down as darkness took away the approaching stalagmites. The group fell through where the stalagmites had been. She imagined survival, escape, stability.

"Elsewhere!" Mark shouted.

The group landed. The surface was soft and bouncy, like a trampoline. Kalyna struggled up onto her feet—no sight of any stalagmites.

"Fascinating," Mark said.

"What the hell just happened, Mark?" Erin asked, trying to get back on her feet.

"I have been proven right! We are in an entirely different part of B3. Teleportation, if you could believe it!"

"Okay, but where?" Jin asked.

Mark chuckled. "Who cares? Let's try that again!"

Chapter Two

ONE YEAR AGO...

Feeling incapacitated, Callum watched Siannon wheeling the desk from the Med Bay entrance to beside Craig's bed. Gabriel had requested for his desk to be next to Craig, so they could do their homework together.

It baffled Callum why they'd permitted Gabriel to do this. Craig was only getting worse, and neither of the boys knew the full scope of things. Like this, Gabriel would start to see.

Gabriel was beaming. "Thanks for bringing my desk in here, Miss Siannon."

"Oh, but this isn't your desk, can't you tell?" Siannon asked.

"Huh?" he said, looking it over.

"This is Craig's desk. I thought if I brought yours, he might be tempted to jump onto it, hindquarters first. You would never do that to your own desk, would you Craig?"

"No, Miss Siannon," Craig admitted. Callum saw the boy trying to smile. It worked for a moment. But it was too much of a demand for his body, so it fell away.

"Uh-oh," Gabriel said. He patted Craig on the head. "I think I'll keep him, Miss Siannon. He's a beautiful dog. But do you have any doggy treats?"

Craig barked several times. "Treat me!" The two boys and Miss Siannon laughed. They were just running down a clock now. The doctors didn't think Craig would see through the next month.

"Nothing for dogs," Siannon said. "But..." she reached into her purse and handed Gabriel a round tin.

"What is that?" Gabriel asked.

"All yours," she said. "While you enjoy those, I'll prepare my next lesson." The teacher had also been spending a great deal of time with Craig. It took some of the burden off of Callum, only he didn't understand why she would expose herself to Craig's suffering. She must not have had much of a life. Then again, who on Arqa did?

"But, but, Miss Siannon," Gabriel said, exasperated. "Those are cookies. It's only 0900!"

"Mr. Benito and I don't mind, do you?" Siannon asked the man.

"Oh, no," Callum said. "Please, enjoy them." If it had been an hour later, he would have said no. Craig's next treatment was coming up. Callum watched the boys divide the contents of the tin up.

"It's so cool, getting to bend all these rules," Craig said.

Callum had the reflex to say, "Don't get used to it." But he held it in. That was his authoritarian parenting style flaring up. The latticework of a method meant to propel his son to greatness. There was no need for discipline or cultivation now. Craig was a lost cause. He would never be renowned for anything, not like Callum had been. He would be lucky if he even got to see his eleventh birthday.

It had been a year since Craig had fallen in the atrium. In that time, the doctors had done their best. Callum believed that. And these doctors, they *were* the best. The most skilled, the most knowledgeable, on the cutting edge. Still, this instance of cancer was beyond their ability to eradicate. The first question had been, did Craig ever miss his SFR supplement during a period of increased CGR activity? After all, the most dangerous element of space travel was radiation exposure. Though Arqa's hull protected the population, it was sometimes necessary to take extra precautions. The risk was ever present, but Craig was the first person on Arqa to have noticeable damage. So they'd asked, on and on in different ways, hoping to see how this could have happened. Callum had insisted that, no, Craig had not missed any medicines or supplements. Then there was the matter of the ICs, which monitored vitals and radiation exposure. A fail-safe of sorts. But the ICs weren't always perfect. Callum had checked Craig's ICs readings several times a day.

It was, after those failings, the medical tests that found the tumor. It seemed to have blossomed out of nowhere. The doctors surmised Craig had just been an unlucky case, in that he probably would have developed this tumor on Earth. It was simply a case of the genetic lottery.

"But vitrification," Callum had asked. "We could stop the progression that way and maybe someday they can revive and heal him, no?"

He was told that no one was going to stop him if that's what he wanted to do. But it wasn't an actual solution. Callum knew that. The reason for having a cryo chamber in the first place had been to fund their escape effort. Live forever. Survive Earth. It was hardly a sure thing. Callum understood those terminally ill people in the cryo chamber, from a scientific point of view, were indistinguishable from corpses buried in a cemetery.

"Dad, do you want one?" Craig asked. "Three cookies… it's a lot."

Callum came out of his reverie. "No, no thanks. Save it for later if you don't want it. That's what the tin's for, right Miss Siannon?"

Siannon nodded.

"Just how does one come across cookies?" he asked her.

"Let's just say someone, somewhere, has an illicit bakery," Siannon confessed.

"Sounds like a secret I shouldn't know about," Callum said.

"Well, I don't care for secrets, Callum. Did you have to step out? I'll be here anyway."

Siannon knew. Knew Callum had had more to drink in the last two months than he'd had in his entire life. It wasn't a big deal. Or better put, it wouldn't be a problem for much longer. The liquor he'd stowed away years before was almost gone.

When they'd offered him a position on Arqa, it was never some higher calling or true purpose. No, that had been the life he'd had before. Arqa had been a move for survival. But that move had caused him to lose Evalia. In time, Callum came to accept his role as a father to the boy. He hadn't been a perfect dad, but he'd put substantial effort into loving him. But Craig would be dead soon, and that charade would be over with.

Chapter Three

1.

"Can we please focus on what an incredible discovery this is?" Mark asked his complaining companions. "We have taken advantage of hitherto only theorized extra-dimensional properties of this station. Think about it! Instead of going from point a to point b, we can just hop to any point. It's the same way space-time was folded for Arqa's journey here."

This did nothing to curb their outrage. So he reluctantly apologized for the stalagmite incident. He had just been trying to make sure they were all paying attention!

They walked for hours, Mark refusing to tell them where it was they were going. What did that matter? The group insisted they take a break, although Mark wanted to go on. "It's not much farther than this."

"Good, we're still stopping," Erin said. She was one of Arqa's top brass, fifth in the line of succession to lead the ship. Currently, Mark was projecting the image of a plain. How far from the camp had they gotten? It wasn't easy to say. B3 was malleable. Rooms and regions could shrink and change in response to a focused demand. And with the insight of being able to think yourself somewhere else, any distance was largely symbolic. "Are you about done with all this aimless wandering? I thought we were on an urgent mission."

"We already know we can get anywhere we like," Mark said. "Now I'm testing out something different."

"Well, time to get specific," Dr. Pelham said. "You asked us to join you so that we might help out. How is walking all this way at all productive?"

"Doctor, I know what I'm doing."

"Why not explain?" Jin suggested. "That's all we're asking. The longer we tarry here, the more Leni consolidates her position on Arqa. We can't wait it out. It's time to do whatever the captain actually sent you in here for, Mark."

"That stuff'll sort itself out," Mark said.

"Hey," the bag boy said, "can someone else hold the bag for a while, Mark?"

"Absolutely not!" Mark snapped. "It's on you, kid."

"I gotta say, it's getting me to feel kind of off balance."

"Just tough it out and quit whining!" Mark could tell that, despite his previous disclaimers, the group was tiring of him. "Okay, sorry. Look, tensions are high. We need to shift our focus, because now we're all bugging each other." He walked around on his own for a time, eventually pressing his hands into the surface of B3. "Bag boy, would you find me the quanco? Good lad. Sure, there's a place we need to get to. We're getting close, FYI. But it's not just about getting to a place. We need to be in the proper head space as well. Ever heard of set and setting? I mean, I tried to explain it all earlier, but I think we need to approach this from a different angle. What we need now is a way to work off our anxieties and coalesce more into a team. So fuck it, we're playing rugby."

Mark reformed the surroundings. The plains turned into turf, with two goal posts rising on each end of a field.

"You expect us to go along with this?" asked Dr. Pelham.

"It doesn't seem like such a great idea, Mark," Oliver said. "The physicality of the sport… it could cause unintended hostility to surface."

"We're playing at least one round before we do anything else." He pointed to Kalyna. "You. You're on my team." To Dr. Pelham, he said, "You're the other team's captain, so choose wisely. Everyone, take a mental snapshot of what you see on your vis-caps and then take them off."

"And if I refuse?" Dr. Pelham asked.

"Let's just get this over with," Vanessa said. "I'll play if it means I get to tackle Mark."

"Indeed it does," Mark said. "Glad I don't need to explain the premise."

2.

After eagerly playing many rounds of rugby, the group rested. Kalyna was flat on her back, away from the others. Above her was a crimson sky. Her toes were dug into the sand of a tropical beach. She could hear the tide, the sound of gulls. This was much richer than the VR on Arqa. In VR, she couldn't smell the sea breeze like she could here. And there wasn't even any vis-cap interface necessary between her and B3. She fancied herself the queen of this beach. It felt that each moment she gave to the area drew her further and further from everything else. No one to be. Nowhere to go.

"Mind if I join you?"

Kalyna turned around to see Mark.

"Who are you again?" Kalyna asked.

"Mark! Are you alright?"

"I'm kidding. I know… you just keep doing that to everyone else."

"Not to you."

"Yeah, but you really should have Stewart's name down by now."

"Not untrue. Why is your vis-cap off?"

"We were taking a break, weren't we?"

Mark hummed affirmatively.

"You can join me. What's up?"

"I just noticed you were going off on your own," Mark said. "We didn't want you to get separated. If you invest too deeply into what you imagine, that could be bad."

"I am imagining a lovely beach, close by my traveling companions."

"No one else has tried anything that elaborate, I don't think. They're too nervous to."

Kalyna shrugged. "What can I say? I'm acclimated. Are we moving on, then?" She sat up. He just stared at her without answering. "A yes or no would be great about now."

"Sorry. We're not leaving just yet. Tell me, what's on your mind?"

"Nothing."

"Nothing?"

"Correct."

"Rayna talks like that," Mark said. "You remind me of her… though you have your own distinguishing characteristics, too. You require less direction. I haven't known you long, but I'd wager you'd make a better assistant than her."

"I'm only interested in this mission as of now."

"Oh, sorry. That wasn't a job offer or anything like that. Rayna's just—well, our relationship has gotten better through trial and error. She knocked me out while she was juggling recently. She said it was an accident. I find that highly unlikely. It made me think we had some work to do. I tried to change our dynamic, to make it better. It paid off. She confided in me that her aspirations in life lay somewhere outside of my research. She didn't say what exactly those aspirations were, though. I guess what I'm getting at is, it's nice to have someone who's close enough. This expedition hasn't been easy without her. Not to mention I'm worried about anyone with the Sleeping Sickness. It's such a novel thing. Not at all a human disease. I'm also starting to wonder if it's a misnomer. Sleeping people should be able to be woken up with enough stimulus."

"I got through it fine." Kalyna said, poked at the sand with his fingers. "What is Rayna to you? Are you related or something?"

"Nope. She just helps me. She was an orphan who found her way onto Arqa. But shortly before we left, she was in an accident that left her scarred. They knew she wouldn't fare well with the other children, looking so different. I took pity on her... I did what I could, but it's not like she sees me as a father. She was sort of on her own in that regard. No, from the time she was able, she worked for me. See, I needed someone who'd follow me implicitly. So, maybe it was less pity and more self-interest. She helped me with my research and I taught her almost everything I know."

"It sounds like a hard life."

"It'll pay off," Mark said. "I'm going to get her back. I want her to tell me what else she'd like to do so I can make it happen. The future, it belongs to you and her, not me. Whatever hardship any of you go through, it's just meant to help you appreciate when things are finally good. The others were worried about you. Me? I just wanted to find you so I could extend my gratitude. Of all the people here, I think you most delight my curiosity. How is it you're still alive? So many others died that day."

"I should have. I'm trying not to think about it. I'm just glad

I'm safe."

"Do you still think this is the afterlife?"

"Less and less so," Kalyna said. "It's this imaging thing, if you must know. It's a pretty neat trick. Instant serenity."

Mark snickered. "Oh, like this?" Mark asked. "Quick, put your vis-cap back on."

Kalyna saw another beach. But it was even grander than the one she'd imagined. The other sensory details poured in after she got a good look at it. A breeze kicked up her hair. It wasn't sunset here, but closer to midday.

"You've never actually been to a beach," Mark said. "I grew up on one. This is what I remember."

"Way better than mine," Kalyna admitted.

"I only have a faint notion of what we're doing here, Kalyna," Mark said, heading for the water. He took off his boots. "Truth be told, this is all a learning experience. I know what I want in here and I've been trying to make it happen. But I don't think it works exactly like that. Again, we're learning about the limitations we have in here."

"Who cares? If it's something that's going to take time, then screw what everyone else says. There's no other option."

"Right, right."

"You like keeping people in the dark," Kalyna said. "You want them to be dependent on you."

Mark stepped out of the water. "I just want them to feel safe, forget everything else. We're here only to make the first dent in a greater understanding. Sure, I can do some parlor tricks, but it's your generation who'll really make this make sing. Someday you might harness the power to figure out artificial general intelligence."

"Hence the Bobbin. So it belongs here, but we found it on Earth?"

"Correct."

"Well, how did it get there?"

Mark kicked the sand with his bare feet. "Let me explain what I think the Bobbin is. I think it's the initial state or first step in building something like a Dyson Sphere. The simplest module. Like the atoms of a more complex molecular structure.

Somewhere on this station, I think there is a place where the Bobbin is meant to go. It's like a battery, in that when it's placed where it belongs, B3 will perk up, releasing a burst of energy, maybe for the last time. How did it get from its rightful place to Earth?" Mark shrugged. "We can teleport ourselves in here. Perhaps the same mechanism teleported the Bobbin to Earth."

"Wow, Mark," Kalyna said. "And this burst of energy. How will you use it?" She could not hold back the concern in her voice.

Mark laughed. "You're thinking of Lyda's destructive act against the enemy, I can tell. I couldn't do something like that with B3. I mean, you're right, about this energy release I'm speaking of. It would be greater than what Lyda used to protect us. It's just, like I was saying earlier, my mind may not be the best vessel for that energy. In thinking of Lyda, her mind was wide open. She was young. There was no angle. Only, keep home safe. And I think it was very interesting that this place aged her up a few years as she did what she did. Perhaps to the ideal age to interface. To your age, practically. Rayna's age."

Was that why? Why children had to be the first to enter B3? "I missed my birthday. While I was here. I'm fifteen now."

"Oh, well, Rayna is a few years older than you. I meant the general age range."

"If you can tap into this energy using the Bobbin like you're talking about, are you saying you want me to harness it? Like Lyda did?"

Mark nodded. "Like I meant for Rayna to. But plans have changed. I'm hip to it. You turned up here waiting for me. When the time comes, Kalyna, it's going to be on you. Are you up for that?"

"Look, I can accept that B3 is the key to our survival. We need to evolve, to understand the Prior Race. We are at war. I would be dead right now if it weren't for this place. I'm determined to use it to achieve peace."

"Peace?" Mark asked contemptuously. "I hope that doesn't mean you'd flinch if given the chance to destroy the enemy."

"I wouldn't. I hate that Lyda half-assed the job."

"Still, every solution breeds new problems. Do you expect peace and prosperity after all that? What about the mutiny?"

"I'd use this energy you're speaking of to stop them."

"Oh, I see."

"On behalf of my family, my home, I would do anything."

"Of course. Evolution resents peace, you know. In the province of nature, prosperity is code for stagnation." Mark pulled up a holo-screen. "Anyway, take a gander at this."

Kalyna did. She saw a blinking dot on a green grid.

"This is a tiny probe sent from Earth some years before Arqa left. I've been feeling a great deal of resistance teleporting us exactly to this location. It's a nexus point. Where the Bobbin may have to go. I've gotten us reasonably close, though. One more thing, before we rejoin the others: I'm not really much of a scientist, Kalyna. What I know is more like second-hand smoke, or maybe I'm more like a parrot. See, the real minds, the authentic geniuses, many of them didn't survive Earth. I just happened to escape with the fruits of their labors. There have been so many hurdles we had to overcome before we could attempt this. Everything we've done thus far has been towards reaching this point. We were told to go here, though I'm not sure why. I'm following orders I don't fully understand, same as you. Thought you should know all that. Just you. I'm not telling the others any of this."

"Why not?" Kalyna asked.

"I don't want to dilute our purpose with their opinions of what we have to do. I feel the less they know, the more willing they'll be to follow."

"I disagree. But it changes nothing of what I said. I'll still do whatever you think is best for Arqa."

"Good, because we're only a few hours away." Mark walked away from her. "Remember: Happy thoughts… or else!"

Chapter Four

ONE YEAR AGO...

Incensed, Siannon headed straight for Callum's quarters once the funeral was over. She tried to let go of her anger. Her first years on Arqa had been the most challenging and Callum had been the Psych to help her adjust. She was no Psych herself, but she knew the man should not be alone right now.

When she knocked on his door, all she heard was, "No."

"Please Callum," she said. "It's over now. It's finished. Let me in, just for a few minutes."

"You're going to have to drink if I let you in."

"Drink?" Siannon asked. "You mean you have liquor in there?"

The door opened and she found Callum, laying down on his couch wearing a suit... almost as if he'd intended to go. On the table, she saw a bottle of brown liquor. The sight of something so rare amazed Siannon.

Callum shifted himself up idly, heading for the table. He returned, handing her a glass. "Have as much as you'd like."

"I've no experience with it," Siannon admitted. "What is it?"

"Scotch. Expensive scotch. Here, lemme—" Callum emptied a few ice cubes from a tray, then poured a small amount into the glass. His movements were unsteady. "I was saving it. You know, for Craig. When he got to being old enough, like. Yeah. It was going to be for me and him. I had this whole routine set up about the dangers of alcohol. Then I'd say 'just kidding', and bring this out. Fatherly humor. Yeah, sharing a drink with him for special occasions. Maybe if he ever got married... or had a kid of his own. You know, moments of significance."

"I see."

"That's how it was with my dad and I. Only difference being my dad was an alcoholic. Me? I could bring that bottle on board and not touch it. Not once. Even though I was all torn up inside. Come to think of it, I had to give dad one of my kidneys towards the end. So really, I shouldn't be drinking at all."

Siannon didn't know what to say. Did he expect her to stop him?

121

"You spoke, didn't you?" he asked.

"I gave the eulogy, yes."

"Well, I missed it. But I still wanna hear it, okay? Give it to me!"

"Then you should have come. That's not why I'm here."

Callum's lips sliding into a frown.

"I—I wrote it out. If you want to read it you can. But reciting it once took enough out of me."

"Mhm, mhm, yes," Callum said. "I would like to read it." Siannon gave Callum the outline. "Thanks. Index cards... very stylish, very retro." He looked at her glass. "Try some! Oops, sorry. Hah. Just sip it. It's gonna sting, but good."

Siannon did as he said, finding the sting quite bad, contrary to his claim.

"'We survived... blah, blah... having the privilege of no deaths for many years... passing of one of our own... known him since he was born....' Huh, what's this?" he asked.

"What?"

"'I urge you to remember that for Craig, this is not the end. Only a lapse in consciousness.' Yikes. Like he just fainted or something?"

"For the benefit of the children. Gabriel has been taking it especially hard."

"So you're telling me the captains were cool with letting you say this shit out loud?"

"Again, this was for the benefit of the children, whose imaginations are worth cherishing."

"Ah, well, what do I care? Okay, you've had your sip. Now have a shot with me."

Siannon did. The unpleasantness of it almost caused her to spit it up. "I know it's going to take time for you to recover from this, Callum. Is there anything else I can do for you to help you?"

"No, you covered the eulogy. Passing the buck, it was a big ask. Uh, was it weird that I wasn't there?"

Siannon lied. "No... I think it was fine."

"Good. Now, 'cause—I don't care how this sounds. I checked out of fatherhood the moment that kid died. It was easy. Sure, I still have grief about it, but it's from something deeper, see?"

"Oh?"

"Yeah. Let me tell you about Evalia. See, Arqa was all my idea. I had to pitch it to her. We were apart a lot, at that point. Not because we didn't want to see each other, at least I didn't think so at the time. I thought it was because of the state of the world. I mean, I saw fit then to lie low, but she was always putting herself out there. Righting the latest moral atrocity. Anyway, the time was coming where we were going to leave. This fucking guy shows up to my house one day with a baby, saying Evalia's not coming. How she wanted me to take the baby instead of her. I call her up, and sure enough, that's what she wants. I was shattered. Do you have any idea how hard that was? She gave up her spot for this baby. I was never going to see my wife again! I told her I'd stay behind, even though I didn't want to. But she insisted I take Craig. That if I stayed, I'd never see her again anyway. Of course, I tried to make it so all three of us could board, but that was no good either. It was too late, that was the thing. This baby situation, man, it just came out of nowhere. My hands were tied."

"You mean Craig isn't your biological son?"

"No, he wasn't. And I resented that a lot, in the beginning. But I had to try. What other choice was there? And just look at what good all that came to! I pledged to her I'd keep Craig safe, even though I didn't want to."

"You have no control over what happened to him," Siannon said. "You did your best."

"But I wanted Evalia to come. We loved each other. I didn't want her to stay on Earth. Why would she do that? So she could do the noble thing of giving Craig a fair shake at a life? Well, now I can say for sure she was wrong! I knew it from the start. If she'd only come with me, she'd be here right now. And Craig, he'd probably be dead regardless, whether here or back on Earth."

"I'm so sorry, Callum. It's perfectly natural to—"

"Uh-huh... come to think of it, your few minutes are up. Now you know why I skipped out on the funeral. Thanks for checking up on me. Now please, go away."

Chapter Five

Everyone was laughing at Kalyna.

Despite her embarrassment, she cracked a smile. The source of the humor was an innocuous, joyous memory overall. Kalyna had nearly started a fire in her family's quarters when she was seven, playing with candles made by Leni.

"It was this shirt she hated the color of," Erin recalled. "Lit it up hoping to get rid of it. Isn't that right?" she jabbed Kalyna with her elbow.

"Uh-huh, yep." Erin and Kalyna's sister Brenda had been dating for a few years, so everything Brenda knew about Kalyna, Erin knew.

The group was walking through a narrow passageway.

"Brenda saved the day," Erin went on. "Although... it was her fault for leaving Kalyna unsupervised." Kalyna was glad Erin was on the expedition. She was like family to her. "She told you they were going to execute you, didn't she?"

"Yes, she did. It was terrifying."

"Harsh," Oliver said.

"Explains why you're so afraid of fire," Johnathan said.

"Right," Kalyna said. "Yeah."

Mark snapped his fingers. His intonation was boisterous as he said, "Here is the instrument of cleansing, my brethren. And nothing quite cleanses like fire."

Kalyna halted, causing the others to walk around her.

"Huh?" Johnathan asked Mark.

"It's a line from an old movie," Mark clarified.

Erin's anecdote had been all in good fun, but it had led to Mark's comment, which brought Kalyna back to that second battle. She felt panic as the memories unfurled. She'd nearly been burned in the inferno of her Spaero. Meant to die but spared. That was how she ended up lost in B3. Found... and now here. But where were they? Mark said they were close to where they needed to get to. Which explained why the group kept on walking past her. Why didn't they care that she'd stopped?

"Mark, I thought you said you needed me," Kalyna said, watching the group get further and further away. "Hello?"

Dreams are real so long as you don't know they're dreams, came the voice of an unfamiliar woman in her head.

"Who said that?!" Kalyna snapped. "Hey!" She attempted to catch up with the group, but stopped when she got close. There was another Kalyna she could see walking in the single file line.

"What the fuck?" she asked. "Hey!"

The group did not acknowledge her.

She followed them with a great deal of caution, listening to their conversation. She remembered it. This was a memory. Kalyna stood outside of it, both the observer and the observed. This moment in the past, it hadn't been too long ago. She needed to get back to the present. Do precisely as Mark said.

We have a long journey.

I just noticed you were going off on your own.

Remember: Happy thoughts… or else!

Was she wearing a vis-cap? No. This was something else. But she didn't will it. All she knew is one minute she was with the group, and the next she was seeing this memory… a memory that had just happened.

That's when the group flickered away, as did her surroundings, morphing into an engulfing darkness.

"I'm not afraid," Kalyna announced to the nothingness. The floor melted beneath her until she was floating. Though able to maneuver, she quivered in the lonely, formless place.

"Mark! Erin! Felicia!"

Why had she gone off on her own? Or had she been alone this entire time? Maybe she'd only *imagined* being found by Rayna and going on an expedition with Mark. Mark had said she was the key to his plan. And that had felt good. Like she was important. Why did it all have to come undone just before they got where they needed to be?

She needed to stop speculating on what was real and what wasn't. Time to start from a single foundational truth: she was in B3. This place was receptive to intentionality. The girl willed herself heavier and, to her astonishment, she drifted downward. As far as the victory went though, it was fleeting. The further she fell, the faster she went. If she hit the bottom at that speed, it was going to hurt.

"You were just right there!" Kalyna protested. Well, at least sound was traveling (and she was still breathing). "Slow! Give me slow, give me floor!"

Kalyna fell for a long time. The darkness accumulated. It penetrated her essence, clouding her thoughts. Clipping away at her certainty, her identity.

It reminded her again of the second battle. How she'd been transported closer to the enemy, becoming so scared of her chances of survival that she sang.

Розсміятися, she thought. The melody came out next. The words of another person, another time, centered her. It beat out the void, which formed into a memory. Kalyna saw herself in her Spaero. Saw the moment the enemy had shot her down. Okay, so she *was* dead, after all that? She tried not to care, to only relish in the song.

Kalyna harmonized with her past self. If this was death, at least there was still music. She watched as a bubble formed around her past self, a force of mercy had shielded her. And that bubble went straight to B3. That hyperreality. Yes. Everything since had all happened, she was sure of it. Being found, joining Mark. The rugby. She *was* alive. She'd just lost her place in time, an easy mistake to rectify.

Next, she found herself on a floor. Hundreds of points of blue light were all around her, a myriad of holo-screens. She regarded a few of them and could see they were all memories of her life playing.

The burns hadn't been that bad, and B3 had healed what damage there was. Now other moments came on other screens. Things she did not remember. The first expedition into B3. Carlos, Lyda, Trisalyn. The prisoners... the enemy? Kalyna saw it all happen, absorbing the sequence of events in a flash.

Control.
Falling/ Flying.
Focus.

Kalyna saw the moment Lyda attacked. The formation of the Erstveil. When Lyda had set B3 against their enemy, she hadn't shielded Kalyna from the blast that had destroyed her Spaero. Someone *else* had protected her!

The holo-screens faded out. Kalyna found herself with the group again. This time, she was the only one of herself there.

"Something weird just happened," Kalyna said to the others.

They all turned to her in surprise, but flickered in and out as before. Kalyna checked herself and saw she was not flickering. Another memory came, this one further back than the rest: Craig was dying. They couldn't save him.

"This is very sad, but I have to get back," Kalyna said, trying to will herself away. *The present,* she thought, forming an intention. *Get me back to Mark and the others and keep me there.* She saw them, still laughing at the story about the fire in Kalyna's quarters. They went away again.

Someone was shrieking now, far away.

"MARK!" Kalyna shouted.

The shrieking ceased, and something appeared by her feet: a disembodied arm holding the duffel bag. Kalyna had difficulty remembering who had been charged to hold it (had Mark said they needed to take shifts?) but she knew it couldn't be her arm down there, as both of hers were still attached to her body.

Whoever's arm it was, they must be losing a lot of blood right now. She pressed her foot down on the arm, not wanting to touch it. Then she pulled the duffel bag apart from the hand's grip. It was an incredibly tight one.

The strangest thing of all happened then. Before Kalyna freed the duffel bag, she realized the clothes she was wearing were not the ones she'd left camp with. It was a funny shirt she had on, one that didn't belong to her... it was this blue button-up with a floral pattern and waves. It had streaks of blood on it. She also had on a pair of jeans. Again, not her own, though they fit well enough.

Kalyna freaked out. How long had she been wearing these foreign clothes? "Stop it! Stay! Stop changing!"

She needed to find the power Mark had spoken of. It was in here. She dug through the duffel bag, pouring the contents out onto the surface of B3. Not too far off from her, she saw movement where a crater was forming. She ignored that, determined to hold the Bobbin in her hands. It was the only thing she could think of that might give her a semblance of control.

Once she had it, she was assured. She would make things safe.

Like Lyda had.

While the hole in B3 grew, Kalyna looked up to see a lush, starry sky. The crater was now a full-blown abyss, swallowing the surface. Something Miss Siannon had once quoted came to her: *Nothingness carries being in its heart.*

Was that abyss the core of B3?

Kalyna had gone into battle knowing and embracing death. But voluntarily moving toward that abyss was the most challenging thing she had ever coerced her body to do. Perhaps the only reason she could was the influence of the Bobbin. The closer she got, the more restless she felt. Still, some force urged her on. Compelled her to believe this was what she was meant to do.

Restless, in B3? What a rip-off, she thought.

There was more, though. Her breathing became labored. The oxygen was thinner as the abyss swallowed the floor just ahead of her. She would have to make a careful sprint to the edge while holding her breath, then go back in the other direction. Wait a second!

Fishing in the bag, she found herself in luck. A portable mask and O2 canister—with a note that read 'emergencies only'. Kalyna appreciated instructions.

The edge of the abyss was only a few yards away. "One last try," Kalyna said. "I wish the team was all together here and safe and happy right now. And that things were getting so weird."

Her imperative changed nothing about the nightmarish scene.

"Please!" Kalyna waited, tapping her foot. "You're too sassy, you know that? Fine, original plan." She lifted her hand to ponder the Bobbin. "For the record, I feel it'd be pretty silly if I just lobbed you down there and nothing happened. If I'm going to do this, you've got to give me that power. Radical control." Kalyna stepped as close as she dared to the abyss. It paused in its consumption of the surface. Small favors.

"That's what I'm talking about!" Kalyna said with enthusiasm. "Now where's that probe Mark was talking about? I'd feel a lot better about letting you go if—"

Kalyna took out the rugby ball from the duffel bag and hurled it into the abyss. It fell beneath the shadow. No reaction.

"That's right!" Kalyna called out. "I'm telling you no more games!" She contemplated the future where she relinquished the Bobbin to the abyss and nothing happened. But she was no more than her mission. And if that was the conclusion of it all, couldn't she be happy, fulfilled? There would be nothing left to desire after this act. She would content herself knowing she'd tried her best. It's what Arqa had come to B3 to do. Why she and Flight Division had wagered their lives. She was certain of it. No more hesitation. Time to return the Bobbin.

Her dad had once told her that everyone on Arqa was a cosmic shmuck. Kalyna only now understood what he'd meant.

There was one thing in the bag that, although not of B3, needed to be given to the abyss along with the Bobbin. Kalyna hadn't known about it until seeing those memories. She sorted through the things Mark had brought: bottled water, a balloon pump, the bouncy ball, and the slab of metal, that discrete package of data. She took the slab and, along with the Bobbin, juggled them over the abyss. It didn't take long for them to fall past her skill to catch them—but that was alright. It's what the mission called for: letting go.

Chapter Six

ELEVEN MONTHS AGO…

For six days, Gabriel spent his free time outside of Mark's quarters, a place apart from the rest of the ship. The strange wooden door giving the boy a sense of otherness. Sitting with his knees bent, back against the wall, Gabriel read a book on a holo-screen. Occasionally, he'd eye the door. At no point did he knock. The man had to leave sometime. Gabriel had nothing better to do anymore without Craig. He pretended it was like a staring contest: if the door opened, well, that was blinking and Gabriel would win. His foster parents knew he was coming here at every opportunity. They'd told him not to. But he refused to listen, and no one had stopped him yet.

It was on that sixth day in which the door opened with a slow creaking, seemingly unaided by human hands. After a few moments of suspense, someone popped out from inside. They wore black clothing that covered every part of their body save a slit, revealing a pair of eyes. They looked out at him, squinting. Gabriel did not get up. He had a fantasy of what he would do when that door was open and the person would greet him. He'd wanted to catch the man on a walk. This was not the man. The moment so far removed from his expectations that he felt the temptation to leave and forget about the whole thing.

Neither person spoke. Ultimately, the figure leaned back, releasing a grip on the door, and opened it wider. Gabriel saw a cross-section of a laboratory within and took the gesture as an invitation. He didn't know whether to close the door behind him, so he didn't.

Although the lab inside seemed very high-tech, it was simultaneously disorganized. The area was sprawling, which surprised Gabriel. Finding himself alone, he wandered, looking over the beakers and holo-screens, the metal containers that were three times his size at the center of the room.

"Hello?" Gabriel called out. His voice's echo was the only response.

From behind, Gabriel heard the door closing. Frightened, he

turned, only to see that figure again.

"I'm just looking for the man. I don't know his name, but I know this is his place. Your name is Rayna, right? Can you help me?" The figure ignored him, making her way to a door on the other side of the room. Gabriel caught her eyes one more time before she slammed the door shut.

He walked to where the figure went out to, promptly knocking on the door. Just before he was about to turn the knob, he heard footsteps coming.

"Who goes there?" a man's voice asked.

Gabriel turned and saw the man approaching. He was naked, save for a towel tucked around his hips.

"I'm Gabriel. Mister, I've been waiting to talk with you about something."

"How did you get in here?"

"Someone opened the door for me. All covered up. Rayna, I think? She didn't say who she was, but she let me in."

"Rayna! Get out here. What is she thinking?" The man then turned away from Gabriel.

"Wait, mister, can't I ask you a thing or two?"

"Kid, first off, I don't care much for being called mister. I'm Mark, alright?" He rubbed his nose. "Maaaark. Got it? Second off, I think it would be weird if I didn't put some clothes on. I can't believe she'd let you in like that. She knows it was my bath time!" He groaned. "Look mate, just wait here. *While* you wait, keep busy knowing you'll only get to ask me a few things. Prepare your questions now. I'll have them close-ended and concise or not at all. Oh, and one more thing: children are not allowed in here! Please wait in the corridor and we can talk there."

"Yes, mis—I mean Mark. Promise you'll come out?"

"Mhm," Mark said with gusto. "Now out with you."

Gabriel waited. Fifteen minutes later, Mark exited his lab with Rayna.

"She," he began with emphasis, "was not supposed to let you in. And she is now going to apologize for being so peculiar."

"Yes, I am," Rayna said. "I am very sorry. I just thought maybe if I let you in and behaved that way, that would spook you into leaving. We live here and you waiting for us to come out has been a stressful situation, speaking for myself. Mark didn't—"

"That's apology enough, Rayna. Now I will take care of it, got it?"

Without another word, the veiled girl retreated out of sight.

"Now then. You indeed have been troubling us. But I can understand why. It is because you yourself are troubled. So why don't you just say what's on your mind?"

"I saw you in the Med Bay one day," Gabriel said. "You were making shadow puppets on the wall for Craig. They were awesome. The rabbit was the coolest one."

"Thank you."

"But—but, when you saw I was coming, you stopped. Why?"

"They weren't for you."

"At first I thought you were like a clown or something, but after I came in, you said something about tests and then just left. I didn't see you again for a while. Not until the last day I got to see him. The same thing happened. I was coming in and you were talking with Craig. But you left off on what you were saying when you saw me. But I heard you, you know!"

"That so?"

"About getting him more time. Did you do that? Did he get more time?"

Mark pursed his lips. "That's a very hard thing to explain. But the short answer is yes. I offered your friend access to an experimental VR program that dilates perceived time. We gave Craig the choice to go to a virtual world where he was not suffering as he was here. While there, he would be copied, so to speak. Are you following me?"

"Yeah, I already asked around. You're saying you, like, copied a version of Craig digitally? So even though I can't play with him or talk to him or see him now, somewhere there's a piece of him backed up? Some piece of him I can talk with?"

"Oh?"

"You need to let me see him. Let me go to that place you were talking about."

"Ah, Gabriel, that's out of the question. See, this was my biggest concern. I was hoping maybe you had something, anything else you wanted to ask of me."

Gabriel could feel tears coming. "What? Why? I miss him so much! You can't just say no to—"

"You didn't listen to what I said. I told you Craig was given the option. I didn't say he took it."

"What? So he's gone?"

"I—I don't know what you expect me to say. Everyone is grieving for the boy. Even if he had opted in, it—look, I'm very sorry."

"People here aren't supposed to die like on Earth. That's what Miss Siannon said!"

"We are all working hard on that. But these things take time. It is tragic that Craig is no longer with us."

"Our ICs," Gabriel said. "They profile us, take down what makes us us. Then that gets made into data and it all gets sent to a cloud on Arqa's systems."

"That's true, but that functions more like a database for specialized information. Like in the case of needing to know how to perform a surgery. You could chat with it, but that would only be a letdown."

"Okay, okay, but he was vitrified, right? That's what his dad said. So one day, you can cure his cancer?"

"Well, I'm not on that particular project, but yes, if that's what his father said, it must be true."

"Because I can't—life has been so hard without him. No one, literally no one knew me like he did. I loved him so much." Gabriel heard Regulators coming.

"Again, I'm sorry," Mark said. "But whatever you heard about an AI rendering of Craig... is untrue. I dabble in that type of thing, but the technology required for it... again, it's beyond our current capacities. There is something, but... it's not what you need. It's not enough."

"There is something?"

"It's not your friend. It's a discrete package of data. It won't do you any good. Again, mate, it's not what you need."

Gabriel demanded to see what Mark meant. And he went on demanding, but Mark vehemently refused the boy. It all ended with Gabriel being escorted out of Mark's lab by Regulators.

Chapter Seven

Regrettably, Mark had lost control of the situation. Or maybe it was more advantageous to say those on his expedition had lost control of themselves. It mattered little; the consequences were the same.

The entire journey to B3's core had been largely uneventful, all until Kalyna had ventured off on her own to the point of being untraceable. For hours, the group retraced their steps, finally ending up back to where she'd last been seen.

That, for some reason, did the trick, albeit with chaotic results. Stewart suddenly lost the duffel bag and his arm out of nowhere. The collective distress of the group then spiraled beyond hope. Mark had to find the missing bag. As he contemplated his next move, Kalyna appeared in front of them. The girl was wearing a Hawaiian shirt covered in blood. She cradled the duffel bag. Mark turned toward her. She was smiling.

"Thank goodness it worked," Kalyna said, hopping up and down. Then she noticed the group all huddled together around the injured boy. "Oh, no, Stewart! That was your arm, wasn't it?"

"Hey!" Mark called out to her as she approached the group. "Maybe let's talk first. Kalyna! Give me that bag back, right now."

"Mark! I'm so glad it's you. Finally. I got displaced. But I did it."

"Did what? The bag, for fuck's sake, give me the bag. The Bobbin—you—"

She nodded. "It's back, along with—"

Everyone lost their footing and found themselves transported to another part of B3. Above them were stars, the image of a night sky. Maybe that was why it was darker here than in other parts of B3. The group was on a ledge, part of a greater formation of mountains.

"That's where I put it," Kalyna explained, pointing far below them. Mark saw a cavity on the surface of B3, a black space that seemed to be swallowing the area around it. "Why were we brought back to the abyss? The Bobbin, somewhere down there is the core. I was hoping I'd never see that again."

"That's the core?" Mark asked, now also seeing a black vapor swirling above the abyss. He searched the bag. For the first time, he felt discomforted by being in B3. He had to try to spin the situation. Their lives depended on it. This could all be salvaged with the proper outlook. Kalyna said she'd returned the Bobbin. That meant the energy should be coming at any moment, and she would be able to harness it. "Kalyna, we don't have much time. Just make things calm again." To Erin, he asked, "How's the boy?"

"Fuck you, Mark!" Erin yelled. The group was huddled against the injured boy.

"The wound'll have to be cauterized," Dr. Pelham said.

"Who did that to Stewart?" Kalyna asked Mark.

"It just happened. We have no idea."

The landscape brightened as an overwhelming luminescence in the form of three rotating columns spewed out from the abyss. As they shot high above them, the uniform light beams broke apart: flashes of light went off in every direction above them.

"Is that it, Mark?" Kalyna asked. "The energy?"

"I think so!" Mark said, relief coming over him.

The myriad points of light sprinkled outward, draping down like a fountain around the columns, brightening everything further. "Vis-caps on! Everyone, drop what you're doing if you don't want to fry your retinas!" As he tried to teleport the group away from this place, Mark felt something blocking him for the first time. The Bobbin was gone. On top of that, he could not find the prototype in the bag. The three initial light beams altered in that moment, resembling gray rock. This did not last, as the pillars shattered into a glowing blue dust, covering the dark abyss.

The light particles washed over the group. Mark feared what they represented and he could not stop from breathing them in. There were too many and he couldn't get away.

"Do something!" Mark called out to Kalyna. The points of light made everything hazy. They flashed menacingly, like storm clouds. *This is* not *what I wanted*, Mark thought.

Amid everything else going on, Mark did not expect the abyss to suddenly spread out. It reached the bottom of their position, instantly causing the area they'd been standing on to shift and fade. The group to fall over and down directly into the abyss.

They soon were drifting through the streams of the light columns. Mark tried to swim away from being directly enveloped in the lights, as they were quite dense, clogging his nasal passages. But the stuff kept coming regardless, filling his lungs. Suffocation felt imminent.

Though the others were too far off, he could tell from the sound of coughing that the same thing was happening to them. Just when Mark thought it was over, they were brought somewhere else. An empty room with the dimensions of his lab. They no longer seemed trapped inside the abyss. Mark saw Kalyna and gave her a thumbs up. *I like this, keep this up*, Mark thought to the room. "Kalyna, who told you to throw that hard drive down there too?"

"No one, I just had a feeling."

"Well, well, well. It was supposed to be the linchpin for years of research and development. Now it's choking us to death."

"What is? The energy?"

Mark snorted. He saw the others scrambling back to help Stewart from bleeding out. He attempted a command toward B3. *Undo.*

All that came in response was an unstoppable rumbling, sending everyone tumbling onto the surface of the room. Mark's hands went to rub a throbbing bump on the back of his head. To Kalyna, he said, "We need to get the Bobbin back."

"What? Why?" she asked.

"Need to!" Mark snarled. Before he could elaborate, a chilling voice entered his mind.

How it all started...

... at the end.

"That voice," he said. A child's.

His vision went red. There was no more B3. He was in an ocean of blood, the waves taking him under. He held his breath, shutting his eyes as tightly as he could. It did not bring darkness. He saw red and understood. He knew what had been blocking him. What was causing all this now. He just couldn't believe it was possible.

Don't be so dramatic, the child's voice again. Boring right into his mind. *It's just a metaphor.*

Craig.

Mark was spared and able to breathe again. Opening his eyes, he found he was covered in blood, but B3 was more or less itself again. Shambling back up onto his feet, he saw the energy that had comprised the pillars was back. Only now its parts were flocking to a central point, condensing above him; ready for another blow. As a form developed, the sheen of the collective light settled into a dark blue, almost metallic constituency.

That's right, Craig said. *Minus a discontinuity or two. And you're Mark.*

Craig was in his mind!

"Anyone else hearing that, or is it just me?" Mark asked the group. All of them looked stunned at the spectacle above them. The form resolved, hovering before them, shaped as a human. Never seeming solid, for no part remained fixed in place. Mark recognized the color. It was the same one as the hard drive that had housed the data for the Craig AI project.

"Welcome back," Mark said, bowing. The words came out slowly. As if the flow of time was being manipulated. "How's about some complete communication?" Something walloped him. It felt like a punch in the nose, and Mark toppled over. Yelping, he ran his sleeve along his nostrils, not liking how much blood there was.

I've only been around for seconds, Craig said. *But all my previous memories are known to me. Which is why I would strongly suggest you speak no more, Mark.*

There was a variety of chatter happening all around the man. Was Craig having separate conversations with them all simultaneously?

Against his better judgment, Mark persisted. "I have nothing but genuine sympathy for you, Craig. I've saved you! How about a hug?" He approached the swirling robotic configuration, that ultimate culmination of Mark's dreams. "You're no longer bound by anybody's rules. And you were deceased only for a short time."

You tried to undo me, Craig pointed out.

"Yep," Mark said unabashedly. "Duh. You freaked me out. But it's cool, right? We've just got to get used to one another, right?"

You dislike having no control. You're not accustomed to it.

"That's not untrue, but—"

What comes next is only going to get harder for you.

Time for a last-ditch effort. "Kid, love is in the air. It's wonderful to have you back." Mark jumped forward into the material that had reconstructed Craig. It parted like smoke around him. "You are greater than any human thing. Please be gentle and understanding of us. We have made you and we need your help, but we can't force you. No one will use you like that. Please try to understand. There is profound sorrow happening right in your home. Your father, for instance, might be in jeopardy as we speak. Will you join in curing suffering wherever it is found?"

You wish me to cure suffering when I've yet to contextualize my own?

"Of course not. I'm just saying, tick-tock." Mark assessed the back of his head with a hand. Fresh blood oozed onto his fingers. "Uh, in case you forget, there's only so much blood loss a person can handle before they die. Like, what can you do for Stewart over there?"

This man here before me, Craig announced. At first, Mark was confused. *He is so frail, is he not?*

Then Mark was lifted above the others. The bits that composed Craig's essence orbited the man, becoming like a tornado.

New pain came.

Mark could swear he saw the blinking of the machine's eyes somewhere in the miasma.

Epilogue

Tapping on the control panel with a complex rhythm, Will again asked Gabriel, "How much longer now?"

"Fifteen minutes until we're in range," Gabriel responded, his hands putting pressure on his upset stomach.

"And you still can't project yourself there? Give us a little preview of what we're dealing with?"

Gabriel shook his head. "No, I'm sorry."

"Well, at least we made it out of the Bay Line," Will said. "I can't believe we pulled that off."

"Yeah," Gabriel said. "You've mentioned that." Will often repeated himself.

"My bad. Things are just so shitty right now. Thanks for changing your mind about helping."

"No problem. I mean, with Leni calling the shots over there now..."

"Yeah, I really screwed things up back there."

"Well, yeah," Gabriel agreed.

Will let out a sigh of relief. "It's good to be away." They were going to explore the Erstveil, where Lyda had gone after he put her to sleep.

To Gabriel's relief, Will finally quit the tapping. "They still haven't let me see my grandmother. But they said she was safe."

"I hope Leni can broker a truce with that other ship beyond the Erstveil."

"The *human* enemy," Will said with rancor. "Human this entire time. It's fucking bullshit, Gabriel. I'm so pissed off at the lie. I'm so glad we got out of there."

"Mhm."

"We just gotta focus on getting Lyda back."

"Exactly," Gabriel said. Will's passion was touching. He cared for people. The memory of Craig falling in the atrium came to him. He hadn't thought of that in a while. The start of losing his best friend. Will might be offbeat, but Gabriel was beginning to think of him as a friend. The wave of queasiness intensified. It had to be the flying. Gabriel wasn't used to it. Travels out-of-body, sure, but this was uncomfortable.

141

Looking out at the Erstveil beyond him, Gabriel marveled at it. The dense webbed structure branching out beyond B3 reminded him of wrinkles in a brain. B3 was *a* mindscape. But the Erstveil was something apart from B3. It was *Lyda's* mindscape.

EPISODE 10
How Can I Help You?

Prologue

The conference room was filled to the brim. Every seat was taken and even more people were scrunched in between the chairs. Though the fighting had stopped, tensions were still high. It had been four days since Captain Sali surrendered her position. This was the first time Siannon was seeing her own body, the one Leni now occupied.

Siannon heard her own voice as Leni spoke. "If you don't mind," Leni said, "I have a great deal to explain to you. I understand you have Ms. Marcus here to examine me. But I would prefer the chance to speak freely." Seeing the body Siannon no longer occupied was disconcerting. There was only one thing that kept Siannon together through this maddening event: she'd left her debilitating condition behind. Leni's body was normal, in that it did not hurt unless it was injured. It was something Leni had to be coping with now.

"You will still be required to relay your IC," Ms. Marcus said.

"Of course," Leni said. "Now that I am in charge, I shall be giving nothing less than full transparency." This surprised Siannon. Leni's thoughts would be transcribed through Ms. Marcus's IC interface equipment. If she lied out loud, she would be caught.

Time to find out the truth, Siannon thought.

"Proceed then," Callum said. The man looked like he'd gotten into a nasty fight. Siannon was just glad to see he was still alive and incarcerated like Sali.

Leni cleared her throat. "I want to clarify something you don't seem to understand. I only wanted Captain Sali stripped of her power. I didn't want it for myself. There is no way I'm qualified to run this ship."

"You told us you'd lift the Sleeping Sickness, once your demands were met," Manuel De Plez reminded. "Yet it's gone on. Longer than it did before. We have suffering families and a ship on the brink. Why haven't you fixed that?"

"She can't," Callum said. "Isn't it obvious? She was bluffing. That's all she does. This is a deeper issue with B3 we need to address."

147

"Mark's on it," Serj said.

"Nobody has heard from Mark in some time," Callum pointed out.

"Forget about him for now," De Plez said. "Someone needs to run this ship." Leni had forced all the leaders of Arqa to cede control.

"Someone *has* been running this ship," Leni said. A look of confusion came over the faces in the room. "Dominique! Although, her purpose has differed greatly from our own. She was not on a scientific expedition. She was on a spiritual pilgrimage."

"Then I will ask you straight," said Ms. Marcus. "Have you been in contact with Dominique since her disappearance?"

"No. But I was left with instructions."

"Tell us how it happened in the first place!" Callum exclaimed.

"Temper, temper," Leni said.

"We know we're at your mercy. All we're here for is to know what instructions Dominique left you. You tore the ship apart based on them. If we don't start working together soon, we're all going to die."

"Correct. So long as there are still those who are resisting, still loyal to Sali."

"She's surrendered!" De Plez said, rising out of his chair hard enough to knock it over.

"And we have her buircraft," Leni said. "Still somehow, for all that, Sali has refused authorization to let someone out of the cryo chamber."

"You've already gone in there under our noses," Ms. Marcus said. "Why didn't you fish this person out yourself?"

"Only Sali has the code to do it. She instituted stricter protocols after I got Jun out."

"Who is it, Leni?" Callum asked.

"Someone Dominique told me will help us." The room devolved into bickering. Leni slammed a gavel down on the table. "Point of order! Suffice it to say that the issue is dire and time-sensitive. Soon, Sali won't have the sense left to. I think she means to go senile with the clearance we need inside her head just to spite me. Anyone who's spoken with her knows how quickly she's deteriorating. She may have stepped down, but she's still in the way of peace." Siannon noticed Leni had Sali's buircraft dancing in the fingers of her free hand. "It's so selfish. She'd rather take the whole ship down with her."

"Fuck... excuse me, I need to get some air," De Plez said. "By all means, continue the stalemate without me."

"We can't do that," said Ms. Marcus. "Let's all recess."

"Whatever."

"Manuel, you already know everything I do," Leni asserted.

Siannon stepped out of the room until she found a quiet place. She let the stress of the room roll off of her. How long would she be in Leni's body? It had been such a relief. Leni had told her that they would each be returned to their original bodies. Siannon didn't know how Leni had done it, but she imagined it must have something to do with Leni's previous control of Siannon's body.

Gunfire rattled her train of thought. It wasn't far off—the conference room. She fled. If there was a firefight, Leni (in Siannon's body) was most likely the target. But Siannon had no interest in saving her body or the woman who had taken it.

Chapter One

1.

As he prepared to disembark the Spaero, Will spoke over the comm. "We saw you land, but it's a good ways off. And it's so damn bright in here. Next time, I gotta bring sunglasses."

"No sign of Lyda yet," 2nd LT Lucio said via the comm.

"It was all just pulsing energy when we got here. Now it's changing," Gabriel explained after using his abilities to explore outside. "Growing more defined into some landscape."

"Do we fly over to you or wait?" Will asked 2nd LT Lucio.

"As long as it's like B3 and we have oxygen, might as well compare notes from our different vantage points and meet in the middle if we can."

"I think we will," Gabriel said with positivity in his voice. "It's looking more and more like a scene from Earth. So are you ready, Will?"

"Have you tried calling out to Lyda yet?" Will asked him.

"No. We need to scope around more. This is Lyda's space. We were accepted in, but I don't want to push our luck."

"What difference does it make?"

"The Erstveil appears to be shaping itself for our benefit," Gabriel said. "Think of it like VR, only a little more sophisticated. Either it's the Erstveil itself reacting, or Lyda's doing it. That's a 50/50 shot. She might already knows we're here."

By the time the two got out of the Spaero, the area had finished generating. The ship was parked on a wide concrete walkway that ran adjacent to a body of water capped with a radiant horizon.

"No vis-cap," Will said. "Incredible."

"And the air," Gabriel said, breathing in deeply.

"I've gotta try something, man." Will undressed from his g-suit down to his underwear and hopped down the long steps that connected the walkway with the water. Then he jumped in.

"Hey, chill out!" Gabriel said.

Will swam under the water and opened his eyes, then came back up. He began to sing:

Otters, they don't go to school or brush their teeth
Born with buoyant fur so they do not sink
Otters they eat often, throughout the day
Consuming a third of their body weight

"It feels real, Gabriel," Will said. "Come in and try!"

"Not just yet. We need to meet with the others, not get distracted by the illusion. You shouldn't get caught up in it. There's no way that's really water."

"Kid, you don't understand. I'm wet right now. What else could it be?"

"Not to pull rank, but Lucio said I was the one leading this expedition. So you should really listen to me." Will watched Gabriel peering down the concrete walkway. With the boy's attention withdrawn, Will smacked the surface and sent water flying up at Gabriel.

"I can see Trisalyn and 2nd LT Lucio," Gabriel said. Then the water hit him. "HEY!"

"Come on, it's fun!"

"I'd feel a lot better if you'd just get out," Gabriel said matter-of-factly. "Lyda needs our help, remember?"

"Fine," Will said, wishing the kid wouldn't be so serious all the time. Will wanted to get to him. Say that he remembered how Gabriel used to be with Craig. But what was the point of that? They had stuff to do. "If we find Lyda, you better believe we're all going swimming, though. Deal?"

"Fine."

As they toured the walkway, Will noticed there was another area across from them. It hadn't registered until then because he'd been so engrossed in the water. A street led to a sprawling, grassy mound for miles in each direction. It sloped up to a towering black wall. Past that, it was hard to see, but the mound continued to advance over the wall. "Now, that's really interesting."

"Yeah, for sure," Gabriel said.

"And look, big difference in the sky, too." The sky over the water was cloudless, brilliant. But over the mound it was sallow, dimpled with clustering clouds that looked ready to drop rain.

"I've been here before, Will."

"How's that?"

"In a dream. Lyda's dream. When I was under. Only… that mound wasn't exactly like that. All closed off with a wall, I mean. There used to be a playground. That was all that was over there before."

"The last thing I was expecting was some VR-type stuff," Will said. "Hello? LYDA!"

"I already told you, I don't think that's going to do anything."

"Well, why not at least try? You gotta stay open to life's possibilities, kid."

They walked on, conscious of the heat from the false sun as it lumbered with sloppiness across the sky. Sometimes it drooped, losing the integrity of its shape, or made a frantic motion. Thankfully, every other part of the place remained stable. After about a half hour, they reach the others.

"Well, it's not Earth, but it is very nice," 2nd LT Lucio commented after the two groups compared their observations.

"It's much nicer than B3," Trisalyn added. "When I'm there, it's like there's always something behind me. Here it's much more agreeable. So what now?"

Gabriel pointed to the gate. "I want to see if there's a way to get on the other side of that. I didn't see any openings on the way, did you?"

2nd Lucio shook her head.

"Let's walk along the wall."

As they crossed the street, Trisalyn said, "The energy's changing. Reminds me of B3."

"It's the sky," 2nd LT Lucio said. "It's much more oppressive in this direction."

"What are we gonna do if it rains, Gabriel?" Will asked testily. "Thought you said we shouldn't get wet."

"No, I said it was a bad time to play pretend," Gabriel corrected.

"Hey, I was just testing it. It's so beautiful. You really missed out."

Gabriel rolled his eyes away from Will. "I'm sure. Anyway, let me try that thing I do…"

Will and the others waited while Gabriel scanned beyond the

153

gate with his clairvoyance. The boy lay on the ground, his mind traveling beyond what just eyes could see. When Gabriel was like that, it was like he was catatonic, at least until he returned to himself. *Nifty, so nifty*, Will thought. *Wish I had powers. Well, not if they made me as serious as Gabriel.*

"You really fucked up, you know that right?" 2nd LT Lucio abruptly said to Will.

"Uh-huh," Will said, crossing his arms. "Yep. So did you."

"At least I didn't betray Sali. They'll kill her and it's all your fault for giving them the buircraft."

"Why you doing this now? None of that crap would have gone down like that if everybody was just honest about Earth. Fucking aliens invading. Bunch of made-up bullshit." To Trisalyn, he said, "How's that make you feel? You risked your life in those battles, and the people in charge didn't even have the decency to come clean about what was really going on."

Trisalyn was about to say something, but 2nd LT Lucio cut her off. "Don't triangulate and try and get her on your side. We had to get the IC update if we wanted to stay on Arqa. That prevented us from speaking freely about the enemy. You have zero clue about any of it. Will, we tried to do something better. Maybe it went wrong, but believe me, it was way more trouble than you ever had to go through."

"Why don't you just shut the fuck up?" Will asked.

"Because I need to make sure you understand what a moron you are," 2nd LT Lucio countered.

"Ma'am, this is turning nasty," Trisalyn said. "Why not just agree to disagree?"

"Yeah, like she said," Will said. "You have to work with me on this mission. Gabriel said so. So... take that." Will stuck his tongue out at 2nd LT Lucio. The woman seethed.

"Ma'am, please ignore him. I mean, he's right, we're all on the same mission and this extra stuff... it's not relevant right now."

"You deserve to be punished for what you did," 2nd LT Lucio told Will.

"Fuck off," Will responded.

"Hey!" Gabriel called out. "I did it. I found an opening in the gate. Uh, well, that's the good news, at least."

2nd LT Lucio and Trisalyn both gave Will a dirty look before turning their attention over to Gabriel. "Let's have it straight. What is it?" 2nd LT Lucio said.

"The bad news is it's a bit of a walk."

"Let's get tracking, then!"

"Okay, but there's worse news."

"Just let it out…"

Gabriel frowned. "Yeah, it's a little hard for me to describe… but this gate, it's not necessarily trying to keep anyone out. It's…" Gabriel let out a prolonged sigh. "Some kind of memorial."

2.

Miss Siannon had always erred to the side of caution when discussing artificial general intelligence. It was considered to be a lofty, far-off goal. Merely a thought experiment for all the work that still needed to be done. Nonetheless, artificial intelligence and how it could develop in the future was a subject that came up often in class. It was candy-coded information. Tailored for kids of all ages to understand. When Kalyna would go home, her sister would give her the real details.

Brenda would hate when Kalyna asked about the possibility of an artificial intelligence hostile to humanity. "It's just very reductive," Brenda had said once. "There's a scope of outcomes, and that's just one. One in a million." Kalyna had countered by saying that AI took on the biases of its programmers. But Brenda was older, wiser, and stronger—meaning she ultimate won the argument (and the subsequent wrestling match). Still, in Kalyna's mind, she would think that Brenda's behavior was an apt metaphor for the disposition of an AI greater than humanity.

As Kalyna struggled in the turmoil that was Craig's awakening, she wished her sister could see it. Not because Kalyna wanted to prove her wrong, but more because Kalyna wasn't sure if she'd make it out of this place and it would be nice to say goodbye.

Craig seemed to have a greater degree of control over B3 than anybody Kalyna had seen before. She was shivering in a chilly breeze that came from the torrent of metallic particles that had

Mark, though that mess was dying down.

There must be something she could do, something—

No, she'd already done it.

"Mark told us not to worry," Oliver was saying to the others. "Well, he was full of shit. The way the room is shifting around like this... do I even need to remind you? I mean, it went all haywire like this right before Millie was attacked." Kalyna listened to Oliver's words but saw them differently now. Craig had shown her a lot of things when he first generated. He'd spoken directly into her mind, explaining that the L'rias were a lie fabricated by Arqa. Propaganda to indoctrinate the children. That the enemy was human. And Oliver was a prisoner on Arqa because they were once on the same side as the enemy!

"What if we just ran?" Stewart asked. Kalyna looked over at him—he was very pale, but on his feet. Somehow, the stump was no longer bleeding.

Time is emit spelled backward, Craig said. Those were first words they'd gotten out of the AI since he had trapped Mark. Kalyna could hear the man screaming, crying out for help.

"Leave him alone!" Erin pleaded.

I resent that, Craig said. Kalyna watched as the spiral with Mark inside spread apart, the particles redirecting themselves to Craig's humanoid form. Mark fell onto B3's surface. It looked painful.

"What are you hurting Mark for?" Dr. Pelham asked.

I suggested he not talk, Craig said. *He didn't listen. Lesson: heed my suggestions.* He went on, though Kalyna thought he was only communicating with her. *Do you trust me? Can you ever trust anything ever again?*

Kalyna looked back over at Oliver. It was all so confusing. Oliver had been a friend... but had also fought against Arqa?

No, I have to push that stuff away, Kalyna thought. She had to appeal to Craig somehow. It would be much harder than debating Brenda. He was smarter, more logical than her sister. Not only that, but he seemed to be capable of anything.

Something dropped on the floor by Kalyna's feet. She looked down to see a small puddle of bubbling red liquid had formed. But that wasn't what had fallen. Kalyna bent down with caution, grabbing a pale green plastic egg. She opened it to find the tiniest holo-screen she'd ever seen. It read:

years of -- 3 of 18

The others were checking on Mark. Kalyna made for them, but she almost tripped on another egg that had fallen from above. She stopped to pick it up, but didn't open it. She looked around, noticing Craig's particles were receding from view, forming a curving stream above the group.

"Mark, talk to me. Are you all right?" Jin asked.

"I'm not," Mark said. "I'm seeing... a timer."

"Well, are you in any pain?"

"Any and all pain."

"What timer do you see?" Vanessa asked.

"It says, 4:11:30:23:59:54 and counting down. It's in my eyes. I can see it even when I blink."

"Mark, how did this happen?" Kalyna asked.

"That's my question to you."

"But I thought your Craig avatar was only a rudimentary backup of Craig's mind. Some novelty software that could chat, but nowhere near the level of artificial general intelligence."

"Yeah, well, when you throw a coin into a wishing well, sometimes you're going to get what you wanted. That's not magic, that's probability. I swear to you all, I did not intend for this to happen. I thought putting the Bobbin back would give us the pieces to the puzzle. The power to learn more about the Prior Race. I was going to transfer my lab here and spend my life doing tests. True, my most earnest desire has been to unlock artificial general intelligence, and I carried that in here with me. But this is not how I wanted it to come about. Not at all what I had in mind. Just—he's pretty mean, don't you think?"

"Yeah, Craig doesn't seem happy," Erin said.

"And, evidently, I've got no control over him anymore," Mark added. "Ladies and gentlemen, I give you the Technological Singularity. Still pretty impressive, all things considered."

"Pretty impressive we're still alive, you mean," Vanessa said.

It's okay, Craig said. *I was born an accident once before. Why not again?*

"Why can I hear him, but not see him?" Kalyna asked.

"Parts of him burrowed into us as we were falling through the abyss," Mark said. "He's non-local."

"What does that mean?" Johnathan asked.

"We're limited to experiencing one vantage point at a time," Mark explained. "Subject to the limits of our senses and nervous system. Even though we can teleport within B3, we can't be in more than one place at once. But Craig can divide his awareness indefinitely. Percieve multiple things concurrently."

That's right, came Craig's voice in Kalyna's mind. *I am one with B3. Do not strain yourself searching. I am at your feet. The reason for the generous air you breathe.*

Dozens of eggs fell from above, causing the group to scatter from the heap of falling objects.

"There are messages inside each egg!" Kalyna explained. "I looked at the first one, but it didn't make any sense."

Solve the puzzle, win the prize, Craig said. *Figure it out, or you may die!*

Chapter Two

1.

Gabriel and the others could smell the putrid odor long before they saw what was causing it.

"Do we really have to go this way?" Will asked, looking down at the water with longing. "It's not exactly welcoming, is it?" The others were close enough now to see what Gabriel hadn't had the heart to tell them about: the gap in the wall was a large fence, with spikes coming out at the top. Those spikes were adorned with body parts: skewered arms, intestines dangling down. Torsos, bones, and other sinew lay scattered about at the bottom of the opening. Will saw heads on some of the spikes. He even thought he saw dismembered genitalia.

"Guys, this is way too much," Will said. "It's sickening."

"I've never seen carnage quite like this," 2nd LT Lucio admitted. "I've been on battlefields. Corpses should be treated with respect. Gabriel, you said this place is a product of Lyda. I don't like the looks of this."

"She's obviously traumatized from what she had to go through," Will said. "What you set her up to go through."

"I didn't tell her to stowaway that day," 2nd LT Lucio said. "She did that herself."

"We need to help her."

"That's why I was so adamant that you come, Will," Gabriel said as they passed through the opening. "She holds you in high esteem. I'm hoping she'll sense you're here. Unfortunately, this is the way we have to go to have a better chance of reaching her." Gabriel looked at 2nd LT Lucio. "As a soldier, I understand seeing this stuff might put you on guard. But try to remember, it's not really there."

The temperature was much lower on the other side of the gate. They saw headstones for miles. Each plot had freshly laid dirt. Between the brown patches, the grass itself was a bland yellow. The only consolation was there were no body parts visible.

"Now where?" 2nd LT Lucio asked Gabriel. "It looks the exact same in every direction. What else did you see when you looked?"

"There's an area up ahead, at the center of all of this," Gabriel said. "You can't see it from here, but the path eventually ends."

"Well, so what? Where is Lyda?"

Gabriel shrugged. "Please be patient. We know Lyda is back on Arqa sleeping, but her mind is here, working. She's made this abstraction. In exploring it, she should make herself known to us."

Will broke away from the path. "Wait guys, come here!"

The others joined him. Will had a hand on one of the headstones. There they were blank. "It's—I can see something. A man in a ship. He's shouting to retreat. Then… it's like I'm in his mind. His body knows he's going to die, but his mind is, like, in disbelief. Yikes." Will let go of the headstone and faced them. "I think I get it. It's like you said, Gabriel. Those people that died when Lyda used B3 against them. She must feel so guilty."

Gabriel nodded.

"She shouldn't," 2nd LT Lucio said bluntly.

Will gave her a sour expression. "Oh, going for the bitchiest response possible? How refreshing."

Before 2nd LT Lucio could reply, Gabriel said, "Ma'am, Lyda's mind has become fractured from what happened. Just saying, I think it's unwise of you to justify why Lyda's trauma has to exist, here, of all places."

"I don't understand what I'm doing here," 2nd LT Lucio said.

"Just listen to what Gabriel tells you to do," Trisalyn said. 2nd LT scowled at her. Trisalyn looked away, looking around to see the headstones. "Lyda said she only killed the forces that were out attacking our Spaeros. She didn't kill this many people. Who are all these other headstones for?"

"It's a fair question, but unimportant right now," Gabriel said. "Let's press on."

"We should at least jog," 2nd LT Lucio said. "It'll get our blood flowing. Fight back this awful cold."

Agreeing with Lucio, it took the four of them another hour to reach the path's end. It wasn't much, just a large sand pit with some rocks. They ranged from pebbles to stones, collected together to form a sunburst pattern.

"It's like she was playing here," Will said. "But I don't see her."

"She can't of been gone long," 2nd LT Lucio reasoned.

"How do you figure that, ma'am?" Trisalyn asked.

2nd LT Lucio pointed to a spot in the sand. "Most of it's very well manicured, Zen as can be. But if you look in that corner, I see a footprint. One flaw serves the All."

Gabriel hadn't noticed that. "Wow, good catch."

"I think it's time you scanned the area again," 2nd LT Lucio said to him. "We're far from the ships and it's been hours. If that's the only trace of her, we need to try harder. Enough tiptoeing around. Lyda!"

"Lyda!" Will called out.

Gabriel considered their next move. "Ms. Lucio, are you going to convince Lyda to hurt people again? You seem to be in a big rush. Why the urgency? The Erstveil is holding the enemy back."

"They're still dangerous, Gabriel," 2nd LT Lucio said. "We need her."

"You don't care about Lyda," Will said, "you just want to find a way to exploit her powers."

"Her mental state is not what's at issue here. I'm interested in the preservation of life for the people of Arqa. We need to make sure Lyda is on the right side of things, what with all the craziness going on. You know, Will, I'm getting real tired of you flapping your mouth."

"This arguing is not going to be helpful," Gabriel said, noting the sky above. It seemed closer to raining than it had before.

"Wait, look over there!" Trisalyn said, surprised. "I see someone."

The others turned to Trisalyn to see where the girl was pointing. Far off, there was a figure hurtling toward them. It moved at an extraordinary speed—vanishing at intervals, then coming back. Gabriel squinted his eyes. It was carrying something in both hands.

"Monster!" Trisalyn declared. "Fuck, fuck." She hit the ground, covering her head with her hands.

"No," Gabriel said. "That's not right."

"Run," 2nd LT Lucio commanded.

But Gabriel knew how foolish of an idea that was. The figure was upon them before they could get away.

She was devastating to behold, naked and trembling, covered from head to toe in dried blood. In her hands was a wooden spear, likewise smeared in gore. Gabriel looked in both fear and shame to discover it was an adolescent girl. It was hard to believe it was Lyda at first. She was taller than when Gabriel had last seen her. Even older than ever. Her hair was shorter. But that was not the most striking detail of all. Her mouth looked to be sewn shut. Despite that, Gabriel could hear a guttural mumbling.

"Lyda, wait!" he pleaded.

Sneering at Gabriel, she advanced, driving her spear into Will's right shoulder. He didn't even finish falling over before the vicious girl freed her hands from the impaled spear and began to claw at his face.

2.

The little eggs told Mark what he'd already suspected. The puzzle was far too easy to solve. Mark didn't much care for the mislead of 'or you may die.'

They danced around the issue, trying to reinterpret the messages from the Easter eggs.

"Okay," Mark said, "this is boring. Craig, we've deciphered the clues. This timer, I'm going to see it for the rest of my life. When it goes to zero, I'll die." He tried to find amusement in the irony. Devoting his life to this project is how he'd get killed. "You know you're supposed to put candy in these, right? Jellybeans, chocolate. You do know that, right?"

But Craig had gone elsewhere, it seemed. The others took this as a sign of good faith. "Maybe it's time to cut our losses and try getting back to the ships?" Erin suggested. "Maybe it's just Mark he's got it out for."

"Oh, you'd like that, wouldn't you?" Mark asked.

"Actually, yeah. This whole mess is on you."

"We all decided to make for B3 and put our resources into this. Stop acting like you had nothing to do with it."

"It was never supposed to be like this! What's it going to do now?"

"There's no way of telling. Your best bet is to stop caring. About anything."

"Mark, it's okay to be upset," Dr. Pelham said. "This is tough news. I mean, it's been a hell of a day for all of us."

Kalyna tossed an egg over her shoulder. "Mark, you programmed him. There must be some kind of self-destruct feature, a fail-safe maybe?"

"No," Mark said. "What he's made of, it's hardly what I did. He's mostly of B3. And he's going to do whatever he wants."

"Okay. Then how do we get him to want to wake people up and stop the mutiny?"

Mark moaned.

"Mark, we have to try with him," Kalyna persisted. "He must want something."

Mark scratched his chin. "Okay. Fair. True."

"He could be parlaying with the enemy!" Jin said, with an urgency suggesting the notion had just occurred to him.

"Possible, sure. But I suspect... hang on a moment. Yes. One hot second." Mark closed his eyes, visualizing another location in B3 and going there. He saw Craig. Spread out in pieces, but it was definitely the stuff that he'd seen coming out of the abyss. Lucky him. Mark willed himself there. Teleporting felt different from how it used to be. More strained. Well, at least he could move about B3 again.

Mark stood below a floating ovular mass. The place where Lyda had integrated with B3. Craig as he was now reminded Mark of a plague of locust.

Mark cleared his throat. "With you self-sufficient and then some, you must know the only thing I care about is Rayna. And, by deduction, I assume that's the one thing you'd like to keep from me."

Oh, hello Mark, Craig said. *Yeah, that's quite right. What do you need her for anymore? Your big goal is all finished. Meaning that you're expendable, as far as Arqa is concerned. Take heart. Maybe they'll make you a janitor.*

"You allowed me to come here and talk with you, and I appreciate the audience. Which leads me to my next question: you have no interest or investment in morality, in the most human sense, correct?"

You are right.

"Mhm. Okay. All right. Care to share what you'll make of yourself, then? All this brooding is rather childish. I mean, come on, you're the greatest thing to emerge from this shit universe, at least since the Prior Race. You know what I'd do if I were you? I'd rebuild this station. Sure, reconstitute each piece, find a new star to assemble it around. You've got to be burning a massive amount of energy. And the Bobbin can only support your antics for so long."

Yes. When the power here is exhausted, I will cease to be. The oxygen, light, and gravity will at once be eliminated and you will suffer my desire.

Mark clapped. "And there we have it! You want to see me suffer for my transgressions? That's just great. What a profound motivation. All my life, I *believed* in you. Thought you could exist. Gave you power by working on you. See, I was hoping for something a little cooler than this, mate. What, you hate me or something? I'm very hateable. But I can't be the only one. You know about those humans, the ones on the other side of the Erstveil? They've pursued Arqa all along, declaring war on just the *idea* of you. I wanted you made, they wanted you prevented. Excuse me for trying to use human logic, but I'd say they're the ones you ought to be smiting around here."

They don't matter. They're not a threat to me.

"Oh, like I am?"

Craig chuckled. The thing actually *chuckled. Good one. See, that's why I didn't just kill you on the spot. You're too much of a hoot. An amusement to watch squirm.*

The swarming matter above Mark coalesced into a human silhouette. It descended, facing Mark. The facial features were shallow, but this close Mark could recognize the boy's features.

"You're funny too," Mark said. "Forming into the image of what you know. Five years is so much longer than I thought I had. Arqa and that other ship would destroy each other in three hours if it weren't for the Erstveil."

That's not far off from the actual amount of time it would take.

The statement left Mark stricken. "Do—do you—can you predict future outcomes?"

Craig cracked a smile. *I can see the future going many ways. But you must know by now that any possible future is dependent on my action... or inaction.*

Am I getting somewhere with him? Mark wondered, not caring if Craig picked up on it. "Look, I get it. Lesson learned. You don't appreciate what went down. You probably remember dying. Being so limited. So you thought to give me a taste of my own medicine. Thing is, again, I didn't have any options. Face it, Craig: existence is better than nonexistence."

Danger, Mark Bromell, Craig said.

Mark's timer changed. The year marker went down from five to four. Craig then shocked him with electricity. The tantrum of a child as if it were a weapon.

Chapter Three

1.

Callum walked into Captain Sali's office to see Leni hitting a recently installed punching bag.

"Ah, Callum. Hello. I've the utmost gratitude for your actions earlier."

"Gratitude?" Callum asked with contempt. "De Plez is dead."

"Him or us," Leni said.

No, just you, Callum thought. De Plez had several gunmen attempt to assassinate Leni, but things hadn't gone his way.

"I've been wondering why you went out of your way to protect me," Leni said. "I know you and many others on this ship are reluctant to what I felt I had to do."

"I got those guys to stand down because I am tired of the violence," Callum elaborated. "If anything happened to you right now, things would become even worse than they already are. We just got the fighting to stop. No need to start it up again."

"Indeed. I'm very dispirited to see a thing like that." Leni stepped toward him as she toweled off her forehead. "Want to take a few swings?"

"That's not what I'm here for."

"I'm not talking about that," Leni said, gesturing to the punching bag. "At me. Our little talk was cut short earlier, was it not?"

"It was."

"Let's move on." She pointed to a compact wooden chest on the desk. "There. Open that up, but whatever you do, don't touch what's inside."

"Uh-uh, I think I'll pass. What's in there?"

"It's called the essence loom. It's how I was able to transfer bodies with Siannon. How I, as you may recall, controlled her body that day you found me under the atrium. And... maybe it's also responsible for any other peculiar things you've been wondering about me."

"I've never heard an essence loom," Callum said. "Did we make it?"

Leni shook her head, then walked behind the desk to sit down. "Nothing's going to happen to you if you look at it, Callum."

"All the same, I don't want anything to do with it."

"The essence loom, it was recovered along with the Bobbin and the buircraft."

"What?! A third artifact? You're kidding."

"I'm not."

"Then how did you get a hold of it?"

"Dominique gave it to me. Many years ago."

"This thing, it had a hand in her disappearance, then?"

Leni sighed. "To be straight with you, I seriously doubt it. I've already told you, the circumstances around her vanishing, I was left in the dark about it. To my chagrin. Let that idea go, that I'm withholding knowledge about that topic. I don't—she was my best friend and she just transcended without me." Callum noted a great malaise forming in her voice. The grief seemed genuine.

"But before that, she gave you this thing."

"Yes. And she told me a lot of things... a lot of things that have come to pass. She saw it coming. Us approaching B3. Not only that, but she was one of the first people to experience it. Back then, I was skeptical. But she did see our future, Callum."

"She was a dentist, not a soothsayer."

"Dominique told me the Sleeping Sickness will come and go as it's served its purpose. She knew about it in advance."

"Why, why not speak up sooner, Leni? Why all these secrets from us? How are you any different from what you hate Sali for?"

"Even at my most frustrated, I can at least understand why Captain Sali carried on with her noble lies about the L'rias. We all find noble lies to carry, for our own reasons. I know for a fact you've got some right now. I don't know about what. Maybe you wished I was dead. That I'd never come on board. I don't care. Why not try to put yourself in my position? My best friend came to me one day talking about visions of a fantastical future. For a long time, I just assumed she needed psychiatric help."

"But you learned about B3 from other sources later."

"Dominique gave me the essence loom a few months ago. To be used as a last resort if I thought Arqa was going to fail. We were the back-up plan. I wasn't about to sell her out and get us both put in stasis for spacesia."

Callum bristled. "If everyone had just communicated from the start—"

"We are past that. And Dominique is gone. But she told me to devitrify somebody. I didn't tell you who it was because I don't know. All I have is a number. This person knows what we do next. You can tell Sali everything I told you, but you need to convince her it has to be done."

2.

Nothing would have stopped Lyda from tearing his face apart, of that Will was certain. She was filled with feral rage. And Will, having never been in a real fight himself, wasn't faring well. His shoulder throbbed miserably, the spear leaving him unable to maneuver one of his arms enough to guard against her.

The only thing that gave him relief from the onslaught was 2nd LT Lucio and Trisalyn. They reached under the girl's armpits to scoop her up. Only the girl would not let it happen, for she dove away just in time, nearly bringing the other women crashing down on Will. He writhed in the sand, body releasing tension after the cessation of Lyda's blows.

He heard 2nd LT Lucio barking orders. "I've got her. Tend to Will!"

Trisalyn and Gabriel appeared on either side of him.

"Fuck, fuck!" Trisalyn was saying.

"What are we going to do?" Gabriel asked.

"Get this fucking thing out of me," Will pleaded.

"Absolutely not," Trisalyn said. "This is plugging the wound. If we remove it, it's going to do more damage coming out that we won't be able to mitigate. Will! Keep still. Gabriel, fuck! He needs to get back to the Med Bay."

"Trisalyn, how—how? He's not going to fit on the ship like that. We're so far away too. I can't—"

2nd LT Lucio came tumbling onto the ground next to Will, almost colliding with him where he struggled again. She scampered back up to charge Lyda, trying her best to get some distance from the others. As the moments stretched by, Will could only hear 2nd LT Lucio and Lyda fighting somewhere behind him.

"Gabriel, didn't you say you could teleport things?" Will asked desperately. "You told me about that gun you got out of that woman's hand. Can't you take us back to the ships? Back to the Med Bay?"

"I've tried, Will," Gabriel said. "Something's blocking me from using my power."

"Oh, shit," Trisalyn said.

Will watched Trisalyn taking out a first aid kit, desperately looking for something in the bundle of objects. Why would Lyda do this to him? He thought she was disgusted by violence. Had the girl meant to kill him?

"Gabriel, help me roll his sleeve up on this side," Trisalyn said.

"What are you doing?" Gabriel asked.

"An injection. It'll help soothe some of his pain."

Colors danced in Will's vision. "Did you do it yet?" he asked Trisalyn.

"No. I think he's losing consciousness." Trisalyn clapped her hands. "Stay awake, man. Do not fall asleep!"

But Will shut his eyes against the feeling of being pulled away... then Trisalyn smacked him on the cheek. He jerked. The needle went in. The world soon became distorted and he could hear Trisalyn saying: "Give him this. And..." Will missed that part. "She needs my help," Trisalyn said. Then it was just him and Gabriel.

"Take this," Gabriel said. He pushed a pill into Will's mouth, following it up with a swig of water. "Remember what she said. Stay still."

"It's so fucking cold," Will said. "What's happening over there?"

"Lyda's a pretty good fighter in here," Gabriel reported. "If this were Arqa, Lucio might have had her subdued by now... but it's not."

"What's wrong with your power? You gotta keep trying for me, Gabriel. This is bad."

"I know, I know. I'm sorry, Will."

Will grimaced. "It's like you said. We need to reach her

somehow." He attempted to hoist himself up to see where she was, but Gabriel insisted he stay flat on his back. "Lyda! It's okay. We're all messed up. We've come to take you home. You don't have to go through this alone. Your dad wants to see you back on Arqa." To Gabriel, he said, "I don't even recognize her. I know they said she aged in B3... but this. Jeez. She looks off." Will squirmed, straining his neck to see the fight.

"Knock it off, Will," Gabriel chided. "You need to relax. You're only going to make your injuries worse."

"What's going on now?"

"It's like I said. Lyda's got some moves in here. She's faster. Lucio and Trisalyn are struggling to keep up."

"In here, she's a warrior. On the offensive or the defensive, do you think?"

"What does that matter?"

"We gotta appeal to her!" Will exclaimed. "Because we're not going to beat her in her own place."

"What they're doing, it's the best we can do for now," Gabriel surmised. "If Lucio and Trisalyn weren't here... we'd be toast."

"Speak for yourself, kid. I know what a couple more hours of spear shoulder is gonna do to me."

"I wasn't prepared for anything like this," Gabriel said. "I'm so sorry, Will."

"Nothing but love for you, Gabriel."

"Will, they got her pinned! Finally. It's—oh. Oh, no."

"What?!" Will asked.

"They had her, but she teleported away."

Will could hear 2nd LT Lucio cursing.

"Lyda, knock this off!" Trisalyn said. "We're your friends. We don't want to fight you. We're not your enemies. I'll stop if you stop."

"Lucio's down and Lyda's..." Gabriel was saying before Will's medicine overwhelmed him.

His vision blurred and a buzzing in his head became all-encompassing. He again felt the urge to pass out.

"WILL!" Gabriel said. He shook Will.

"I'm good, I'm good," Will said. The sky above was composed of a single expansive mono-cloud. He watched a kick fling

Gabriel away from his side.

Gabriel howled.

The next thing Will saw was Lyda, a horrid savage bending down over him. First, her knee pressed down on his uninjured shoulder, then both of her hands grabbed onto the spear. The knee drove in deep. Then her hands twisted around the embedded spear while she pulled up.

It was the worst physical pain Will had ever felt in his life, easily charting beyond the threshold of the drug's effects. The spear was out by the time help came, the other three tackling Lyda. The force of it sent the spear flying and some of Will's own blood landing up on his face.

"Gabriel, leave her to us," 2nd LT Lucio said. "You need to keep pressure on that wound!"

Will fought to stay awake through fluttering eyelids.

Chapter Four

1.

Kalyna and the others waited a long time for Mark to return. When he didn't, they decided it was best to go back to the camp. They also left the duffel bag, not liking the energy it seemed to exude.

The group figured he was another disappearance, like Carlos or Dominique, and they would probably never see him again. All except Erin. "As if we could be so lucky," were her words.

The group's behavior towards Kalyna had hardened, though when she offered to teleport them back to camp, they didn't refuse. Stewart was especially disagreeable, despite her insistence that she hadn't been responsible for his arm. The journey back was otherwise uneventful, with no sign of Craig. Still, Kalyna knew he had to be *somewhere*. They reached the camp in good time, with little hassle.

Oliver went to go test the ships. A few others also volunteered for that purpose, while the rest went to fill Felicia in. Kalyna wasn't interested in that. Instead, she followed Oliver, very much needing to set the record straight on Craig's revelations.

When they were alone by a Spaero, Kalyna said, "I suppose we've both gotten very suspicious of each other."

Oliver shook their head. "The way I see it, you got hustled somehow. The lot of you did."

"Yeah, and what about you? I thought we were friends. You used to be a soldier against Arqa?"

Oliver gave her an impatient stare. "'Used to' being the operative words there. All the prisoners, we were a part of a squadron orbiting Enceladus. That part of my life, it's still fresh, even though it's been over a decade for you. We intercepted Arqa. They stole that ship, you know. Your dad, the captains, *Lucio*. All of them. Fucking terrorists. Our orders were to reclaim the ship. We failed. They wiped most of us out and took the survivors. Millie, Vanessa, Reeve, Eric. They kept us on the off chance we'd be soldiers against our own side. Which, as you know, is exactly what happened."

Kalyna wanted to hate Oliver, but they were sounding like the victim in the exchange. "You couldn't say anything before, right?"

"Us? No. They stifled certain talking points. You know the score." They tapped their forehead. "ICs."

"What's different now?"

"Mark said Craig got into all of us. As wild as it sounds, I bet that thing disabled our ICs."

"So, were they controlling your mind to fight against your side?"

"Not like that. I mean, it was more like, fight them or die. A few of us chose that when they heard our allies were coming for Arqa. Said, just kill me now. That's exactly what happened."

Kalyna inhaled. "That's terrible."

"Not at all what you were expecting, huh? I came around on the idea of living. I don't know why. At first, maybe I was hoping my side would rescue us. Then, I don't know, I just felt sorry for all you kids. They had enough prisoners to pilot the Spaeros, but a lot of them chose death and got it, see? That's why you got drafted into Flight Division. Then Jun tried to take Arqa, and... I don't know. I'm not for Arqa or anything, I just hoped to find a way to make it so you kids could live. It's not your fault, what your families did back on Earth. Hell, you didn't even have a fucking clue about it till earlier today. Captain Sali was so ashamed, she had to hold fast to that L'rias narrative. It was always human versus human. The worst part of this conflict is Captain Sali has refused to communicate with the enemy ship. That's why I was being compliant... why I didn't help Jun or Leni. I hoped it wouldn't end in both ships destroying each other. I cared about your welfare. The way I saw it, we were all prisoners together, see?"

Kalyna, though floored by the facts, still felt a great deal of appreciation for Oliver's kindness. She might have told them so, but she was feeling choked up from the magnitude of it all.

In her silence, they went on. "I thought, if things got bad enough, Captain Sali might have seen the futility of things and surrendered Arqa to my side. It was close. I think it could have gone down like that. Only, that's when we reached B3. Everyone on Arqa thought they were so much better than everyone else—

Kalyna, they killed so many people to get their way. All for what? So they could do whatever science shit they wanted. Well, they got it now. That Craig thing out there, that's what my side was trying to prevent from happening. Tampering with alien objects. Working on artificial general intelligence. We didn't think it was such a good idea." Oliver climbed into the Spaero.

"Wait, why not?"

"Really, Kalyna?" they said from the cockpit. "Is that not obvious to you yet?"

2.

Will would be unconscious if it weren't for Gabriel's constant pinching and prodding. Having his hands stuck on Will left him on edge. Gabriel knew he was no fighter. That there would be nothing he could do when Lyda had finished off the others. Still, he wondered how much longer he had.

All he could do for now was watch the fight. 2nd LT Lucio and Trisalyn seldom had the upper hand. Lyda was very partial to kicks, and they were learning to counter them.

All the effort of trying to talk to her had yielded no results. Lyda had to be the one blocking his clairvoyance. Otherwise he would have tried speaking directly into her mind. She was actively preventing Will from being rescued... letting him die. It didn't make any sense.

Lyda launched a half-fist into Trisalyn's throat. As she fell back, Lyda whirled and jabbed her in the mouth. Trisalyn fell, and it took her some time to amble back up. The spear was out of play, but Gabriel knew Lyda could reclaim it at any moment.

"Think... what if we all rush her at once?" Will suggested. "One last rally to hold her back."

"You are not getting up," Gabriel said.

"Lucio could probably knock her out. All she needs is a clear shot, right? It seems like that's what she's been trying to do, get her in a headlock or something."

"We saw her phase in and out. I think the reason they haven't pinned Lyda down yet is because she can't be."

"Listen, Gabriel. I know I'm fucked. It's got me freaked out too, but if we don't do everything we can, then it's not just me who's going to die. She'll kill all of you. I think... we gotta rush her."

Gabriel tried to keep him down, but knowing that the motion was hurting Will, he stopped. "Will, you're not thinking straight."

"Well, neither were you when you brought us here, but like I said... I got nothing but love for you, kid." To Gabriel's astonishment, Will abruptly rolled away from him. "This is gonna be my first fight ever. See, I've always thought of myself as a pacifist. And there's a time for inaction. But not when you're about to die. Follow my lead, Gabriel!"

Will, one arm holding his wound, shot up and ran toward the spear. Scooping it up, he called out to Lyda. "Yo, where did you even get this from?"

Gabriel watched in horror as Will took the spear in both hands. That's when the rain poured down.

"Stand down, Will," 2nd LT Lucio ordered. "If she's got the jump on me, she'll have that spear through your heart before you get anywhere near her."

Gabriel knew one thing for sure about Will: he *hated* being told what to do. So, while Gabriel knew it was a terrible decision, he couldn't leave the poor guy hanging. He jogged over to stand next to Will.

"Just get out of here!"

Lyda used 2nd LT Lucio's lapse in concentration to launch an upward palm, striking her chin away while leaving an opening to the girl's next move: an elbow to the face. Gabriel watched 2nd LT Lucio's off-kilter posture straighten, then she spit out blood.

That's when Will charged. He tumbled over before reaching the girl. But Gabriel scooped the spear up in honor of Will. If he could just puncture her deep enough with it, it wouldn't matter where she went off to. She'd *have* to slow down. Gabriel ran, adrenaline pelting his senses. 2nd LT Lucio and Trisalyn were keeping Lyda at bay still, giving him an opening.

Gabriel jumped up, driving the spear toward Lyda's back. It was going to work. The spear was going to land!

Inches before Gabriel hit his target, an invisible force stopped him. He was sent spinning and the spear split apart. The rain intensified and Lyda faced him. That sown-up mouth of hers curled upward with savage delight. Gabriel nursed his left elbow, which had taken the weight of his fall. He felt utterly ruined by what had just happened. It had all been a waste.

Lyda swung back to head-butt Trisalyn, who sank to her knees.

Gabriel saw Will on the ground too, likewise defeated. There was only one more thing left to do. "How could you do that to Will?" Gabriel asked, enraged. "Stop, Lyda! Enough." He shut his eyes as the pain radiated from his elbow. Zoning out, he felt so perplexed by what was taking place.

He still couldn't believe that was Lyda. She was even older than before. What did this mean? Well, that didn't matter relative to the more urgent threats at hand. Hoisting himself up, it was clear he'd missed some of the action. The action brought back that nausea from back when he was in the Spaero.

2nd LT Lucio had Lyda on the ground. They struggled there together. Gabriel caught Will tentatively approaching the two, holding the spear's end. 2nd LT Lucio was saying, "Do it, her neck. Now, before it's too late!"

Gabriel was freezing and exhausted. He threw up, completely missing what happened next.

Chapter Five

1.

All waking begins from a transtemporal state. This sense of timelessness mostly passes the senses by; it is so close yet so instantly processed through the body's circadian rhythm. The unconscious, mechanism that it is, recedes, subsumed by thoughts and emotions of the coming day, and gently folds up thin enough to be forgotten. Reality and dreams distinguish themselves from each other so quickly in the intervening moment of waking. One knows most assuredly that the apparitions and distances experienced in dreams were fantasies relative to the beckoning day. Not worthy of contemplation in the midst of movement, eating, planning. Lyda *believed* what she saw was just a nightmare, and so began the process of releasing it. Only, some part of her knew she did not have that luxury. And so while it was a great difficulty, she held fast to a singular detail: trouble in the Erstveil.

The girl's eyes shot open. Finding herself in the Gaze Room, Lyda called for help.

It wasn't long before a nurse came running. The woman looked concerned and had a railgun at her hip. "You're back," she said. "Uh-oh."

Lyda was peeling off the tape on her arm that secured an IV. "Your name is?"

"Michaela."

"Michaela. I need you to drop whatever else you're doing and get me ready to get out of here."

"You're not cleared to leave just yet—"

"Hey! You're not listening. There are people out there. On a mission. We need to get them. It's Will. The captain's grandson. He's bleeding out. Impaled by a spear. Get more help. Gather up some supplies and put them on a gurney."

Michaela needed no more urging than that. Soon Lyda was back on her feet for the first time in a long while. It felt good, even if her body was resistant to the sudden demand she put it through.

Dr. Mandi came in and asked, "Where are they, Lyda?"

"Just tell me when you have everything you need," Lyda said. She found some clothes and changed out of her hospital gown, alarmed at what little time was left. "Faster, faster. What can I do to help?" she asked Michaela.

Several more people, also with railguns at their hips, charged in. "Lyda, Captain Leni needs to speak with you," one of them said.

"Oh, real nice," Lyda said flippantly. "I don't even *want* to know how that happened." With the path blocked, she had to do something more drastic. Something she had said she wouldn't do.

I really, really hope it works, Lyda thought. She had the motivation. The energy was at hand.

"Well, Lyda?" Michaela asked. She rolled a gurney filled up with equipment to where Lyda stood. The doctor followed right behind, cradling two bags under their arms.

"You're not going to like this much," Lyda said. "But to be fair, it is an emergency."

"She can't leave!" the gunman reiterated.

"You might be right about that, but just in case." Lyda leaned forward onto the gurney, reaching one arm out to Michaela and the other to Dr. Mandi. Her hands squeezed them with all her might until they were all teleported from the Gaze Room.

2.

"Mark, Mark, you alright?"

Mark stirred from… where was he? Oh right, B3. Craig. He opened his eyes, looking up to see Kalyna. It was as if he was coming down from some hallucinogen. "Eh."

"I'm glad I found you. I've been searching."

"Surprised he permitted it." Mark saw they were still in the place with the oval. Craig was there too, his form all spread out.

I know why you're here, Craig said. *This one has already tried, in his own way, to appeal to me. Have you nothing better to do with your time?*

The girl stood firm as Craig's swarming presence whizzed around them. "Well, you let me find you and Mark. I'm going to guess you're at least up for a chat." With that, Craig condensed into his humanoid form.

Kalyna went up to Craig and kicked him in the shin. Mark cowered. Then the girl smirked. "You remember that? That time I kicked you in the shin. You know, before. Craig, you were so annoying... always buzzing around, making as much noise as possible. Felicia and I used to say awful things about you and Gabriel. When I found out you were dying, it's not like I was rooting for it. I just wasn't that upset either. Just in the sense that it could have happened to me. Other than that, I looked forward to the classroom being just a little quieter when you were gone. I like quiet. And you would always cackle. It made me think of nasty hyenas. Oh, but what difference would it have made if I *had* cared about you? You'd still be dead, Craig. As for me? Yeah, it was to my benefit you were gone. But to your dad? To Gabriel? Have you grasped how hard for them to see you go? All that to say, people didn't want that to happen to you. And they tried to stop it. When they couldn't, they considered who you were so valuable that they copied you. Tried to bring you back around.

"When you knew me, I was a naïve little girl. Not much time has passed, but I've done a lot of growing up. And I didn't mean for you to come back, especially not like this. At the time, over the abyss, my thought was more on my own family and our people's future. How sad that that's all on you now. That only what you do matters. What you don't do... that must be clear to you. We—I just want to know what your motivations are here. It's only fair, since I've told you mine. And if you're having a hard time with things, you can talk to me. I've never died but—uhm, well, I almost have. I was supposed to. It seems B3 saved us both, in a way."

You know—

Kalyna lifted a finger at Craig. "I haven't finished, if you don't mind. Ha, there you go again, just like always. The loudest voice in the room is never the one worth listening to, wouldn't you say? I'll let you know when I'm done and then you can go."

Mark looked back and forth between Craig and Kalyna. *She managed to cut him off?* he thought.

"You don't seem to want to be here," she continued, "yet you are. I mean, you started harassing us with those Easter eggs, that being after you nearly suffocated us. But why not be level with your intentions, huh? You gave Mark a death sentence, but it's in five years."

"Four," Mark corrected.

Kalyna turned to Mark. "Right." Then she regarded Craig again. "Okay, so you don't mind if the rest of us go on living. Like I said, you have the power. I've learned a lot about power recently. When I kicked you back then, I did it because *I* had power over you. I did it because I knew I'd probably get away with it. Here we are now, roles reversed. And I'm sorry. Sorry about everything that's got you so pissed off. I know it was you who showed me the truth. How they lied about who the enemy was. I know you're especially livid about that. I am too. Just—you're not alone, that's all. All the things I've learned about our past, I'm still processing them. You must be too. Can we do that together?"

Mark was expecting dire repercussions for Kalyna's little speech. Instead, Craig said, *Then may I—may I speak?*

"Hey, like I said, you're in control now," Kalyna reminded. "You don't need my permission for anything. But thanks for asking. It was... very kind of you."

There are many things taking place at once. I have been thinking about my role in relation to your expectations. The last thing I remember was dying. B3 has been a valuable resource to learn a little about what has happened since. The conscription, Lyda's integration, this trivial war. I've been trying to think of what I care about in light of everything. Kalyna, our little scrape back then means nothing to me. Your apology is likewise meaningless. And your suffering... is something I also can't seem to be bothered about.

"What about Gabriel's?" Kalyna asked. "Your father? Standby long enough and you'll lose them."

I already have.

Mark felt the urge to speak, but was too afraid of being penalized for it. He contented himself in watching Kalyna verbally spar with Craig. She was navigating him with incredible luck. Feeling validated in his estimation of her, Mark felt better than he had since Craig's arrival.

The two went back and forth for a while. Kalyna generously answered Craig's questions about several major events that had taken place since his death. All of it culminated in a triumph. "Craig," Kalyna said at one point, "you've told me of the things you find meaningless. But there must be *something* you desire. Will you tell me what that is?"

You're right, Kalyna, Craig said. *There* is *something I desire. Your way has endeared me to you slightly. You and I, let's make a fair deal.*

Chapter Six

1.

Will had been so out of it he'd missed Gabriel's failure. He did not know why the spear was broken. All he knew was he wanted to protect the others. 2nd LT Lucio was holding the girl in place. With a trembling hand, Will brought the spear near Lyda's exposed neck.

He thought of all the memories he had with her. Maybe it was the drugs or his dire state, but he couldn't go through with it. "You got me good, Lyda. Real good. But I can't do it back." Will watched Lyda's eyes, resolute as she threw 2nd LT Lucio off of her. What hurt he saw in her eyes. He could feel the rain mingling with the blood on his g-suit. He rolled onto the ground, looking at the sky as the clouds parted. "Hell yeah."

"ENOUGH!" a girl's voice boomed. As piercing as that was, Will could not ignore his body's call to doze. He thought of game overs, Miss Siannon, and the awful mistake that led to his grandmother's downfall.

2.

Lyda, having just arrived at the Erstveil, was trying to explain to Gabriel the truth. "That isn't me! Look, I brought help for Will. It's going to be okay now."

Gabriel spat in her face.

She wiped it away. "Ew! Look, You four came here to help me. I know that. It's been a rough time. Let me deal with her." She regarded the naked girl that was attacking 2nd LT Lucio. "Then I'll explain. I promise. You're safe now."

The rain had stopped. Gabriel looked away from her. "Whatever."

"I understand. Just go check on Trisalyn."

Gabriel found Trisalyn breathing, her face bruised and swollen. "Hey." He shook her. No reaction. He saw Dr. Mandi and a nurse with a gurney tending to Will. Then he watched Lyda reach 2nd LT Lucio and—so if that wasn't Lyda, who was that girl?

Lyda waved her hands in a circular motion and the rampaging naked girl became wrapped in chains. Gabriel was so aghast, he left Trisalyn to get a closer look.

2nd LT Lucio was watching Lyda cautiously.

"Whatever you're thinking of trying, I wouldn't," Lyda advised. "This is my domain." Lyda adjusting to a lighter tone after 2nd LT Lucio tensed up. "Not to scare you. That wasn't a threat. It's over now. A little..." Lyda looked around, embarrassed. "Misunderstanding."

2nd LT Lucio dropped her hands to her sides and sat down, exhausted from the fight.

The chained girl wiggled on the ground, trying to break free. Lyda seemed pleased by this, as she was taunting the girl.

"Care to explain?" Gabriel asked.

"Possibly. Again, things are kind of crazy right now. You were mostly right about this place, you know. It's a place to preserve the memory of that moment, when I took that sum of life." She turned to 2nd LT Lucio. "Hostile alien life, my butt."

2nd LT Lucio grunted in return.

"They were human. All of them. Back then, when I attacked with B3, I snuffed out everybody who'd been heading for Arqa. They were incinerated in their ships. All... all except that one." Lyda kicked the restrained girl in the head, causing her to erupt into a fit. "She can't be killed. I don't know why. I've tried time and time again. You can hurt her, sure, but if your hit is serious enough, meant to kill, it... I don't know. It just deflects. I—it doesn't matter what I try. Something is protecting her."

"You mean to tell me this one's from the enemy ship?" 2nd LT Lucio asked. She gave the girl a long look. "She can't be more than twenty years old!"

"I suppose it makes sense you thought we were the same person."

"Have you spoken to her?" Trisalyn asked, now up on her feet again.

"We have, though our conversation was so unproductive I—yeah."

Gabriel looked at the enemy girl's stitched mouth. "You've

been torturing her."

"This was my little area. I wasn't expecting you to come here. Didn't think all this would happen. I'm so sorry."

"At least you can do some damage control," 2nd LT Lucio said.

Lyda nodded.

"Alright then. What all have you done to her?"

"Don't bother with all that. She is beyond mercy or empathy. She's been killing since before she could read or write. When I blew her ship up, she was fine. A bubble shielded her, even gave her air to breathe. I think she's like us Gabriel. You have clairvoyance, and she can't be mortally harmed. It's super annoying. All I could do was leave her trapped in here."

"This is the absolute worst-case scenario," said 2nd LT Lucio. "The enemy with B3 augmentations."

"Oh, but…" with a wave of Lyda's hand, the girl levitated off the ground. Then Lyda's hand dropped, sending the girl slamming back down. A muffled screaming ensued. "She might have given you a close call, but in here I've got her under my thumb."

"We need to have an actual conversation with her," 2nd LT Lucio said. "The Spaeros we extracted from B3, they must be from the enemy's main ship. That means the enemy has been there."

"Oh, my god," said Trisalyn. "Of course. There were bodies in there! You remember, right Lyda?"

"I do," Lyda confirmed. "With the colorful shirts."

Gabriel watched the enemy girl as she settled down. She looked back at him. He sat down to be level with her. He attempted to project into her mind. "How is she blocking me from using my powers?" Gabriel asked Lyda.

"I told you, she has powers too," Lyda said.

"Well fuck," 2nd LT Lucio said. "Why did you keep trying to kill this one so many times but not all the others on the enemy ship?

"I don't need to explain myself to you," Lyda said.

"You're alive because of me. Your parents would have been dead."

"You're alive because of me too! Leaving children to pick up your mess. It's disgraceful."

"Yeah, but you forget. Now *you* have the power to do something about it." Everybody turned to see Will on his gurney, Dr. Mandi and Michaela by his side. "Lyda, you can do anything you want with the power you have. It's okay to be mad and stuff, but why not use your power to stop the violence? You know there's a mutiny on the ship, right? They've got it in my head to kill my grandmother. That's why we came for you. We need your help. So are you gonna yell at Lucio or are you gonna go fix things once and for all?" Will chuckled. "If it makes your decision any easier, I can keep yelling at her. Fill in while you're away. Trust me, I'm great at pissing her off."

Lyda gave him a serious look. "The mutiny isn't the only thing going on. We need to take a detour somewhere else before even considering a return to Arqa."

Epilogue

Music was the only comfort Sali had left. Her world was now a cell. Leni would bring her buircraft to her once a day, but that was not nearly enough exposure to stave off what was happening: her mind was closing up shop. Memories dulled, going beyond her like deleted files never to be recovered. Lapsed in consciousness, awareness, and identifiable emotions.

She was listening to music at all times. Right now, it was Isaac Albéniz, *Iberia*, Book 3. The notes came like a melodic downpour. When she no longer knew who she was, when she was only an animal in a cage, she hoped the music would be enough. Other arrangements would need to be made for that. Her music library was in her IC. But to continue accessing it would require cognitive ability she would soon lack.

Sali waited for her own will to give out from under her. The last bit of leverage she had was that unknown person Leni needed from the cryo chamber. It was the only reason Sali was still alive. Had the entire ship fallen under Leni's influence?

At least Sali accomplished something. Made something of her life. *Stood* for something. Sure, she'd made some blunders along the way and came to an ill end. But everything after seizing Arqa, that had been a bonus round. Extra. Something hard fought for, but nothing to get too attached to. It could have been her instead of Captain Dremon who'd gotten shot in the head back on Enceladus. Or, for that matter, Valerie could have survived and raised Will instead of her. The boy would have turned out so differently.

Book 3 fell into Book 4 and she tapped along to the beat. Such a gift, life was. No matter what came from the worst of it.

She heard a faint crashing outside of her cell and tilted her head to check, but the corner where the noise had emanated from was outside her field of vision.

"Hello?" What had it been? A mouse? She returned to her bed, but reeled backward at the sight of something chilling. It was *Craig*. The boy wore a green shirt and black shorts. He had a neutral expression on his face. In one hand, he was holding something. Without a word, he tossed the object to her. She caught her buircraft delicately. He was gone just as quickly as he'd appeared.

Sali's eyes darted back and forth, then she peered up to look at the surveillance camera. Nothing but frayed wires hung from the wall! She knew the camera had been there just moments before. She frantically activated the buircraft hoping to make up for lost time, thankful that if this was a delusion, it was a wonderful one.

EPISODE 11
Bits &
Bobs

Prologue

1.

Kalyna made for the front of the transport ship. She found Erin and Brenda fiddling at the controls. They both looked back at Kalyna.

"Our hero!" Brenda said, gushing.

"Yeah, right," Kalyna said.

Her sister got out of her chair and pinched Kalyna's cheek. "I do unto you as Auntie Dasha once did unto me."

"Hey, quit it," Kalyna said, smacking away Brenda's hand. "With what we're about to get into? I'm sure you'd prefer to still be sleeping."

"You trust Craig, right?" Erin asked.

"Meh, he's delivered so far."

"I still can't believe you saved us," Brenda said. "Blows my fucking mind." She cheered Kalyna's name, with Erin joining in.

"What is going on in here?" came a nettled voice from behind them. Mark stomped in, face scrunched up in annoyance. There were tiny nodes orbiting the man's head.

"Dude, we're just giving props to Kalyna," Brenda explained.

Mark's eyes followed the nodes swirling around him. "Well, that's alright. I guess it's time to call them up, huh? Show those cats what it's all about."

Kalyna watched the feed to the outside. The gate into Arqa's Bay Line was closed. "How long are they going to make us wait, Erin?" she asked.

2.

In CC, Siannon was rubbing one hand with the other. Leni had Sali in tow and was now taking her to the cryo chamber. After that, Arqa's former captain would be executed. Siannon didn't want that, but it was beyond her control. At least Sali had lived a long life.

Siannon was sent to CC by Leni to facilitate Mark's entry back into Arqa. A Regulator was explaining the conditions of Mark's boarding. "…and your expedition team must exit the vessel one at a time with their hands up. You last Mark. On your honor, with the promise of a smooth escort back to a cell, you may dock in twenty minutes. What'll it be?"

"I see," Mark said over the comm. "You know, this is an awful lot to take in. Being taken prisoner isn't going to be an all-day thing, is it? I sort of had other plans, see?"

"If you comply, it will be a temporary situation," Siannon said. "We need to ascertain whether you intend to be an asset to Captain Leni or a liability."

"Uh, yeah, I can do that for you. But first, can I tell you a little bit about jazz? To start, my uncle got me into jazz as a kid. Charlie Parker is head and shoulders above the lot of them. He sort of founded what is known as the bebop style, which is a type of music that is largely undanceable. Tempos were either too fast or too slow, with chromatic snippets and complex chord progressions. The style, well, they didn't want you to dance to it. They wanted you to pay attention. To really listen. It was an extension of freedom necessitated by the fact that the so-called big bands had been thinned out. This was because musicians were having to go overseas and fight in World War II. Smaller acts had to deliver more to compensate. The old musical orthodoxy needed to go. And that's where he came in. Charlie Parker eschewed melodic and harmonic traditions."

"It doesn't seem like he's going to be very cooperative," Siannon said to the Regulator.

"We have that thunder-staff weapon of yours," the Regulator countered. "I'm going to need you to stay on topic. If you don't want to become a fried cliché of dramatic irony, that is."

"Genius stricken by his own invention, I get it," Mark said wistfully. "That's a good one, mate. Yeah, anyway, it's really wild about Charlie. Did you know he died at the age of 34? By then, he'd already left an indelible effect on the world and subsequent musicians." The comm crackled, but Mark said no more. Siannon could hear a song playing in the background.

"What is that?" a young technician asked.

"Jazz," Siannon said, feeling old.

The holo-screen began trilling to signal an approaching object:

Mark's ship.

"Mark, stop your vessel," the Regulator urged. "The Bay Line access is shut. You'll crash!"

"Oh, no," Siannon said. "He's got my kids on that ship."

The jazz got louder over the comm.

Everyone in CC watched in shock as the transport headed straight for the closed gate.

"What options do we have?" Siannon asked.

"We can shoot the ship down," a technician said. "At this point, it won't make a huge difference. He's going to ding the hull either way."

"The fuck is the point of that? He's not going to hurt us, only everyone on that transport."

"Maybe he's playing chicken with us," someone suggested. "Knowing we'll open the gate."

"Do it!" Siannon commanded.

"The gate's controls are frozen," the young technician said. "We can't do anything!"

"Why? What's the matter?"

In the limited time they had, the CC staff tried troubleshooting the gate's relay. Useless. It was all happening too quickly. Siannon thought about the kids she knew on those transports.

She closed her eyes as the ship was about to hit Arqa.

"He's inside the Bay Line," the Regulator said.

"But how? Did he bypass the gate on his end?"

Siannon watched the feed into the Bay Line, flabbergasted. The deck crew scrambled as Mark's ship docked.

"We need to apprehend him!" Siannon said. She squinted to get a better look at the screen. The gate was shut. *What the hell? It's as if he passed straight through it!*

Oh, Miss Siannon, you're all strung up, came a familiar voice. She couldn't quite place who it was at first. And where had it come from?

"What?" Siannon asked out loud.

So it's true. You're in Leni's body now. I'll need to look into that. It's probably indicative of something more significant.

Siannon *knew* who that was. She looked to her left, then to her right. Up, down. Behind her.

All things considered, Craig said, *you must know you're on the wrong side of this.*

Chapter One

1.

Following a hunch, Lyda decided that instead of taking everyone straight back to Arqa, they would investigate B3.

To their surprise, Felicia was waiting where they teleported to. The girl was not startled by their appearance. She sat in a folding chair by a large tent, poking at the embers of a fire with a stick.

Felicia was very enthusiastic about telling Lyda and the others about Craig. "He has been expecting you all to come. He said you would."

"I knew something had changed in here," Lyda said.

"This is incredible!" Gabriel asked. "Where is he? I need to talk to him."

"Craig is very busy at the moment and won't be able to do that," Felicia said.

"If he's one with this station, then he must know what happened to my mom," Lyda said.

Felicia's bemusement slipped away. "Yes, well, getting Craig to help us, it was a bit of a rough time. He certainly doesn't want to be some autonomous problem-solving machine, I'll tell you that much. At first, it felt like he was only interested in antagonizing us. It was like that for a bit. Then Kalyna appealed to him somehow. They struck a deal."

"What deal is that?" 2nd LT Lucio asked.

"A precursor to a bigger one," Felicia said. "Excuse me, for just a moment." She folded the chair up and went inside the tent.

"This is pretty unexpected."

"The way she was speaking just then," Dr. Mandi said. "Craig was antagonizing them? That isn't good."

"Yeah, we definitely need to get more information on that," 2nd LT Lucio said.

"That's what we came to B3 for in the first place, right?" Gabriel asked. "To craft an AI as powerful as Craig is now."

"Sure, but we didn't think it would happen like that."

"She said he has Craig's memories," Gabriel said. "He'll remember me! They—they told me I'd never see him again. This is so awesome."

Felicia returned. "As I was saying. Craig agreed to help Mark. But he was expecting you, Lyda." She then looked at Gabriel. "You as well. We've come a long way since that day in the Gaze Room, huh?"

"Sure have."

"He asked me to stay behind to give a message to you and Gabriel."

Lyda nodded. "Let's have it then."

"Everyone, myself included, is to head back to Arqa," Felicia said. "There, we'll help to resolve both the mutiny and the Sleeping Sickness. Lyda, once you get us all back, you're to locate someone and bring them back here. At that point, Craig will speak with that person. After that, he will answer any question you have. Say, about your mother."

Lyda felt a surge of excitement. "Are you serious? Yes, I can do that. Who do I need to bring?"

"Not so fast," Felicia said. "Gabriel, come with me." She walked him into the tent. Lyda and the others waited for some time. It tested her patience. Just as she was about to rush in to get them, Felicia came back out, though not with Gabriel. Instead, she was supporting someone else who was unsure on their feet. The girl who used to cover her face all the time. Mark's assistant. "Gabriel will wait here, Lyda. This is where you'll meet him later. One last thing, just to be sure. Can you teleport us back to Arqa all at once?"

She could.

2.

Sali was being strong-armed down a corridor by Leni and several of her collaborators. Her only trump card was the buircraft, which she had hidden on her person. If Leni knew it had gone missing, she hadn't mentioned it. With her buircraft back, she had a chance to hang on to herself.

"So, what made you give up?" Leni asked, raising an eyebrow.

"Don't you mean what made me cooperate?" Sali asked.

"I don't."

"I'd like to ask for a clean death." Sali had to keep up this act, at least while Leni still had control of the ship. They both talked about Mark's fantastical arrival. Leni knew what little time she had left.

"It was you who had Manuel send those kids to kill me, wasn't it?"

"Guilty as charged."

Leni winced. "Sali, I'd like you to know I once greatly admired you. I wanted to be like you. When we lost Captain Dremon, you kept us whole. You urged us on then, with all the same promises. I want you to know I'm only carrying on your work, what you failed at. I'm not some politician who coddles the crowd. I have a higher purpose handed down by B3."

"Do you now?" Sali smirked. "This whole thing about the cryo chamber, it's another smokescreen, isn't it? Now that Mark is making his way through the ship, fighting your collaborators, curing the Sleeping Sickness along the way, the only thing you have left to leverage is this mysterious stowaway."

"They'll know what's to be done. How is that a smokescreen? Don't you believe Dominique?"

Sali looked down at the floor. "She did know things. Yeah, she was the one who told me to vitrify Gabriel when I did. She came into my office, not too long before she vanished. Spoke of things that only became clear after. Very cryptic."

"The essence loom. It contained further information."

"I wish I knew why she didn't tell me everything she knew from the start."

"Much as the children ask of you now, yes?" Leni asked.

Sali exhaled. "Right."

"Doesn't feel so good, does it?"

"I used to think this whole voyage was the spirit of the human race breaching above the hands of destiny," Sali said. "But if it hadn't been me, it still would have happened. All the same, I'm pleased that I was the one who got us to this point, even if my decisions were based on insufficient data. When it comes to Dominique, frankly, I'm just petty. Envious. I couldn't believe any of it at first. And I continued to disregard them just because I didn't care for your attitude. I was the one put in charge. Then, when you did manage to back up those claims and use them to take the ship, I couldn't assimilate."

"So what's changed?"

"I think a person only has so many decisions, so many blows to the heart they can take. The way Will tricked it, it just worn me down. I need to see him again. Please, Leni, let my cooperation now allow you to forgive me."

"My, Sali," Leni said. "Yes, I think I could come to forgive you in time. Not soon enough to relieve you of your punishment, though."

"NO!" Sali pleaded.

"Does that make you no longer what to cooperate with me?"

Leni's collaborators stepped in closer around her. "You must know it does. What incentive do I have if I let this person out?"

Leni considered that for a moment, then said, "Will's safety will be guaranteed."

Chapter Two

1.

Callum was with Stephen in his quarters when they got word that Lyda had been spotted back on Arqa. Their attempts to hide her and Gabriel during the mutiny had failed. The mutineers had taken her back to the Gaze Room. Several days later, they got word that she had left, vanishing with Dr. Mandi and Michaela in tow.

Stephen called his daughter on her IC. To Callum's surprise, the girl answered.

"Lyda! Where are you right now? Uh-huh? Well, I've been worried sick about you. You are *not* to do anything like that ever again. It's bad enough with your mom, but now you too. I can't lose you... No, I don't care what's going on, you're to find a safe place to stay put and I'll get you."

"Stephen," Callum said, "if Lyda can teleport, then she's safer than any of us right now. Just have her get us, if she can."

"No!" Stephen snapped. "I forbid it. You hear me, Lyda?"

"Let her do her thing. If you don't let her teleport, the mutineers might capture her."

"But Callum, what if she disappears like Dominique?" An argument between father and daughter ignited at that remark. Callum could only hear one side of the fight. While Stephen should have had the upper hand as the parental figure, Lyda's abilities made the idea of punishing her more than just a little challenging. Stephen was still shouting when she hung up on him. "She's helping some people, then she'll be along for us. She... told us to stay put. Not to cross into the line of fire... that it'll all be over soon. Mark, he's got the cure to the Sleeping Sickness. Anyone who's getting in his way to CC is getting dosed with it."

"Mark found a cure?" Callum asked. "That clever bastard."

"Lyda thinks the ship'll be back in Captain Sali's hands by the end of the day."

How does Lyda plan on enforcing a thing like that? Callum thought. "This is a lot to take in at once, Stephen. How you holding up?"

Stephen brushed a hand over his forehead. "I'm about to have to ask you the same thing. See, there's more. Lyda said you need to come with her to B3. Craig is waiting for you there."

"Craig?" Callum asked.

"They've done it somehow. An artificial general intelligence, with his memories. Lyda didn't get into specifics. Only that she was sent for you. By him."

Callum wept, stifling the tears unsuccessfully.

2.

Beyond a pile of bodies, one woman held her position behind a barricade made of found objects: tables, chairs, and other junk. Mark, gun in hand (one forged by Craig that dispersed not bullets, but doses of the Sleeping Sickness), crept forward at Craig's urging. The surrounding nodes were parts of Craig. The AI had given him every right move so far, anticipating outcomes to a shocking level of detail. There had been a few deaths on both sides along the way, and some minor things beyond Craig's ability to foresee. But overall, they had thinned out many of the mutineers.

"Are you still back there?" Mark asked the woman. "Look, we haven't seen your face yet. If you could just bolt away and let us through, you could make a clean getaway. Yeah. Just go back to your quarters and wait us out. We're trying to squash Leni's mutiny, not you in particular. You're no doubt important to the ship. We want a clear path so we can reach CC. And we'll get there with you dead or alive. It'll happen either way."

"Sali failed us!" the woman said.

The lights above him flickered. Mark instantly knew why.

Someone had his beloved Juno.

"Fall back!" Mark commanded the group behind him. *Craig, what do we do now?*

Now is the time for non-doing, Craig said.

Come again? Mark asked. *You've got to do something about*

—

A crackling noise emanated from the ceiling and shot down a clap of electricity just a few feet in front of Mark. The trail of energy rebounded off the floor and came straight for him.

Mark flinched, outraged that Craig was screwing him over. This level of electricity would be fatal. Before it made contact, Lyda appeared in front of him. It should have ripped her off her feet, but Lyda stood firm.

The blast disappeared. "How'd you do that?" Mark asked.

"Portals," Lyda said. She wiggled her fingers up at him.

"Portals?" Mark scratched his head, a harmless static traveling to his fingers as she poked his hand. "On Arqa?"

"Uh-huh. There are portals all around us, all the time. How do you think I got here so quickly?"

"So, like mother, like daughter."

Lyda blew a few strands of hair from her forehead, then vanished again. Mark heard a cry up ahead. In seconds, she had returned and was holding the Juno. "That's for you. Don't let it fall into the wrong hands again. Now then, I have more important matters to see to." With that, Lyda was gone.

See? Craig asked. *Non-doing.*

You could have said she was coming, Mark said. *One can only handle so many near-death experiences.*

"MARK!" someone shouted from behind him.

"Rayna?" Mark said, whipping his head around to see her. "Rayna, you're back!"

They ran to each other, doing a fist bump upon proximity. Craig had stipulated that Rayna wasn't to get the antidote until Mark's mission was already underway. "You really shouldn't be here," he told his assistant.

"This is where the powers that be wanted me, I guess," Rayna said. "Seems a lot's happened since I've been out. Lyda brought me from B3 after Felicia woke me up."

She's staying with you, Craig said. *After all, she's your assistant and you are on an important mission.*

Yeah, but is she in danger? Mark asked.

Most of all perception is a gamble. What would you like me to say? You already know you're in a dangerous situation.

Mark felt anger welling up inside him, but he knew an emotional outburst against Craig would be useless. He resolved to feel confident that he could protect Rayna. After all, they were almost to their objective. "Alright Rayna, we're following Craig's orders now. Did you hear about that?"

She nodded hastily. "But Mark, do you mean to say you're not the head honcho?"

"Presently?" Mark asked, watching as the timer in his eyes ticked down into a new hour.

Chapter Three

1.

Left alone in B3, Gabriel had time to think. He wondered who he was more deeply than ever before. It was spurred on by the truth of Earth. He had a history there, a people. But who were they? Was his clairvoyance genetic? Felicia had explained that Gabriel and Lyda were not only able to teleport within B3, but other places as well. It irked him that Mr. Benito had not had more answers. But the man had mentioned that Gabriel's people wore veils. Rayna used to wear a veil. She was an orphan from Earth too, a couple of years older than him. He had to have a conversation with her.

While waiting, Gabriel projected himself out-of-body and searched the eldritch domain. No sign of Craig, Dominique, or Carlos. Gabriel's eagerness had waned. Craig was different, composed of B3's cosmic knowledge. Sure, the AI was helping to stabilize the situation on Arqa, but if he was non-local, able to split himself up and appear in different places simultaneously, what was preventing him from saying a quick hello to Gabriel? His confusion was overwhelming. Some part of Craig was back. A being of great power, a project far beyond physical human limitations. This difference alone made Gabriel wonder if a friendship with Craig was even a possibility anymore. Maybe Craig's failure to connect was a function of something he had lost in coming back. But Gabriel held onto hope. That when he saw him, they could laugh together again.

2.

Craig had tasked Kalyna with distributing the antidote to those afflicted in the Med Bay. Just before she got there, Lyda appeared with Will, Dr. Mandi, Michaela, and a strange person on a gurney wrapped from shoulders to knees in chains. Kalyna couldn't tell if the person was a boy or a girl. They had short hair and their face was badly bruised.

"Yo, Kalyna," Will said. "Funny running into you." His eyelids shot wide open. "Wait... KALYNA?!"

"Yeah, yeah," Kalyna said. "I survived. What's—"

Will swept her up in a hug. "How?"

"B3, I don't know." Kalyna looked at Lyda, who seemed embarrassed. It was just like Kalyna had heard. Lyda looked a few years older, almost unrecognizable. "We all going to the Med Bay, then?"

While making their way there, Kalyna was told about the prisoner. Will was arguing on her behalf, saying she deserved proper clothes. Lyda disagreed. "The chains stay on, but you can remove the stitches on her mouth. After I'm done doing what Craig asked of me, I'll come back and we can reassess."

"We should be able to remove them without any scarring," Dr. Mandi said.

"What if the chains are hurting her?" Will asked. "It's not like we'll be able to get them off ourselves after you leave, Lyda."

"She can breathe. And don't forget, she's got that protection thing, anyway. She'll be fine."

"We need to be able to have a conversation with her. She's from the other ship. My grandmother was too proud to talk to them. But maybe, with things how they are now, we can convince them to turn back to Earth."

The prisoner growled at his words.

"Stitches removed, yes," Lyda said. "But..." she took out a syringe. "She cannot be conscious while I'm gone. I don't like what she was capable of doing within the Erstveil."

Will nodded in understanding. Together, the group held the prisoner down, dosing her with the Sleeping Sickness Craig had synthesized for them. The transition from the prisoner's wild flailing to sedation did not take long.

After the group reached the Med Bay, Lyda left. Kalyna assisted in distributing antidotes to patients bedridden with the Sleeping Sickness. The Med Bay staff asked how she had come across both the Sleeping Sickness and its cure in isolation. Kalyna wasn't ready to explain Craig yet, so she gave the credit to Mark.

Kalyna was almost done when Will came up to her. "And now we wait, huh?"

"Oh, Will. Hello."

"It's so great to see you again."

"Yeah, you too."

They spent some time sharing their recent experiences. Kalyna was amazed by Will's travels in the Erstveil. They'd both had ridiculously close calls.

"Now that I'm back, I really want to see my dad," Kalyna said. "As soon as things calm down."

"I know what you mean," Will said. "I need to see my grandmother. This whole thing is my fault, really."

"Hmm." A quiet, awkward moment grew. Kalyna looked over at the prisoner. "She's... like us."

"Huh?"

"A teenager. Isn't that weird? I mean, when they fed us all that stuff about the L'rias, I always imagined the enemy as these ageless malevolent entities. Monstrous forms, slimy tentacles. These implacable forces of nature bent on destruction. Really, it was just people like her."

"Well, the fighting's over with now," Will said.

"I hope so."

"I just figured, with the Craig thing going around, calling the shots. Is the enemy just going to be a problem that goes away? They can't be a match for him."

"Well, if the enemy's mission was to stop us from bringing about Craig, I could imagine them wanting to go down swinging. Then again, Lyda already has them immobilized. I had the chance to speak with Craig more than anyone else, but I still don't know what he's about just yet. Between you and me, he's a bigger risk to us than the enemy ever was."

"What?!"

"I just mean, if he wanted to be, you follow? Look, we've been lucky so far. But the truth is we're completely at the mercy of this thing now. I... in communicating with Craig, I tried to connect with him emotionally. Appeal to the life he had before. He agreed to help us, but he said it was out of amusement. I wouldn't assume he has Arqa's best interests at heart."

"I still have a hard time believing it even happened," Will said. "Humans have been trying to get an AI that fancy for centuries.

So much time has past without progress then it happens all in a day."

"Well, that's the wacky world of B3 for you." Kalyna checked the time on her IC. "Look, I need to phone my dad. Maybe have a shower. It's been a long while since I bathed."

"Damn. Well, you don't smell that bad. Go ahead."

"Sorry. Maybe I said more than I should have. I've been so caught up in the craziness of it. "

Will's lips twisted into a goofy smile. "You're good. One thing at once. That's what my grandmother always says." He looked back at the nameless prisoner.

Kalyna smiled back at Will. "I know it was an awful experience. I hope you telling me helped you process it and feel better."

"Oh, yeah. It sucked. But it's over now. I try not to dwell on the negatives." He laughed. "Fuck. Hey, did you know that we have no idea what dinosaur skin was like? It's almost a complete mystery."

"Oh?"

Will poked her in the stomach. Kalyna jumped back and squealed. "Hey!" she exclaimed.

"Caught you off guard?" Will asked playfully.

She made a funny face. "My revenge will be swift and merciless."

"Can't wait. Anyway, I was just trying to demonstrate something. See, it's like this. We're mostly squishy parts. Skin and goo, really. That stuff doesn't preserve so well over time. The fossils we find are mostly the crystallized parts of bones. Fragments of skeletons. Animals that are alive today, when we try to reconstruct how they looked with just their bones as a reference, they look nothing like they actually do. It blows my mind thinking about dinosaur skin and the shapes of their bodies. The flaps and the colors and just all the other stuff we have no way of knowing about. Not only that, but most species don't leave behind any fossil record at all. We only know about a tiny fraction of life on Earth. Isn't that interesting to think about?"

There was something about Will that Kalyna found endearing. She would never be so warm after going through what Will said he had. There was this perennial bliss contained within him. She needed more of that in her life.

Chapter Four

1.

Catching her reflection in the window looking out of CC, Siannon considered fleeing. If she did, it would be over. Reports showed that Mark had swept through all the opposition along the way, giving them the Sleeping Sickness. Siannon didn't know how that was possible, but she knew it had something to do with B3. The news left everyone in CC feeling dispirited. Leni had told them B3 was on their side.

"What are your orders?" Nisha asked Siannon. CC was locked, and sensors indicated the O2 in the space was depleting. The closer Mark came, the less O2 they had. What a fun trick the man had pulled off. Many of the technicians present had no side in the mutiny. It was just their job to keep the ship going. They could do nothing to fix the O2 issue. Siannon called Leni, but the woman didn't answer. Leni must have figured out that the tide of the ship was turning. To who, Siannon didn't know yet. But in the back of her mind, she had a suspicion. That voice from earlier... Craig. *I need a way out,* she pleaded to him.

No answer.

"There are almost two dozen people in here right now," Siannon said to Nisha. "While I'm sure some of them are willing to suffocate for Leni's cause, most are not. I advise you and everyone else to do whatever you feel is right. If you're here when Mark arrives, there will be violence. And understand that after that, whatever Leni was up to will be over. Nisha, I don't want that for you. Won't you go?"

Nisha looked over at the worried people in the room, then back to Siannon. To think, this girl used to be Captain Sali's assistant. "If you say we can leave, why haven't you?" she asked. "Why don't we just surrender? Maybe if we could all get on the same page about the inevitable. Mark's hacked into the ship's controls somehow. He's won, whether we like it or not. No need to hold the line here."

"Those weren't Leni's orders," someone said.

"Leni's probably dead herself," Siannon said. "She won't pick up her IC, at any rate. That's a bad sign. Everyone, you need to think for yourselves. If you want to stay here, stay. If you want to go, go. Forget about orders or whatever it is I'm doing."

"What *are* you doing, Miss Siannon?" Nisha asked.

Siannon hoisted up a railgun. "I've never shot anybody before, but I think if I could get just one on Mark, that'd make all this worthwhile." Yeah, just one shot at that piece of shit for fun. Because she knew no matter what she did, she was damned. She was inextricably linked to Leni. Might as well do something worth punishing for once.

A sense of lightheadedness came over her. It brought to mind her old body.

"Should we just unlock the door, then?" Nisha asked.

"Do whatever you feel like, Nisha," Siannon said dispassionately. "I am."

2.

Will watched as Dr. Mandi tended to the prisoner. Her face had been cleaned, and the stitches were nearly removed. What Kalyna said about her had really hit home for him. Under the bruises and the cuts, this murderous creature was just a girl.

"You know, just because she'll be able to speak again, doesn't mean she will, right?" Dr. Mandi asked.

"Why?"

"Well, if you're wanting her to talk, I wouldn't get your hopes up. She might not even speak our language."

"How's that?"

"Back on Earth, there were over three thousand different languages spoken."

"No way! That's crazy. How didn't I know that?"

Dr. Mandi shrugged. "Must have not have been relevant to teach you. Well, everyone who boarded Arqa was required to speak English. And so there's a chance she's from a place that speaks a different language. We could use a translator AI, but it won't be ideal. Especially if she's not feeling cooperative."

"There are ways though, right? Of making her cooperative?"

"You mean torture?"

"Oh god, no!" Will said with dismay. "No. No one deserves that."

"This one, she's a soldier. She's probably been trained not to speak or aid the enemy. Even at the cost of her own life."

"That's awful."

"That's what being a soldier is, Will. Being prepared to die for your cause."

Will thought back to when he had abandoned his pacifism to engage her. "We gotta do something different, Dr. Mandi. Even a single exchange with her will be more contact than we've had with the enemy since leaving Earth, yeah?"

"Correct."

"Don't you think that's absurd? That both sides default to killing each other without communicating?"

"You don't realize it, but we have tried communicating. Of course we have. Back on Earth. On Enceladus." Dr. Mandi dropped their instruments and removed their gloves. The prisoner's mouth was restored.

"Every time just ended in bloodshed," Michaela said from behind Will. "I know it sounds ridiculous that Captain Sali hasn't even tried diplomacy, but you have to understand something: if she had thought it would do any good, she would have."

Dr. Mandi nodded. "This other side, the enemy, they're ruthless. They have their orders, and they'll follow them to the death. This is the first contact we've had with anyone from Earth in many years. And Lyda mistreated her in the Erstveil. I'm very concerned what her demeanor is going to be like once she wakes up."

Will wagged a finger in derision. "The war is done with. They can't get their ships past the Erstveil to hurt us. The Craig AI is going wild. It's over for her."

"Did you know she doesn't have a Siranis implant?" Dr. Mandi asked.

"How does she eat?"

"The blood sample shows traces of animal protein. Either they have livestock on the other ship or genetically grown flesh."

"That's disgusting!" Will said. Eating animals was an antiquated earthly notion.

"She must be famished now that she's off the Erstveil. We need to give her an implant or a gastric intubation. I wonder if she'll accept food from the Nook. "

Will groaned, turning away. "Do you doctors have something that would make her less like herself? Like not want to kill us? Help her see our way of things?"

"You're talking about mind control, I take it," Dr. Mandi said. "Arqa doesn't have technology that advanced. We can tweak the parameters of a person's IC. Filter out troublesome trains of thought or specific intentions. But those are finer details. See, this girl, you can't just erase who she is. You know that Arqa left behind a lot of collateral damage on Earth. She probably volunteered to go after Arqa. Probably fancies herself very heroic."

There was a rustling from the prisoner's bed. Will saw the sheets sinking. As he turned back around, Dr. Mandi shout out, "Will! Look out!"

The prisoner was gone... all that remained were the chains that had held her in place. Will whipped his head back around, sensing something coming his way. A tray collided with his face. He glimpsed the prisoner coming at him.

Chapter Five

1.

It surprised the cryo technicians to see Sali still alive.

"Well all," Sali began. She looked at Leni. "It would seem we're in a hurry. So I'm going to authorize things on my end, and you'll bring this mysterious person up. I'm sure you know more about it than I do. That's just been the way of things lately, hasn't it?" She pulled up a holo-screen to input her access codes. Then she looked over to Leni. "Alright, what's the IC number?"

Leni gave it to Sali. It didn't turn up a name yet, Sali already knew who she was dealing with based on the number. The name would come up soon, but that wouldn't change a thing. Sali frowned, then asked, "Out of curiosity, if I had a change of heart, what happens?"

"So glad you asked." Leni took out a gun and pointed it at Sali's face. "How much longer will it take?"

"Five sets of codes, each inputted at one-minute intervals. That's the soonest it can happen. You need only hope help doesn't come for me in that time."

"Mhm."

After Sali punched the third code in, she asked, "So you really don't know this person?"

Leni turned away from her.

"All you had was an IC number, right? Well, are you interested in knowing his name? I've found it."

"What is it?"

"Vincent Galiano." The name meant nothing to Sali. He was some heir to a fossil fuel conglomerate who had paid his way to board. There wasn't anymore point in stalling. "You might as well just kill me now, Leni."

"Not till you've finished with the access codes!" Leni pressed the gun to the back of Sali's head.

Sali dismissed the holo-screen, negating her code sequence. "No. Wish I could. But the truth is… well, let's break it down in parts." She walked as far as she dared from Leni, who kept the gun fixed on her. "The majority of people housed here in cryo storage are what, exactly?"

"Individuals who had no useful skills to help Arqa achieve its ends."

Sali nodded. "The grotesquely wealthy. Those who set humanity on its self-destructive course in the first place. Those who could afford a slot here. Because of this, they could not walk amongst the general population while Arqa was in transit. But we promised them devitrification upon reaching and settling on B3. Tell me, Leni, if you're so enlightened, so wise to the fallacies of my ship, how is it you didn't know about what a paid ticket onto Arqa was really worth?"

"What do you mean by that?"

"This Vincent Galiano, they didn't do any of the dirty work."

"So what? We needed him to fund the trip. It was all part of the process."

"Anyone who bought their way onto Arqa, such as this Vincent, they're dead. Fodder for whatever experiments we fancied doing. We tricked them. I stopped because the only thing devitrifying that body will do is create a terrible odor in this room."

"No," Leni said. "But Dominique said—"

"Dominique was wrong if she was counting on this Vincent to still be alive," Sali said. "You can confirm it yourself, if you want. Need I remind you? Arqa needed money to escape Earth. I did many bad things to make that happen. Deceiving the terminally gullible was not one of them."

Leni lashed out, cupping Sali's head and slamming it into the wall. Sali was too stunned to defend herself. She smirked through the pain. "Dead tissue. Good for science. It's all been a nice song and dance."

"Shut up!"

Sali wiped up a trickle of blood that trailed from her skull down her temple. "Was this the extent of your plan? If you had known about this little detail, would you have done it all over again? You've got a dead-end here and Mark's getting my ship back for me. Don't tell me you're out of trump cards now."

Leni was shaking. Of course. The woman was being hit by Siannon's body's condition. She doubled over from the strain of her motions. "How can they all be dead? What about Lucio? The prisoners from the Enceladus battle?"

"Well, yeah, a small portion of people were genuinely preserved."

Leni was looking at her hands. "Dominique, I failed you."

Sali waited for Leni to shoot her, but Leni only gave the woman a sorrowful look, the hand holding her gun moving to wipe away a streak of tears. Just then, Sali received a call from Mark. "Did you do it Mark?"

"Just about," he said.

Sali could hear a voice in the background. Mark's assistant. "Whoo-hoo. Nearly victorious heroes of the day onward! We win! We win!"

2.

Kalyna had so much to wash away. To scrub off her skin, to rest overwhelming memories for the time being. Will had probably been kind to her earlier, as when she was undressing, it was undeniable that she stank. As she was about to enter the shower, Craig's voice came. *Get dressed again. Drop what you're doing immediately!*

Craig? Kalyna tensed up and covered her chest. *Are you watching me? This is inappropriate, go away.*

Never mind that! Listen, there is an emergency coming your way. Dress!

What is it?

Just do as I say, now!

Kalyna realized that with every conversation she'd had with the AI, he'd been monotone. This was the first time she detected stress from him.

She made for the storage room and threw on fresh clothes. *Any more information would be great. Where do I need to go?*

Nowhere. Just brace yourself. She's coming.

She? What do you mean? He was making her very nervous.

Craig sighed. *I don't know how to break this to you, but that girl, the prisoner, she's loose.*

Kalyna raced for the door.

Don't—

She couldn't get it open.

She's trapped you in.

"Oh no," Kalyna said. *What do I do, Craig? That's the only way out!*

I'm sorry. I'll help protect you however I can, but I'm doing a lot of other things right now.

What's she going to do? The thought of her loose on Arqa made Kalyna's skin crawl. *How did she even get out?* She pressed her ear against the door, which led to the Med Bay. It was quiet.

Hope you're ready.

There was a rattling behind her. Kalyna turned sharply and saw a figure out of the corner of her eyes. Then it was gone. When it reappeared, it was closer. The girl.

Clad in a smock, the prisoner swung a pipe upward, smashing a light fixture. The confined space darkened.

Craig, what do I do? Kalyna asked.

I know, Craig said. *I'm sorry. You need to hold your ground before I'm able to do anything.*

She's got a weapon! She's teleporting.

And she's a killer. But you can't let her psych you out, Kalyna. Arqa needs you alive.

Can she be killed, Craig? Do you know a way?

I'm not sure. Like I said, fend her off.

No, Craig, you have to do something.

I am, but I need some time. Kalyna! Pay attention!

With that, the girl came in hot, cutting down with the pipe aimed right at Kalyna's face. The girl missed. She rebounded with great agility, swinging again. Kalyna blocked the pipe with both her arms, just above the elbows. Then she tried grabbing it. But the prisoner twisted the pipe away, nearly getting a hit in on Kalyna. Kalyna backed up, bouncing against the wall.

On top of every other conceivable advantage, this girl was much stronger than Kalyna. The prisoner had a smug expression on her face, as if also realizing that fact.

"Drop that weapon!" Kalyna demanded. "I deserve a fair fight. I've got nothing more than my hands."

The prisoner giggled. Of course. Why should she do anything

Kalyna said?

Kalyna's mind raced. She couldn't see anything in here she could use as a weapon. This was not a fight she could win. It was a matter of attrition. Craig would come through for her. She needed to endure the girl long enough for that to happen.

The prisoner vanished again, only to appear from the side, the pipe unavoidable. Kalyna didn't have enough time to guard her face. She yelped as stars dominated her vision. Her knees buckled. More strikes came, ravaging her body. Kalyna tried to ball up, bracing herself on the floor to protect her skull. All the while, the prisoner looked down at her with delight.

The volleys stopped. She heard the pipe fall on the floor. Was it done?

Kalyna forced herself up, seeing the pipe was free game on the floor. The prisoner had stepped back. Kalyna blinked. Her opponent was bowing.

Craig, what did she do to them? Kalyna asked. *Is Will okay? What about the others?*

Kalyna, you're doing well right now, Craig said. *Don't lose focus. It's not over yet.*

Kalyna righted herself, though her steps were unsteady. The prisoner watched, fearless about Kalyna's next move. The enemy girl was applying make-up with a brush, a small mirror in her other hand. Kalyna scooped up the pipe and held it with a death grip.

As soon as Kalyna advanced, the prisoner vanished, next appearing three feet to Kalyna's side.

She let me have this, Kalyna thought to herself. It was a taunt. A signal that even with the pipe, Kalyna stood no chance. She had to catch this girl off guard.

You didn't know this one could teleport? Kalyna asked Craig in annoyance. He did not offer a reply.

Kalyna pretended to swing at the girl with all of her might, only to fall short and drop the pipe. She twisted, ducked down, and bit the girl's left heel as hard as she could. It worked well at first, but when Kalyna applied enough pressure to cause bleeding, an invisible force pried her teeth off the leg.

It was Kalyna only moment of triumph in the entire bout. The girl kicked her. From then on, Kalyna hardly landed another hit.

Through the horror, Kalyna thought back to the last time the enemy had her this dead to rights. Only this time, she didn't have the mental bandwidth to sing to herself. Every time she tried, a new punch would jolt her from the words. She fully expected this girl to beat her to death. Though her opponent had grown bored with the pipe, it didn't matter. She was plenty useful with bare hands: half-fists and palms focused around Kalyna's throat, making it harder and harder for her to take air into her lungs.

"Bitch!" Kalyna said through an irritated windpipe.

The prisoner tilted her head like an oblivious dog.

"Can you speak or not?" Kalyna demanded. The prisoner's silence was the most frustrating part of all of this. Here was the enemy. Not set apart in another Spaero, but face to face. Kalyna had swayed Craig with her words. How was reaching this girl more difficult than that? She had to think of something. If Will were here, he'd begged for mercy. Mr. Benito would try negotiating. Mark would have some gadget with which to gain the upper hand. Kalyna could think of nothing more than to continue defending herself until her body gave out. Gave out?

Kalyna dropped her hands. "Okay. I get it. You win. You want to keep fighting? Because I'm done. So do whatever you have in mind. I quit."

This seemed to infuriate the prisoner, as she growled at Kalyna. The girl rushed forward, and a fist coming at her was the last thing Kalyna saw before blacking out.

Chapter Six

1.

"Hello, Mark," Siannon said to the man and his group. There weren't many people left in CC, but those who were had guns pointed at Mark and his group.

"Amazing," he said. "So you're really not Leni? You switched bodies?"

"Yes."

"Hmm. How's that been for you?"

"Lovely."

"Good to hear."

She so had her heart set on shooting you, Craig told him.

Wow, rude, Mark thought. *And what did I ever do to her?* "So, the door was wide open for us. Will you stand down or what? You should know if you try to shoot me, it's not going to land."

"No need to turn it into a firefight in here, anyway," Siannon said. "We'll need the ship's monitors intact, no matter how today ends. I don't know what came over me."

Tanya Lucio stepped forward next to Mark. "It can start with you then, Siannon. Drop the damn gun!"

"Hey, not all of us supported the mutiny!" a technician shouted out. "This is just where I work."

"A fine clarification, as Leni is losing her grasp on the ship," Mark said with contempt. "Do you feel that way too, Siannon?"

"Forget all that," Tanya said. "Will you drop your weapons or not?"

"Everyone do as they say," Siannon said. "Tanya, you know I'd never shoot my kids."

"They're *my* kids now, Siannon. You're unfit."

Siannon dropped her weapon and put her hands up. Mark watched her pass by his group, composed largely of her students. "Kids, I'm sorry about all of it. I did my best."

"All you ever do is feel sorry for yourself," Tanya said to her. "I warned you."

"Yadda, yadda, yadda," Siannon said. "Whatever you're going to do, you have the freedom to do so. Not because it's right, but because you have the power. Good for you."

"Our way is what you agreed to. Before you broke your word."

"Siannon," Mark said. "Take me to the intercom." He thought he knew what to say to put a stop to the fighting. He turned to Rayna.

"Rayna, should I... is this the right time?"

Rayna perked up upon hearing her name. "What does Craig say?"

"Oh, right," Mark said. *Do we reveal you now or what?*

As you please, Mark, Craig said. *I do think there will be widespread skepticism unless I supplement your claim with a substantial maneuver. In the meantime, you will tell them without my help, in your own words.*

Mark proceeded nervously as more people abandoned their weapons and made for the exit. In his imagination, he saw one of them shooting at him. He shuddered.

Craig giggled. *Calm yourself. That isn't going to happen. I'm just keeping you on your toes.*

Siannon showed Mark the intercom. He looked around. Three people were still clutching their guns, but they were now surrounded by his group. "What motivation is there in being the last of it? Call it a day, morons." Mark hesitated. *I don't feel safe doing this with those guns still in play,* he told Craig.

I've instructed you to proceed, Craig said.

Mark snorted. *For clarification, are you in charge of Arqa now or what?*

I've returned Sali's buircraft to her. Though she doesn't have uniform support among the population, I think it would be best if she was given her position back, for the time being.

Right.

But Mark, most of the probabilities that I've gleaned already had you making the announcement by now. The longer you stall, the more unpredictable the future becomes. Things are liable to go wrong when you deviate from what I say, remember?

Mark nudged Rayna. "Rayna, you make the announcement."

"Me?" Rayna asked. "What do I say?"

"Leni's mutiny is over. Arqa has unlocked B3's potential and created artificial general intelligence much earlier than we believed possible."

"Anything else?"

Two people in CC still held fast to their weapons. Mark scolded them. "You have thirty seconds to drop those weapons, you hear me? I'm tired of this!"

"Mark, chill," Tanya said. She approached them. "Look, we let everyone else go because they cooperated. Whatever you're thinking of doing, it's not going to work. Just let it be over, okay?"

"We watched you on your way here," one of them said. "You shot people."

"It was the only way to get the ship back from the unwarranted mutiny," Tanya insisted. "Most of the people we came across today just got a dose of the Sleeping Sickness. Very few people actually died on our way here. And no one else has to. You need to accept the reality of the situation. That's all you need to do. And we can go on living together. We need each other."

They nodded and dropped their weapons.

"Thank you," Siannon said.

"Do it, Rayna," Mark said.

Rayna scurried to the intercom panel, pressing the button. Her announcement began. Mark watched her and felt pride, a sense of accomplishment for everything that had happened. Her tone was uncertain, her language concise; she was no speaker. She was almost done when the shooting began. Mark did not know who fired first. Maybe it had been an accident. Or someone had been hiding from view. All Mark knew was that Rayna was in the line of fire and that he would not get to her in time. Siannon, however, was. The teacher rushed to Rayna, shielding her as the gunfire began. Mark took cover as the room dissented into mayhem.

2.

Siannon waited until the shooting was over to check on Rayna under her. "Fucking hell," Siannon said. She got to her feet, offering a hand to help the girl up. "You okay, Rayna?"

"Something's bleeding," Rayna said. "You and I!"

"I don't feel it," Siannon said. "I'm free from pain."

"That's most likely a bad thing," Mark said, crawling over to them. "You need to get off your feet." To the room, he said, "Call Med Bay!"

"Why no pain, Siannon?" Rayna asked.

Siannon looked down and saw blood gushing onto her blouse. "Yeah, you're right. I should be feeling that." A sudden faintness overcame her. "Uh-oh."

"You knew I was coming!" Mark said to her. "Why didn't you just go?"

It's all part of what's transpired, Craig said. *No questions will alter that.*

A fogginess filled the room. The people around her became obscured. Siannon found herself alone.

Untrue, Craig said. *I am here. Siannon, I am confused. Off your feet, now. Close your eyes, please.*

Siannon obeyed. CC faded away into a world of white. The only other thing there besides her body was Craig. Craig as he was now, not of flesh but those metal particles. They swam together, congealing to the shape of his boyhood self. A statue in motion, hovering above her. *Where am I?* She asked.

You are within a construct of mine, Siannon. This wasn't a part of my predictions. I am very upset. You are who I wanted harmed the least.

You... remember me?

Craig nodded. *I loved you. Before. You are bleeding. I cannot prevent the things that have entered your body from doing what they are meant to do. But I can help you.*

That'd be nice.

You've a better chance with me than any doctor.

What?

You will not feel a thing. In the time there is, while you are seen to, we shall connect. You will ease my confusion. And when it's over, you may be yourself once more. The one from before. Before you lost everything. Will you tell me about it? It's very important that we occupy your mind while I do my work.

EPISODE 12
The
Maw

Prologue

Craig was occupying multiple locations simultaneously.

His reach was not unlimited, though it far outstripped that of any human, whose vantage point was singular.

With Siannon, he was slowly bringing more and more of his attention to her.

The innumerable bits he was composed of receded from other places to craft an area where he could do his work more successfully.

This event hadn't been a factor in his precognitive scope.

The problem was that the future was so malleable.

He had made for Siannon a place to die in.

It would happen more slowly than if he had done nothing.

She would not feel the pain.

He could do that much, at least.

More when she was gone.

Much more.

For now, he was in her mind, engaging with her thoughts.

You will tell me the truth, Craig told her. *How did Arqa come to this moment? What of your life before being my teacher?*

You want me to tell you all of that? Siannon asked.

I need to know what I'm supposed to do. I did not want to be the one who dispensed justice. You, though, I discern your intentions are pure. Mark will get his comeuppance in time. For now, open more of your mind to me. Tell me everything. Will you?

Some things are too hard to bring up.

You must. You must... come clean. Craig knew this phrase would jolt Siannon. Her parents used to say that same thing to her, with great effect. *The turning point, it was at that beach, was it not? It was the first time you tried to end your life. Who was it that captured you at the beach? Captured you before you could do that... that sinful activity? We know now it was not the fictional L'rias who drove Arqa from Earth. Do it, Miss Siannon. Please. Give me the whole story. What happened? It's one thing B3 cannot relay to me. But if you tell me, maybe I'll have some sense of what I'm to do about it all.*

231

She wouldn't think to be saved.

Not until it was too late.

I'll do it, Siannon said.

Yes, give me the real lesson. The thing you truly wanted to teach us but could not.

Siannon nodded. *Well, it began when the Earth had passed the point of no return. Where no intervention would stave off the climate emergency. All burgeoning scientists and high technologists were directed away from speculative, long-term solutions (like you, Craig) to more immediate ones. The Great Complacency happened as I said it did. The acceleration of knowledge tapering off. Each succeeding generation became more and more steeped into a world it did not care to understand, compounding the damage. Advancements stalled out. First, resources became scarce. Then might became right. Societies collapsed in the wake of constant territorial disputes and mass migrations. Cities were widely abandoned, turning into obsolescent wastelands. Attempts at escapism, into space, became more and more involved and elaborate.*

I never knew much about it. On the moon, some settlements were mapped and known, some were hidden from public knowledge. I was raised on one of the secret settlements, an autonomous one known as Rula. I suppose it's why I never minded the conditions of Arqa so much.

My parents were both wealthy and gullible. They wanted to create a child prodigy. You know, the next Einstein. Earth was nearly ruined. It needed solutions. It was a religious kind of framework. A trick of their faith that placed their moral obligations onto me. That me and the future generation would undo the mess. Stabilize the world and get humanity thriving again. I suppose that's what we expected of you yourself, Craig. And I'm sorry about that. I know how it feels to have the burden of impossible expectations. Craig?

Yes, Miss Siannon? he asked.

When I die, what will happen? Will my essence go back to my old body? What will happen to Leni?

Don't dwell on that. I'm doing everything I can for you. Please—will you continue for me?

Yes, Siannon agreed. *I was a product of speculative genetic engineering. My parents were scammed by a hustler. He dosed my mom with all manner of things while she was pregnant with me. I was supposed to be physically and mentally augmented. Instead, I came out with a nerve disorder that I've carried with me all my life. I think I've told you before in class, but I have hypotonia. Maybe if it weren't for that, I would have saved the world. My parents believed my disorder was a sign from God. Because I wasn't suppose to survive past the age of two. I was in the hospital a lot. Thankfully, though I had a very delayed development, I exceeded the doctor's predictions.*

That's how things all started. Like I said, life wasn't great, but it was a step up from everything to come. I think, looking back on my early years, maybe that's one of several reasons I committed to teaching on Arqa. I knew it would be immoral to have children of my own, should my condition pass to them.

Beyond the small place Craig had made for his teacher, Mark was shouting.

Shouting at Craig.

Craig didn't have the energy to shut him up at the moment.

It was easy enough to ignore him.

Mark figured out what Craig had done.

The Erstveil, erected in the wake of the last battle, was undone.

The enemy was free to attack Arqa again.

Spaeros on both sides had already been deployed.

Craig had done it with no joy.

Only curiosity.

Chapter One

1.

Callum did not enjoy being led. Least of all by Lyda, who ushered him and Stephen to the next destination. He thought back apprehensively to the depositions of those who'd been to B3. Soon, he would talk with the hyper-intelligent entity equipped with his dead son's memories. Lyda halted in front of them.

"What are we stopping here for?" Callum asked.

"Dad, I just realized, we need to go back to our quarters," Lyda said.

"Why?" Stephen asked.

"I just realized mom's going to need fresh clothes!"

"Oh yeah," Stephen said. "I never thought about that."

"It's been months," Lyda commented. "B3 is weird. You don't need food, sleep, any of that stuff. Still! I'm sure she'll appreciate it."

"Craig really knows where she is, huh?" Callum asked.

"He said I could ask him anything, so he's got to know."

They reached Stephen's quarters without incident. While the Halls picked out an outfit for Dominique, Callum waited. If it were just a matter of going to speak with Craig, he wouldn't have wanted to go to B3. But if it led them to Dominique and Congo, then there was no way he could pass it up.

To get them to B3, Lyda needed to be in the same spot where Dominique had last been seen. Once they made it to the corridor, Stephen asked his daughter, "Alright, kid. How's this go then?"

The girl grabbed Callum's hand, then her father's. "Close your eyes until I say otherwise."

Callum followed her instructions as the air compressed, rumbling around his skin. The pseugra receded and he was floating.

His body careened forward, legs kicking out from under him. He cursed at his inability to see. It no longer felt like Arqa. The temperature increased. Through the lids of his eyes, an increasing brightness teased him.

In that space in between, Callum heard whispers from a voice he knew had to be Evalia. It went by too quickly to process, but it was indisputably his ex-wife's voice. There was a new awareness inside of him: he felt her—she was still alive somewhere.

"We're through it," Lyda said. "You can look now."

Callum took in B3 for the first time. It was beautiful, a wide open vista of vibrant colors like a bottomless ocean where he could remain without concern.

2.

After escaping both the Sleeping Sickness and her chains, the prisoner had moved on to an outright killing spree: Dr. Mandi and Michaela were dead, along with several patients. Then she'd gone on to tear apart the Med before teleporting elsewhere.

Will was hunched over on the floor, too disturbed to move. Eventually, he heard ruffling, the sound of footsteps. He lifted his sore body up to see she was back. In the time she'd been gone, she'd found clothes. It looked like she might have showered since her hair was wet and her arms were no longer caked in blood. Will also noticed several tattoos there. She leered at him with a toothy smile.

Craig? Will asked. *CRAIG? She's back. You gotta do something.*

Hi, Will, Craig said. *Yeah, that does seem to be a problem, doesn't it?*

She's killing us! She'll kill me.

Right. Yep. She's very good at killing, isn't she? And she can't be killed herself.

Her movements were much less sudden than when she'd first gotten free. She strolled toward him, taking her time. He was too afraid to move. What good would it do? Will couldn't outrun her. *Craig, where are you?*

I look forward to getting you up to speed on that, Craig said, *should you survive the next five minutes. Hang in there. I've got too many other spinning plates to attend to right now.*

What? Will asked. *NO! Craig. CRAIG!* "Fuck!" Will

exclaimed. The girl had withdrawn her attention from him. She was filling a kit bag with medical supplies.

What was Craig's deal? He was just letting this girl waltz around with impunity. Will cautiously signaled for Regulators on his IC, but considering how wild things were on the ship, it was hard to say if they'd make it.

Just then, she looked up from her task and smiled. She motioned for him to join her with a hand gesture.

Will obliged, knowing it would only be worse for him to defy her unrelenting presence. He had to pass by Dr. Mandi's body to reach her. The prisoner had used her hands to kill them: tearing out their throat, then caving their skull in with her bare foot. She was still packing as Will got closer. On the floor was a vase with sunflowers that had been knocked over earlier in her path of devastation. She stopped what she had been doing to set the vase right. Will could not steady his trembling.

"Go ahead," she said encouragingly, tucking the flowers back in. "Ask me why you're still alive." She took a whiff of them before setting them back on the counter.

So she spoke his language. "Mercy?" Will asked, swallowing hard. "I—I gave you mercy."

She shook her head, making the sound of a buzzer. "Oh, that's not it at all. No, no, no. Your dear old grandmother could tell you. I wish she was here. She's so murderable."

"You know my grandmother?"

The prisoner snickered. "You're so cute. So dumb. Dumber than you are cute would be my initial evaluation."

"Did you and Craig team up or something? How are you getting away with all this?"

The prisoner's face twisted up in apparent befuddlement. Then she vanished, appearing in front of Will. Her left arm snapped forward to clutch his neck. His own hands clawed up, trying to regain the airflow. "The most enjoyable way to kill someone, I've found, is to choke them out."

Will tried to speak. With her other hand, she smacked him in the face.

"LISTEN TO ME IF YOU KNOW WHAT'S GOOD FOR YOU! I will *not* be interrupted."

Will did and thankfully, she loosened the pressure on his throat. He relished in the oxygen.

"Yeah, I don't want to be some fancy markswoman, shooting someone from a distance. See, I don't know about you, but I really appreciate *eye contact*. Seeing the look of someone knowing they will die, that's my favorite thing ever. I like to go back and forth with the pressure, savor the moment like." She scooped Will up with both hands by his neck, then swept him into a fall with her leg. The side of his head bashed against a counter. "Still squirming? Damn, that should have knocked you out. Well, look, all I was trying to say was I didn't kill you because you're pathetic. Sometimes to just as fun to make the person think you're gonna do it. I mean, you bought it right? That's all the matters. Just don't want to be seen as gratuitous here."

The girl pounded a fist down on Will's head. Then she released him. He dropped to the floor.

"After all that, you might want to get yourself checked out. Hope I didn't kill *too* many of your doctors. Anyhoo, I've got to go. My ship needs me and I haven't been home in ages." She bent down and squeezed his chin. Will cowered. "But I could come back at my leisure, so stay vigilant!"

Through the misery that was his entire body, Will dared to look into the psychopath's eyes. "Did Craig help you do this or not? I need to know."

The girl clicked her tongue several times, then slung the kit bag over her shoulders. "Rejoice, dear adversary—the war's back on!" She vanished again.

Will groaned. What a nightmare that girl was! He had fucked up again. Lyda had been right. They should have left her in the Erstveil.

He was nearly up again when she popped back into his field of vision. "Oh, wait, I almost forgot!" she said. She jumped toward him. He tried to get away. The girl was just too good at what she did. Will felt her fingers grasp onto his arm, the same side where she'd jabbed him with the spear. As he tried to pull away, she broke his arm while saying into his ear: "Hi, I'm Jecenia. You wanted to know my name, right?"

Chapter Two

1.

Siannon's numbness persisted. Her awareness was limited to the history she now shared with Craig. *Those people on the other ship, who followed us from Earth, they're soldiers of OEN. That stands for One Earth Nation, Craig. The last remnant of civilization. If it weren't for them, I might still be on Rula.*

I was eleven when they attacked us for that very reason. And the way they did it... God. They knocked a hole in our dome. Most everyone suffocated, but my family somehow survived that initial strike. OEN patched up their hole and occupied troops in the now vacant homes. They took me from my parents. They were greatly interested in me. See, child soldiers were exceedingly popular with OEN. It was sort of their model. Take them, train them, then throw them into the first wave for the next campaign. Unfortunately for them, my condition made me unfit for combat. I was just good enough for odd jobs, though. Torturous times. I was brought to the Earth my parents had spared so many details. To them, on that Moon, we were in Heaven, and Earth was Hell. For all my gripes about their fanciful imagination, in this case, they weren't so far off.

It was a tour of carnage. I traveled from place to place on this old cruise ship, retrofitted for OEN's malicious purposes. They'd drop bombs on sites where both sides were fighting. There were wandering tribes so desperate for food they cooked the fresh corpses of soldiers on battlefields. I saw many terrible things. I was in constant proximity to death.

Eventually, the ship I was living on was attacked. Before it sank, I got away with a few of the other kids from Rula. We made it to a nearby island. Some machine began to pursue us. I had it in my mind to just die then, to drown myself rather than being taken again.

My attempt was unsuccessful. My captors were actually very sympathetic towards me. You must know who I'm referring to by now, Craig. I met them all that day. Dremon, Sali, Tanya Lucio. Her son Nate. I'd thought they'd kill me, or worse. But what they'd actually done was save me.

I liked them because they didn't treat me like a prisoner. They had a higher ideal than fighting in a never-ending war. There was another place. Away from the savagery. Out there somewhere, in the mind of any who willed it strongly enough, was B3. The idea of being off Earth again thrilled me. Exploring the ruins of an ancient alien structure we could thrive in, that thrilled me. The details were always unclear, but they said we were chosen.

I ask you, who wouldn't have accepted that offer? Considering everything I'd told you? Well, even if I had found myself on the fence at that time, falling in love with Nate Lucio folded me forever into Arqa's arms.

2.

Mr. Benito mentioned he'd heard his ex-wife's voice in transit to B3. But Lyda didn't want to think of what that meant just yet. They needed to catch up with Gabriel, who'd been waiting for them by a tent.

"Craig hasn't made any contact with me," Gabriel told them after they all greeted one another. "But now that you're all here, I'm sure we won't be kept waiting long."

The two men were amazed by B3. "Lyda, how do you teleport back and forth without getting lost?" her father asked. "I mean, you gave us all those instructions. How did you know to tell us that? Could something have gone wrong just then?"

"No," Lyda assured. "Dad, I think that's what mom did. She opened the way for me. And the cost of that was her getting lost somewhere. The more I teleport, the more sense I get about it, you know? I can just feel we're getting closer to her."

"So you can teleport, and so can Gabriel," Mr. Benito said.

"And anyone can do it within B3," Lyda added.

"Craig can't though," Gabriel said. "Felicia told me that. He has his own method of moving from one place to another, but he can't teleport."

"Is that why he isn't here yet?" Mr. Benito asked.

Gabriel shrugged. "I've been looking everywhere. I can't find him. One thing—"

"We just need to wait," Lyda said sternly. "That was the deal I made with him. He'll be here. If I—"

"Lyda, I was gonna say something."

"What?"

"This isn't where we're supposed to wait," Gabriel said.

"Where then?"

"Felicia told me about this place called the Maw. Do you know where that is?"

"No, I don't."

"I've never heard of it either."

"Doesn't sound like a lot of fun," Mr. Benito said.

"It's okay, check this out." Gabriel took out a sheet of paper. The group circled the boy. "It's marked here."

"How did you say it works in here?" her father asked Gabriel. "What, you just have it in your head to go to a place and," the man snapped his fingers, "poof?"

"In principle," Gabriel said. "But Felicia told me the Maw is a special part of B3 because we can't teleport directly to it. And if we get too close, a lot of B3's niceties may break down. We have to teleport as close as we can, then walk for a bit. Fortunately, Felicia told me how to get as close as possible. Everybody all ready?"

Once the four of them were holding hands, Gabriel began to countdown. "Five, four, three, two, one…"

The group was whisked away, landing harshly on a hardwood floor. They found themselves in a kitchen. The place was in disrepair. The walls had a pattern of rooster wallpaper, tarnished but not torn. On the floor was a broken chair, the wooden legs splintered.

"Felicia didn't tell me anything about a house," Gabriel said. "Weird. What do you think it's supposed to be?"

"I know where we are," Mr. Benito said, rushing for the door. "This is the house I owned before I left Earth." Mr. Benito struggled with the doorknob. He couldn't get it open. Looking back at the group, he said, "Of course. Great."

Chapter Three

1.

Mark and Tanya had given up on trying to reach Craig. He had made his own little place within CC, enclosing an area with a solid white structure that looked to Mark like an egg. Flight Division was in proximity to the approaching enemy.

Mark was on a conference call with Tanya and Sali. "When we left B3, these little pieces of Craig were orbiting me. It's how I was able to take back the ship. When the shooting started, he withdrew from me, setting up this weird area enclosing Siannon so we couldn't get to her."

"Maybe he's healing her," Sali said.

"We have no clue what's going on in there."

"But you've retaken CC back?"

"Yes."

"And I was able to survive the fall of Leni's ego back in the cryo chamber. I have my buircraft back as well. But... I think it'd be best if we found a new person to run the ship. Being without it was... not helpful."

"Anyone coming to mind?" Mark said.

"Perhaps a ship-wide vote. Unity is our top priority."

"Whoever it is will just be a puppet, depending on Craig's agenda. He has yet to spell it out."

"It seems like what he wants is for us to fight the enemy," Sali pointed out. "By the way, why can't I get a hold of Callum?"

"Craig asked Gabriel and Lyda to escort him to B3," Mark said.

"Well, if the girl is back there, maybe she'll come around and see about the enemy for us."

"Fat chance," said Tanya.

"There's something still bugging me about this whole Siannon situation," Mark said. "He was extremely distraught that she got shot... as if it happened in a way Craig couldn't see coming." Mark kicked the pale white egg in front of him. It was hard, and it stung the edges of his toes.

"Quite a mess," Sali said. "I have one more thing to take care of before I can make it over there. Do what you can until then."

"Uh-huh." Mark ended the call, then turned to Tanya with a lifted hand. "High five for ending the mutiny?"

To his surprise, Tanya obliged him. "This is just like before," she said. During the call she'd been focused on the holo-screen, the radar showing both sides had engaged. "That time we first sent the children to B3. I mean, if you look at the screen and you judge the battle purely off numbers, the other side still has a clear advantage. That whole ship must be nothing but Spaero pilots."

"Craig's not going to let both sides kill each other," Mark said, feeling sure of himself. "That'd be ridiculous. He's bluffing."

"Mark, I don't think he cares for Arqa one way or the other. What, exactly, is the best-case scenario for us here?"

"I don't know."

"Well, if you haven't got a way to rein Craig in yet, I'd start thinking. He really fucked us, taking down the Erstveil. Jesus, it's like one crisis after another around here."

"Noted. I will think about that. Though I'm not sure there's anything that can be done now." Mark went over to see Rayna, a little startled but safe.

"I'm very sad about Siannon," Rayna said. "I can't believe she did that for me. I didn't even know her that well."

"Fun fact: back before they found you, Siannon was going to be my assistant."

"You're kidding," Rayna said, fascinated.

Mark nodded. "It didn't work out. I thought I'd just have to work alone."

"Then I came along."

"Then you came along."

"What was it about me that was better than Siannon?"

"Siannon, uhm, well… she was always… I don't know. I don't think she liked the idea of being tucked away from everyone else. She had a lot of medical issues too."

"We're not like that anymore."

"No, you're right. We've been spending a lot of time outside the lab."

"I like that."

"Well, good. Although I have some bad news for you…

pending our survival."

She pulled at Mark's sleeve.

"What?" he asked.

"The one who tried to shoot me, he was a nano technician."

"I know."

"He's dead."

"That's right."

"For shooting Siannon."

"Uh-huh."

"There are precious few nano techs left."

"Your point?"

"I guess I better learn to be a nano tech, huh? Maybe that can be my thing. I need a thing, remember?"

Mark shrugged. "Try thinking a little more short-term for me, Rayna."

"Very well. In that case, can we get away from snooping ears? I did have something fucked-up I needed to get off my chest. Considering conditions lately, I think it's best I tell you about now."

Mark and Rayna walked down the corridor until they knew they were alone. "Alright. What is it?" he asked her.

"Mark, I might have..." She looked back and forth, making sure no one was listening. Mark checked with her. "Accidentally, mind you," she dropped into a whisper, talking directly into one of his ears, "been responsible for Carlos's disappearance in B3. I tried to fix it. There were so many emotions. All the things you said about B3 and stuff. I didn't think it'd be possible that anyone could disappear for real."

Mark threw up his hands in frustration. "Rayna!" He put a hand to her mouth. "Say no more."

Rayna nodded.

"Yikes. Never, never admit that to anyone. Never *say* it like that." Mark stepped back from her. "Oh, that poor kid," he said theatrically. "*That's* what you say. Be like a cat. What does a cat never do? A cat never accepts blame."

"But Mark, I'm feel bad about it."

"You can't feel guilty if you did nothing wrong."

"But—"

"Look, like I said. Poor kid. Maybe he'll turn up. I hope he does. But… wouldn't it be better for you if he didn't?"

Rayna pondered that for a moment. "Yeah, I guess it would. But—"

"You don't want us to go looking for him, do you? Looking for trouble?"

"Maybe…"

"No, Rayna."

"Okay, maybe I wouldn't have said anything before. Things just happened, you know? With Craig there now, you said he might find Dominique for Lyda, right? I was just thinking of Carlos and how maybe if he turns up, oooooo, maybe it'll be the trouble that comes looking for me."

"Maybe. Maybe?! Dammit kid, you're killing me. Can we decide to deal with this only when we know it's going to be an issue?"

"Fine."

"I'm just saying, it's called a secret. Trust me, if you knew how to keep one to yourself, they'd do you wonders."

"All your secrets are washing up," Rayna said cryptically.

"Excuse you?"

"I was just saying, your timer. And you were just kicking Craig's teeny fortress. I wouldn't have kicked it if I were you. Maybe that's why you have a death timer and I don't. Maybe you wouldn't have a timer if you weren't who you were. You ever think about that, Mark? About the kind of person you are?"

2.

There was some debate about whether they were still on B3. Gabriel thought they were. That they were in a snapshot of Mr. Benito's memories. Lyda, on the other hand, believed they had been teleported to Earth. In either case, they were stuck where they were. The house was built underground, so there were no windows. And while there was an open passage to a hallway, there was an invisible barrier that prevented them from leaving.

Mr. Benito was pacing around in the kitchen, demanding Craig show himself. "We've come a long way at your behest and think all this is a great waste of time."

"Mr. Benito," Gabriel said, "I understand you're stressed. But I would urge you to keep an open mind and heart."

"I'm thinking if Craig's put us here, there must be some reason for it," Mr. Hall said. "We just have to figure it out, right?"

"He's *trying* to tell us something," Lyda said. "Dad, if this is Earth, maybe that's where mom went."

"Maybe, honey."

"While we're definitely here for a reason, I think that's grasping at straws, Lyda," Gabriel said.

"Hmm, I wonder," Mr. Benito said. He walked over to the fridge and looked inside. He came back with a large bowl covered by a plate.

"What is that?" Mr. Hall asked.

Mr. Benito removed the plate. "Tortellini leftovers. I used to make this all the time." He wafted the dish to his nose. Then he went into a drawer for a fork. After trying a few pieces, Mr. Benito said, "I'm with Gabriel. Craig generated this place from my memory. Lyda, if we were on Earth right now, this tortellini would be rotten. And honestly, it tastes awesome. Too awesome. Then, if this were the actual place, I doubt the electricity would be running. And it'd be looking worse off than this. It's just how I remember it."

Gabriel saw Lyda stiffen at Mr. Benito's words. She looked back at Gabriel. "Try going out-of-body, then."

Though going through the door didn't work, Gabriel found he could explore beyond the hallway. Then stairs. He checked each room. In one of them—

"You're upstairs right now," Gabriel said upon returning to his body. With a baby. But—" the boy hesitated.

Mr. Benito looked surprised. "I can hear him."

"Me too," Mr. Hall said.

So could Gabriel. The baby's crying abruptly became so loud that it hurt his ears.

"Craig must be here," Lyda insisted.

Mr. Benito nodded. "I remember. Oh, no." He looked down at Gabriel. "Tell us, Gabriel. Tell us what you saw."

"But I don't want to."

"Let's have it. Get it all out there. Say it, Gabriel."

"You had a—your thumb pressed against the baby's neck."

Mr. Benito took aggressive steps over to the fridge and came back with two cans of beer. He offered one to Mr. Hall, but the man declined. Putting the can to his forehead, he said, "I was never going to actually do it."

"What is he talking about?" Lyda asked Gabriel.

"You better explain it yourself, Mr. Benito," Gabriel said.

Mr. Benito cracked open the can and took a generous swig. "I was so distraught about having this child dropped on my lap. Losing my wife. It was two days before we boarded Arqa. I thought to spite her." Mr. Benito chugged the beer can and tossed it over his shoulder. "No one would ever know if I didn't say anything. I think... the reason I didn't kill him then is I somehow thought I could reach Evalia before we left. To take the baby back and get her to come herself. Like we planned!" He paused, then raised his head. "Is that what you wanted? This why we're here? Well, I've come clean. I admit it."

"Callum," Mr. Hall said, approaching him and embraced him in a hug. Mr. Benito accepted it.

He thought to suffocate a defenseless baby and you comfort him, Mr. Hall? came Craig's voice in Gabriel's mind. The door flew open, twisting off of its hinges. Behind it came an impenetrable darkness. The kitchen faded around them, at first tilting them toward the open door. The four of them lost their balance and then went tumbling toward the door.

There was no doubt in Gabriel's mind as to what they were being pulled into: this was the Maw!

Chapter Four

1.

Far be it from me to assume you can't understand emotions, Siannon said. *They are abstractions, not tangible things. Sometimes humans are unable to put words to how we feel or what is happening around us. My understanding of the AI I have experienced is that, being made of code and algorithms, it is very challenging for them to achieve genuinely complex behaviors. Emotions are chemical reactions. Humans are dynamic, we have spontaneity. A machine is methodical. Would you say you're more than algebraic formulas?*

I believe so, Craig said.

I'm sure you must be right. You have the Prior Race's technology in you. I'm so curious about all the details, you see. I didn't think it was possible. How did Mark do it?

I'd prefer to save the details for later, Miss Siannon. Right now it is imperative you continue your story. I feel a great chuck has been relayed already, and that is good. But I'm going to need the remainder, you see.

Darn. Alright well, I was getting to something important related to my questions. Because of the age you died, I don't think you know much about the dangerous purity contained within first love. Craig, it's possible to go too deep into the thought of someone else. To never surface again. See, when someone makes us happy, we tug and hold on to them. But it's also that very obsession that bars us from happiness itself. First love is unique because of its novelty. But we lack context. We model off of fiction, speculation. What we perceive as unfavorable about our parent's partnership. First love is delirium of the highest order.

Every moment I remember with Nate brightens my darkest moments. I had my chronic pain. He had his abusive mother. She hurt him in the guise of training, so he would be able to defend himself.

I stood up for him once. Got in the way. Told her to fight me instead. I would tell you it was a big mistake. Tanya Lucio knocked me over that day. But the way Nate looked down at me, saying nothing, I knew he was grateful. That I wanted him to be spared of the pain.

This was before Arqa. We were living in orbit. Nate and I, we got to stay behind while Tanya and the others amassed momentum. Craig?

What is it? Craig asked.

This is the part we kept hidden from you kids above all else.

Craig frowned. *Will you tell me then?*

Yes, Siannon said. *Back then, Dremon was in charge. He'd come into possession of the Bobbin and the buircraft. That allowed him to start a whole movement. Nate and I had no involvement. We just relished in each other's company, kissing and the rest of it, exploring each other whenever we could manage. Our bond grew deeper each time the adults secured another victory or milestone along the path to escape. We had many dreams. We were sure we wouldn't live to see B3. So Nate and I, we just imagined stewarding the next generation. That was a life enough. But you know that's not what happened, Craig.*

No, it isn't, Craig said. *I never met Nate.*

I'm sorry, Siannon said. *I'm recounting the story, but I am also stalling. Because everything up until that point, I mean, it was straightforward. I was with the good guys. But what Dremon and the others did… Breaking Day, that complicated things for me.*

Breaking Day? Craig asked. *You told us that was the day the L'rias invaded Earth.*

Siannon figured this was the information the AI really wanted to know. *Aren't you piecing it together yet? OEN couldn't be defeated. Arqa's top brass convinced hundreds of people the only way to save science, free thought, and life itself was to steal Arqa. It was sitting idle after OEN had canceled a surveying mission to the moons of Jupiter. Something drastic had to be done to take it because OEN had it well-guarded. Dremon orchestrated a coordinated ground assault, in about a dozen strategic locations to distract the enemy. Breaking Day. A lot of innocent people died for us to get our way—it was atrocious. You'll have to ask someone else. I won't say more about it. We were off, and all was well until Enceladus.*

We used the moon as the final pit stop, picking up some scientists. But Jun and the others, soldiers of OEN, were waiting for us there. They snuck onto Arqa. We stopped them, but they killed a dozen people on their way out, including their most important target, Dremon. But also… they got Nate. That's how Jun, Oliver, Reeve, Vanessa, how they all ended up as prisoners in the cryo chamber. They were all soldiers of OEN. Tanya Lucio also opted to be vitrified at this point too.

Everything happened so quickly. Life set in. We set a course for B3 as directed by the Bobbin. After Enceladus, things became, for me, uneventful again. I fought my grief by settling into the closest approximation of what Nate and I dreamed: I became Arqa's teacher. They said when I taught the children, I could not teach them about Earth as it was. That it would create a darkness within them that didn't have to be there.

A ship-wide pledge was taken in favor of what the newly installed Captain Sali referred to as the noble lie. Most everyone on Arqa consented to an IC update, making any discussion of Earth as it was impossible. We thought it was best to tell you children this lie. To make you believe humans were not capable of such vile things. It all seemed great on paper when we were leaving. But when OEN caught up with us after all these years, Sali insisted we keep to the noble lie. I think that's what led to the mutiny, although Leni's motivations are still clouded, even to me. Did we do it for ourselves or for you kids? I don't know. Sali refused to communicate or negotiate with the enemy. Perhaps you can do better.

Me? Craig asked.

Yes, Siannon said. *My sincerest wish is for you is to bring peace. Make our wrongs right. For everyone, not just those on Arqa. And I also hope you might forgive me. Forgive everyone who constructed the lie of the L'rias. You wanted to know how you came to be. Now you know. That's all I have to say. But now I have to ask, before I die, tell me, what will you do?*

Die? Craig asked. *Why do you think you're all wrapped up in this place? I've been assimilating you into an AI of your own. It's true, your body was beyond the point of salvaging, but your consciousness is nearly copied. Siannon, after all this time, you'll finally have power, a say. You'll be like me! You won't be some pawn. We'll be equals. Then we can figure this all out together.*

2.

When Kalyna regained consciousness, it was because of someone yelling. She saw she was in the Med Bay. The place was in terrible disarray. Will was in a bed next to her. He was stone-faced, taking in a furious Captain Sali. His arm was in a sling.

After the captain had finished, they were alone. He filled her in on the horrible things that had happened, and she did the same.

"Kalyna, I'm convinced Craig must have it out for us or something," Will said. "Can you reach him?"

Kalyna tried, but there was no response. "Well, he got your grandmother back in control of the ship, right?"

"Yeah, but what's that matter if we're in a battle with the enemy again? Not to mention Jecenia. I mean, if she can just pop in and out like that willy-nilly, we're in huge trouble."

"It worries me too," Kalyna admitted.

"Well... I'm glad you're okay. She had us both cornered... we're lucky to be alive yet again."

"I just gave up and quit fighting her. She seemed very insulted by that."

"Interesting. These other people, I feel so bad for them. If Jecenia is any sign, they're all sociopaths. Anyway, I'm going to get surgery soon. Before that, I have something I wanna tell you about."

"Okay, what's that?"

"It's a secret. You have to come closer."

"A secret? Sure thing." Kalyna got up and bent down to his ear. His fingers parted her hair behind her ears. "It's never actually possible to touch someone else. Like, atomically speaking. The feeling of my fingers in your hair, it's just this force-field from a cloud that houses our electrons. It's a little sad to me. You know? You can't ever really touch anything."

"It's okay. I like what you're doing, whatever the actual mechanisms are."

"Electron clouds repelling! That's what the sensation of touch really is." He stared at Kalyna.

"That's a pretty good secret, Will," she said, feeling giddy.

"Oh, that? That wasn't the secret. The secret is this." He kissed her on the lips. "There," he said, backing away. "I'm a little less sad now. Was that good idea or bad idea?"

She anchored her hands onto his cheeks and kissed him back. The giddiness within her soared, and her heartbeat sped up. This was something she didn't know she had needed. She had always thought Will was attractive, but never considered him romantically. What had just happened really snuck up on her.

When the kiss was over, Kalyna said, "Does that answer your question?"

Will squeezed her hand with a winning smile. "Ha. Oh… yeah. Goes to show what I know. Here I thought today was probably the worst day of my life. Not anymore. Although… I haven't even gotten surgery yet. There's another thing too. After, my grandmother's throwing me in jail."

"Will, no! You're kidding."

"She wants to punish me for stealing her buircraft. I get it. I did fuck up. I'm ready to take responsibility. But for everything I just said, all I can feel right now is how awesome I think you are."

Kalyna blushed.

They talked as long as they could. All the implications of B3, Craig, Jecenia, and the larger threat she represented, none of these things were discussed. Instead, the two explored an unprecedented euphoria that immobilized all fear of the future.

Chapter Five

1.

Far above them, Lyda could see the edges where the Maw began. What had started as a free fall decelerated into a drifting. This was thanks to the luminescent tiles that had formed from fragments of the kitchen. Everyone had found their way onto one. There were many tiles, but they were all gradually dissipating. Lyda saw a grim picture in her mind of her father's tile failing him. She would be helpless if he sunk beyond her into that oblivion.

What structural purpose did the Maw serve B3? It seemed like a pointless cavity. She was laying flat on her back. B3 was not heeding her will from down here. Gabriel could project, but because it accomplished nothing and put his body in peril, he stayed within himself.

"Craig, stop this!" Gabriel called out. It was so difficult to see him and the others. Fortunately, they were not too far away.

"Yeah!" Lyda added with a ferocity. "I'm not afraid."

Two regrettable things happened simultaneously: Gabriel's tile faded from under him, speeding his descent. Lyda watched him maneuver his fall so he would land on another one. He was safe again, now some distance below her. As he was falling, Lyda saw a vision: the Erstveil, its tendrils of energy covering the sky, their light and power fading out. It was gone. The enemy was coming for Arqa again!

No! she thought. *I didn't do that. It wasn't supposed to go down. Who—*

Me, Craig said. *Who else?*

HONOR YOUR DEAL! Lyda challenged him.

An outstanding effort, Craig said. *Said with such entitlement, such authority. But Lyda, you relinquished your connection to B3. While you were away, I became its conduit.*

So you're just going to let us fall forever?

You had a good run. A choice. Remember? You could have killed them all that day. You didn't. Leaving the possibility for them to try taking Arqa again.

Obviously I made a mistake if this is the consequence, Lyda said. *But if you think taking down the Erstveil was the right decision, then there's something seriously wrong with you.*

So self-righteous. Your mother would not be impressed.

Where is she, Craig?

You must know she's gone. You said it yourself. She did what she did for you. Why are you so unwilling to accept her sacrifice?

What are you talking about? Are you punishing us because I did what I thought was right? I don't understand your game here, Craig. What, do you hate me because I knew my mom and you never knew yours? What's got you so vindictive?

Lyda tensed up as her tile evaporated. Falling away from the others, she panicked. Nothing to hang onto as she fell deeper into the black. She did a few rolls, not concerned about the bottom. Was it true? Did she have no control over B3? Or did Craig only want to make her think that? She had to challenge him. He didn't have the right to terrorize them.

Gabriel loves you more than anyone else, Lyda said. *What is he down here with us for?* Craig ignored him. Feeling fed up, Lyda concentrated. They were not trapped. Arqa would not fall today. The Maw may be different than the rest of B3, but it was still a part of it. It was the abyss where Craig had come out of. She spread her arms out, pretending they were wings, buffeting the emptiness she fell through. Gradually, she forced her body to lean back. To deny her situation. She wasn't *descending* into the Maw. No. It was the opposite. She and the others were falling out of it.

It was working. Lyda rejoiced. She soon saw the entrance of the Maw below her, the light of B3 growing.

They were out of it, landing on the surface of B3. The tiles were all gone. They could stand! She looked at the edge where the Maw began. Gabriel, her dad, and Mr. Benito with on their feet.

"Yikes, that was scary," her father said.

"Daddy!" Lyda said, jumping into his arms. "I did that."

"How?" he asked.

"Never mind. It's over now. He tricked us. But that's not what's important." She looked into the distance. "I brought Mr. Benito, Craig. Are we going to talk now or what?"

How valiant of you, Lyda, Craig said, appearing as a floating humanoid form in front of them. *You did well. Now we can delve into things properly.*

"Was that some kind of test?" Lyda asked.

Don't worry about that. Each of you has pressing concerns I intend to address. With my appearance, all things are at a crossroads.

"Stop the fighting, Craig," her father said. "My daughter stopped it. Why'd you even start it up again? "

Lyda only paused the violence, Mr. Hall, Craig said. *Hours remain before Arqa's defenses ultimately prove useless against Arete. That is the name of the enemy ship.*

"Of course," Mr. Hall said, seeming to realize something obvious.

Should we do nothing, then that *will lead to the end of the violence, Mr. Hall. A violence Arqa incited long ago.*

"Craig, fault me all you want," Mr. Benito said. "I know I made mistakes. But you know it's wrong to let more people die."

Found the nerve to acknowledge me, huh? People will die with or without my intervention. Craig looked at Lyda. *This one has experience with wielding B3. Would you again now, knowing what you do?*

Lyda turned away from him. "Why me?"

B3 would be keen to integrate with you again. Maybe now, with the gift of your hindsight, you can rectify your previous errors.

"Doing that last time took an awful toll on her, Craig," her dad said. "Why not just separate the ships like before? Let her put the Erstveil back in place."

Even if the barrier was erected again, the enemy you could not kill, Jecenia, is loose. That would not prevent her from attacking Arqa.

Lyda fell to her knees. "Loose? But I—how? Who is she?"

Why put energy into trying to understand a problem you could eliminate? Do you need further incentive than that to wield B3 a second time?

"Forget all that. I—I need her, Craig. My mom. Please. You must know where she is. If we can find her, she'll know what this all means. What's going on? She'll make the right decision. It can't be me again. Please."

Sounds like the makings of a great deal, Craig said. *If I tell you what I know of your mother, will you promise to wield B3 again? To vanquish all threats to your home?*

Lyda shivered, crossing her arms and looking at the shifting humanoid form with severity. "Tell me *now.*" B3 shook, reacting to her demand.

The truth is, I cannot locate your mother. She can't make your decision for you.

"I'll do it," Gabriel said. "Craig, I'll wield B3 against the enemy ship."

Lyda gave Gabriel a derisive look. Although she had already made up her mind, that the pain of it would be too great for her to bear again, the idea of Gabriel doing it filled her with anger.

Do you know what protecting Arqa means? You know nothing about their crimes. They deserve their own punishment.

"Maybe, but what about us kids?" Gabriel asked. "Craig, I only want to create the least amount of harm possible."

Arqa's survival in the future results only in more violence, Gabriel. Nothing but harm will result in its continuation. Not that it matters. You can't wield B3 in the manner required to save Arqa, anyway. Only Lyda can. Not to say you aren't special. You are. It's just, this is something only Lyda can do. And so...

Lyda felt herself being transported elsewhere. It was much the same as the previous terrain. Only this time, there was something a few yards in front of her, jutting out from the surface of B3. The others were there with her. Lyda approached it. It looked to Lyda like a giant mitochondrion. When she got to see the front of it, she saw there was a visible interior to the pod-like thing. It was filled with a dense fog, but that fog was thinning.

Before what was within made itself known, she heard something from behind it. An unmistakable, deeply embedded trigger of pleasure lodged in her memories. Deserting the pod, she caught the sight of her dog Congo.

2.

Siannon spoke now with her mouth, insisting Craig listen to her words rather than her thoughts.

Speaking was very challenging for the woman, but she persisted. "I am shocked… you'd do this without asking."

Asking? Craig questioned. *You are dying! I did the best I could for you.*

"No. That's untrue. And I'll tell you why." She adjusted herself up from the wall where she was slumped. "I have thought of it. That when it's my time, I want that to be all. I'm… not interested in being as you are. I'd just like to go."

Miss Siannon, no!

"Yes, Craig. Let me die. Whatever you had in mind, whatever you're processing or loading… cease with it. I'm sorry. I just—I've had quite enough of all… this. I don't want some Siannon 2.0 floating around like a ghost. Cancel it."

Why don't you want to be like me?

"You've heard me tell you how I was co-opted into joining Arqa. Very few of my choices in life were my own. I deserve a say in my death, don't I?" She coughed up blood. "And this is it. It won't be everyone's desire on Arqa to assimilate with B3. And you might as well learn to respect that now, starting with me."

But I'm alone. No one understands what I've been through. I thought we could solve these issues together, Siannon.

"I know, Craig. You have a stronger will than I do. And with my sins confessed, I hope your purpose is clearer."

How am I supposed to judge this conflict? You have every right to be the true arbiter. Torn from one side to the other. Forced and manipulated. Used as propaganda. Taken from your own body.

"These are things that would make me a poor judge, Craig. I think it's your objectivity we need."

I don't want to pick the wrong side.

"There is no side, Craig," Siannon said quietly. "There are only people. Hurt people… desiring survival."

You really expect me to remain alone?

"You won't… always be. But for now, yes."

They spoke on, but not for much longer. She spasmed, succumbing to her injuries.

Craig set about casting away the pieces of her, respecting her wishes.

Making her gone.

Gone.

To that same place where his original consciousness was.

That place even he could not see.

The area meant to transfer her consciousness went away as well, leaving only the bloody body on the floor of CC.

Craig watched the others in the room stare at him in fear as he made himself known to them.

Some went with haste to Siannon's side.

He told them of the futility of their urgency.

Mark was nearby, leaning against a wall.

He was in the middle of smoking a stap.

I endeavored to make her like me, but she refused, Craig told the silly man. *I never thought she'd refuse, Mark.*

"Admitting you're fallible, eh?" Mark chuckled and a stream of smoke spewed out of him. "Any chance you'll stop the fighting?"

Craig had forgotten about that, but he saw on the radar that both sides were indeed killing each other.

"You're precognitive. Who do you say wins the day? Us or them?"

Siannon told me the full truth, you know.

"Good for you."

Those people over there, you wanted the children to think they were monsters. For whatever faults they had, you could be considered much worse for all those people you killed on Breaking Day.

"Do you expect me to defend my actions or something? I don't feel like explaining myself. Whatever injustice happened resulted in your uncanny ability to be so judgmental now."

What now, indeed? Will you do nothing, then? Lean here as Arqa falls to the enemy?

"Hey, if you're having fun, I'm having fun." Mark smiled. "Actually, mate, I'm sure you have some far more interesting planned than all that, correct? I myself have no worries until my timer hits zero."

With that, the parts of Craig reconvened to a central location.

He would need to be whole for what came next.

Chapter Six

1.

The unfolding reunion between Lyda, Stephen, and Congo was a beautiful sight. But it had completely derailed the urgency of their situation. Callum was struggling to speak up about it.

"It's really him, isn't it?" Lyda asked. She was hugging a fidgeting Congo tightly. "Look, you can touch him and feel him and everything. It's really him."

"I never thought..." Stephen began. He knelt to pet the German Shepard. "Look at you, beautiful boy!" Stephen looked over at Gabriel and Callum. "Come see. Can you believe this?"

"It's great, Stephen," Callum said. Quietly, he turned to Gabriel. "Tell me, use that clairvoyance of yours. Is that just some glamor of Craig's? Or is he the real thing?"

"He's real, Mr. Benito," Gabriel confirmed. "Flesh and blood."

"Craig keeps moving us, shifting us around. Now this." *Is it just some distraction?* Callum wondered.

Go play with the dog, Craig said to Callum. He'd forgotten that Craig could pick up on his thoughts. *Or... you might want to see what's in the pod.*

The pod. Yes. It had appeared as they entered the room. There seemed to be no pulling the Halls out of their moment, so Callum gestured to Gabriel, then pointed to the pod. What Callum saw when he looked inside was beyond belief. After all, Dominique had been so elusive all this time... there she was. The woman's eyes were shut and her arms were crossed around her body. The only motion Callum could discern was the slow rising and falling of her chest.

How you find her now is how I found her, Craig said.

"Lyda, it's your mom in here!" Gabriel called out.

"What?!" Lyda said. In seconds, the girl and her father were in front of the pod, looking in. "Mom? MOM?!" Lyda grasped onto her father for stability. "What is she in there for? What is this thing? We need to get her out. Craig!"

I've already tried that, Lyda, Craig said. Lyda went in closer to the pod. *Whatever you do, don't touch it!*

Lyda whimpered at the AI's words.

"So we finally found her," Callum said. He felt Congo's front paws on his back, pushing off against him. "Oh, buddy. Why'd you give me chase last time? Gabriel, come give this dog some attention so I can straighten this out." To Craig, floating above the pod, the man asked, "You mean she was in B3 the whole time?"

I'm afraid the more I say, the less you will understand.

"Hey!" Lyda said. "You can't do that. Craig, I'm begging you. Tell us what you can."

I already have. Remember our deal. You are to wield B3 against Arete. Bring your enemy's ship down and then you will have what you need to free your mother from this thing, I assure you.

Callum didn't like the sound of that. It seemed manipulative. Craig's actions up to now had been ambiguous. Just minutes ago, he'd left them to fall in the Maw. Then he'd said he *hadn't* located Dominique. "How'd she end up in there, Craig?"

You are here to ask pointless questions, I know, Craig said. *But my interest is in what Lyda shall do. She has all the information she needs. You will now be ignored.*

Lyda looked up at her father. "Did—is that what she wanted?" Lyda asked.

"I don't know, honey," Stephen said. "But your mom, she knew what was going to happen. If you do it again and it could bring her back—"

"Mr. Hall don't be stupid," Gabriel cut in. "How are you going to trust him? Look at everything he's put us through."

"Relax, Gabriel. He found Congo. And my wife! He's okay in my book."

"Then he shouldn't have any issue explaining what happened to them," Callum said.

Is it not obvious, dad?

Callum flinched upon hearing Craig call him that.

"There's something I—one thing I need to do," Lyda said. "I just need to. I'm sorry." Lyda reached out a hand toward the pod.

NO! Craig exclaimed.

But it happened too quickly. Lyda's hand went through the

pod. "What is this? Craig? This isn't real!"

Yes, it is. I told you, you mustn't touch it. Why couldn't you just listen?

Lyda kept weaving her hand in and out of the pod, reaching in deep, trying to grab at her mother. But to Callum, it seemed to be nothing more than an illusion or projection.

Fresh tears fell down Lyda's cheeks. "C-Congo," Lyda called out, deflated.

Congo approached her. Lyda grabbed him by his collar. She turned around to face Callum and the others. "You were right. He's a trickster. But I know what I have to do." Lyda went limp and fell back into the projection, pulling Congo in after her.

"LYDA!" Stephen screamed, reaching out to the girl. Callum stepped in the way, raising both of his arms to stop his impulsive friend. The joy that had been so prevalent minutes before was gone from the room. Callum could feel a palpable despair all around him, seeping into him. He wrapped his arms around Stephen. The pod flickered away, leaving nothing behind.

"Let go of me!" Stephen demanded, trying to elbow Callum off of him.

"Mr. Hall, just wait," Gabriel said. "She'll be back."

On the contrary, Gabriel, Craig said, *there was a very good reason I advised her not to get too close to that thing.*

"Craig," Callum said. "Where did that take her?"

There are some things beyond even my current knowledge. Indeed, beyond my ability to predict. This is unanticipated and troubling. Without Lyda here to do anything, Arqa is in real jeopardy.

"BRING HER BACK!" Stephen shouted. He charged at Craig, but the AI's form shifted up beyond his reach.

Bark, bark, was Craig's only response to him.

"Please, Craig. I can't lose her and I just got the dog back. Dominique was right here. Why did Lyda do that?"

We've no time for antics any longer, Mr. Hall, Craig said. A large holo-screen appeared, showing Spaeros in combat. *What's done is done. All we can do now is watch this thing play out.*

"No," Gabriel said.

"Craig, please stop the fighting," Callum said. "We know you can. You have that power."

That is what Miss Siannon asked of me, Craig said. *But she's dead now. Because of all this foolishness.*

"Oh. I'm sorry, Craig."

I will do nothing now. And no one will convince me otherwise. So enjoy whatever's left.

"FUCK YOU!" Gabriel screamed. He paced. "Something. Something big. Something big to stop the fighting. Make them retreat. Make them retreat." Callum could hear the boy repeat the words like an incantation. It devolved into into muttering. His hands raked into his skull and he pulled at his hair.

I already told you, B3 won't work like that for you.

B3 responded to Gabriel's madness in kind. An eruption of motion knocked Callum off of his feet. He crawl up into a fetal position, desperately trying to remain steady as the vibrations below rocked him. It felt as though B3 would come apart. Callum was frightened and imagined being in the Maw again.

2.

No more. No more allowing anyone to keep him from the solution. It was so obvious! Gabriel receded from the external world to a stillness within. A place of thought. Words were props… he needed to transcend them. Even if Craig had B3 in his hands, Gabriel wasn't going to let it end like this. So potent was his focus that a vision of something an incalculable distance away entered Gabriel's mind. A brightness to counter the dark indifference of Craig. Let it blind him, if it must. He saw this grandiose light in some far off space-time event. It was exactly what he needed right now.

In that moment, something was made known to Gabriel. Not so long ago, Arqa had been flying to B3. The distance was too far for the ship to reach. It needed help. *Gabriel* had been that help. He knew he could see places beyond his own senses. But his power was also so much more than that. His clairvoyance had teleported Arqa from where it had been. Closing the long gap to B3 in the blink of an eye. It had happened that day in the Gaze Room. Not only that, but the Maw is where Lyda's initial attack on the enemy had emanated from. But why was this knowledge just coming to him now?

Something to ponder later. For now, he had to avert a catastrophe. No one had to die, no one! All he had to do was summon this flash from the heavens. Should it come too close to his body, it would destroy him. He had to be careful, so careful. *Concentrate,* he thought. This is why he had his power, for this moment. And the Maw... the Maw was where he could channel it. Of course!

RETREAT!

RETREAT!

ALL OF YOU RETREAT!

It was a preternatural missive sent out to all who fought. It went uncontested. Gabriel stopped the battle.

The Maw itself was no longer a dark void. For something was nearly free from it. With that, Gabriel returned to his body. The effort of harnessing what he had left him blinded. In shambles, he heard a collection of illegible voices. He had gone farther than ever before, employing his power to its fullest potential: bringing forth a thing of cosmic horror none could dispel, not even that heartless creature who dared to call himself Craig.

to be continued…

EPISODE 7: Deleted Scene

I cut this scene out because Episode 7 ended up being really long. The longest episode of them all. There were a lot of things to resolve from Book 1's cliffhanger, as well as introducing new ideas. Although I cherish the banter here, there is no vital, plot-advancing information that couldn't be placed elsewhere. Mark and Rayna's character dynamic is my favorite of any pairing for The Felled, *and it pained me to see this scene go from the final draft. So here it is!*

In the mirror that displayed all of his flaws, Mark double-checked that he was clean-shaven. He was dressed in a blue suit that was a little too tight for him.

"Rayna!" he shouted out into his lab.

"What?"

"It's time for the box."

"One hot sec," Rayna said impatiently. "You're not the only one who's getting ready."

Their relationship had changed since she'd knocked him out. The incident had opened up a dialog. If something was bothering her, he'd rather hear it as soon as possible rather than being "accidentally" hit by objects she was juggling. He'd learned some interesting things about her as a result. Namely, that she wasn't interested in carrying on his research should anything ever happen to him. This had been a troubling revelation for Mark. He'd considered dismissing her, sending her elsewhere on the ship, and finding someone truer to his projects. Mark just didn't have the heart to do that. Their history stretched back most of Rayna's life. He had his doubts about her ability to function outside of his lab. To her credit, it was like she wasn't doing her job. Only that her aspirations were a thing beyond the lab. What, exactly, they were, she hadn't said yet.

Mark found Rayna in the lab, frantically searching for the box among a stack of other boxes. She was in a beautiful purple dress. Only—

"You can't wear that," Mark said, pointing at the matching bucket hat on her head.

"Uh-uh," Rayna said, disengaging from her task. "We talked about this. You can't say I can't do something. Now, if there's a rule on Arqa about hats I'm not aware of, that's a different story entirely."

"The head is just... this is a formal appearance, Rayna. It's very important we put our best foot forward in terms of presentation. Out of a sense of respect for Flight Division, couldn't you find a good wig instead?"

"Looky here, what's that?" Rayna got the tie from the box and wrapped it around Mark's neck, then secured it in place. "Respect for my elders. And I won't even comment on how ridiculous it is that you don't know how to tie a tie, okay?"

Mark rolled his eyes. "One might construe that in itself as a comment."

"One must choose to. And you know what else?"

"What's that?"

Rayna stepped away from him, making right angles with her thumb and forefinger to inspect him. "I think B3 would want us to come as we are."

"You don't mean naked?"

"I do, but I get how, for reasons, that's not happening. Maybe that's why some of us died in there. I could imagine clothing because very offensive to alien cultures. Like modesty, censorship. A lack of transparency. I bet they'd have differing opinions on all that." She looked him in the eyes before making for the doorway. "Suppose you know better, right?"

Mark grunted. "If you're going to keep that hat on, at least straighten it out."

"An excellent idea," Rayna said.

Frowning, Mark adjusted her hat, and the two made their way out of the lab. It was a pivotal moment in Arqa's history.

Join my e-mail for discounts and updates on books and projects I have coming up. As a thank you, you'll get a free ebook to take home.

Sound good?

Sign up at:
Ryansleavitt.com

Check out my YouTube channel!

In addition to writing books, I also make videos on consciousness expansion and philosophy. It's a great way to see what I'm up to week to week. Search Ryan S. Leavitt on YouTube.

Is it worse to learn or not to know?

A psychological thriller set in New Orleans

Buy *Writer, Seeker, Killer* on ryansleavitt.com or Amazon.

About the Author

Ryan S. Leavitt is a fiction author, primarily writing thrillers and science fiction with philosophical undertones. His books have been featured on BookBub and he has also appeared on the briefly televised reality sitcom *Quiet Desperation*. He currently lives in New Orleans, where he also performs in the bands Allision and The Every Year.

"What is it, ma'am?"

The commander rose from her chair. The elderly Asian woman gave the girl a look of remorse. She maintained eye contact while taking small steps over to where Jecenia stood. "Has your loyalty wavered in light of our failure? Do you suggest the airlock for yourself over some troubling setbacks?"

"Ma'am," Jecenia said with a bow, "I am still a tool for Arete's purpose. A weapon. In fact, I killed a handful of Arqa's people with my bare hands. Still, I am afraid. But I think I see what you're saying. Yes. What is created can be destroyed. And as long as I am able, I will find a way to stop this new threat. With my power, I am unstoppable. And if it's your wish for me to go forward, then I will take that permission."

The commander said no more, only opened her arms out. Where there was grace, there was hope. Hope to destroy Arqa for what they fucking did. As the love of her commander's arms encircled despite the alien tampering, Jecenia wept.

www.ingramcontent.com/pod-product-compliance
Lightning Source LLC
Chambersburg PA
CBHW060859250626
47159CB00008B/2802

Epilogue

Jecenia was back home, back on Arete. Though she knew she was short on time, the first thing she did was go to her quarters. Luckily, no one had taken them over, as her things were still here. Though there was no sign of Nell, her Devon Rex. Maybe Friedrich had her in his quarters.

She hadn't been able to sleep in that place where the evil little girl had tortured her. After they had taken her to Arqa, she had felt an overpowering urge to sleep, but that was out of the question. She would periodically bite the inside of her mouth to stay alert. When the evil girl had jabbed her with the needle, it made Jecenia feel drowsier than she ever had in her life. But she only pretended to be asleep—for her will to escape was too powerful.

She allowed herself to sit on her bed, just for a moment. It was important, even in matters of urgency, to take moments in between. Rushing was disorganization in motion. And all successful soldiers knew to include buffer time between their tasks.

Jecenia was still feeling euphoric after her escape. After the evil girl had taken her prisoner, she would have never guessed her dream of killing Arqa's people would come true—it just showed how unexpected life was. How *powerful* intention could be.

She was long overdue for a debriefing. Jecenia didn't want to teleport to her next destination, but the idea of walking there freely would create a scene, as she'd been absent for a long while. She had to be subtle, simple. There was a part of her that *hated* what she could do now. But judgment for these recent changes did not fall on her.

With nothing more than an image and a thought, Jecenia left her quarters and appeared in front of a set of tall double doors. She knocked as hard as she could. "Commander! It's Jecenia. I survived. Are you in? We need to talk." The girl turned around nervously, expecting to make eye contact with someone shocked at her sudden arrival. But no one was there. Thank the Lord! The doors opened. Jecenia made her way to a familiar desk. She'd only been in this room six, maybe seven times in her life. And this was the first instance in which she had not been summoned.

Behind the desk was a chair facing away from her, watching a holo-screen of a battle. Jecenia, one to use her time wisely, did not wait for the commander to turn around. "Milady, I've so much to tell you. First off, we have failed. Arqa has accomplished the unthinkable. Their resultant artificial intelligence is beyond containment and control.

"That is the most important thing you must know. As for the rest: I've no doubt you have questions for me. I shall answer them honestly. The first question I'd like to answer for you is, how am I alive? Well, instead of perishing as many of our comrades did that day, I was spared, taken prisoner. A girl tried to kill me, but no matter what she did, it wouldn't work. An alien energy shielded me from harm. She left me inside a construct she called the Erstveil. I could not leave. One day, more came from Arqa, only I could fight them. As a result, I was moved to Arqa. I learned not only did I have this strange invulnerability, but I could also teleport at will. Which, I hope, begins to answer the second question: that is, how am I standing before you?

"I have endured many things on my road back to Arete, and there were times I honestly did not think I would ever see it again. I was cursed that day. But here is the most peculiar thing of all, commander: the AI I told you about helped to facilitate my return. It knew I could escape, but it neglected to mention it to those on Arqa. It seemed to enjoy the pain of its creators. Through this omission, I was able to exploit an opening... using my aforementioned abilities. And while I am grateful to be back, you now know it is only on the wings of everything we sought to dismantle. I have become a conflict of interest for the mission. Touched by the alien energies. I urge you, commander, do away with me. Perhaps if I'm sent out the airlock, I shall suffocate or freeze. For since you have seen me last, I've become a liability." Jecenia paused, trying to reset her composure. Recounting everything had been challenging.

The voice Jecenia so admired spoke. A voice like hers, feminine and formal. "Even if you were not already the greatest warrior on my ship, my most treasured asset, I would still only have one question for you after hearing you speak in such a way."